fly on the wall

nonfiction by Michael Hirsh

*PARARESCUE—The True Story of an Incredible
Rescue at Sea and the Heroes Who Pulled it Off*

*NONE BRAVER—U.S. Air Force
Pararescuemen in the War on Terrorism*

*TERRI—The Truth
(with Michael Schiavo)*

*YOUR OTHER LEFT
Punch Lines From the Front Lines*

*THE LIBERATORS
America's Witnesses to the Holocaust*

*PIRATE ALLEY
Commanding Task Force 151 off Somalia
(with Rear Admiral Terry McKnight)*

fly on the

wall

a fly moscone mystery

MIKE HIRSH

ANTENNA BOOKS
BROOKLYN

Antenna Books.

Fly on the Wall. Copyright © 2012 by Michael Hirsh. All rights reserved. Printed in the United States of America. For information, address Antenna Books, 156 Prospect Park West, Brooklyn, New York, 11215.

www.antennabooks.com

Library of Congress Cataloging-in-Publication Data

Hirsh, Michael
Fly on the Wall : A Fly Moscone Mystery / Michael Hirsh.—1st ed. p. cm.

print ISBN 978-1-62306-000-8
ebook ISBN 978-1-62306-002-2

1. Private investigators—Fiction. 2. Punta Gorda (Florida)—Fiction. I. Title

First Edition: July 2012

10 9 8 7 6 5 4 3 2 1

Contact Michael Hirsh at:
flyandjinx@gmail.com

For my brother Sam Hirsh
And my brother-in-law Richard Aronson
Thanks for listening.

"You live for justice. You die in despair."

—Paul "Fly" Moscone
(with apologies to Charles Dickens)

fly's nightmare

The sound of the storm scares the hell out of me. Just opening the glass door from the sheriff's office to the parking lot is a struggle. The second we stepped outside, we were both soaked to the skin. As we fight our way to Wayne's two-and-a-half ton, four-wheel drive behemoth, it never dawns on me that a Ford Expedition would have difficulty moving forward in a seventy-mile-an-hour headwind. But from the moment Salladé turns the car south on Golf Course Boulevard, it's apparent we're going to have a problem.

"Wayne, ya might want to give it more gas!" I shout over the roar of the wind and the sound of rain pounding the car. Wayne is director of Charlotte County's Office of Emergency Management. I thought he would have had this all figured out.

His response isn't comforting. "I got it floored and we're going nowhere." As he says it, something slams into the windshield on my side, caroms off the glass, and blows past us, leaving a spider-web pattern and cracks in front of me. We both cringe at the impact. I reach out and put my hand flat on the center of the web.

"It'll hold. How much farther we got to go?"

"Farther isn't the problem. We have two choices, both bad. When we get to the stop sign, we either go right and drive a mile to the jail, or turn left and head for the airport terminal. Either way, we end up broadside to the wind."

"You think you can keep us on the road?"

"I'm going to try."

"Try is not what I want to hear from you. Try is what I ask my grandkid to do when I put her on the potty."

"Look, the airport is closer, but the jail is probably going to do better in the storm. Besides, all my people are there and they have generators. What do you think?"

"They're payin' you the big bucks to be the manager. So manage."

"Then hang on. Things are about to get interesting."

Out of force of habit, Salladé signals for a right turn, which causes me to snort. It would prove to be my last laugh for nearly an hour. The wind catches us broadside as we come around the corner and the 5,000 pound SUV leans so far over to the right that the two left tires are way off the pavement. If he isn't strapped in tight, Wayne ends up in my lap. For an eternity, it feels like we're going to be tossed on our side. Not that big a deal inside this beast, until I see that we're sliding toward the swale which is now a fast-flowing creek, maybe five feet deep. If we go in, drowning becomes a distinct possibility.

"Bafongool! Do something, Wayne!" I yell over the roar of the wind.

He doesn't answer. He just keeps wrestling the wheel. The look on his face scares me—'cause I can tell he's as terrified as I am. For a second the wind slacks off, and the Expedition bounces back onto all four tires. And then it feels like afterburners kicked in. He still had it floored and we shoot ahead till another blast of wind hits us. It's like we slammed into a brick wall. Once again, we're barely inching along, occasionally getting pushed toward the shoulder and the swale, but somehow, he manages to keep us on the pavement.

After what seems like enough time to watch the Godfather Trilogy with commercials, he throws the wheel to the left and we shimmy into the road that leads to the county jail parking lot.

Thinking the adventure is over, I take a chance and start to exhale. Big mistake. Another missile crashes into the windshield, this time creating a spider web on the driver's side. If I hadn't been strapped in, my Vietnam legacy startle response would have had me hitting the floor. Between the cracked glass and blinding rain, the only parking technique that will work is one taught by the Braille Institute. We slam into the concrete barriers strategically placed around the jail.

"We're here," my chauffeur announces, then he lays on the horn for several seconds, hoping the people inside will respond and open the lobby door. The thought of standing there, pounding on the locked door while getting blasted by wind, rain and seashell fragments from the unpaved parking lot is not comforting. But getting the jail door open is not our immediate problem. It hadn't dawned on either of us that just getting out of the car is going to be a test of strength. The Expedition's large front doors are like sails and the wind slams them shut every time we try to crack them open.

Finally, I come up with a plan to get us out of the car. I put my shoulder against the inside of the door and muscle it open, and then I turn sideways and jam my legs down to the ground. For a second it seems as though the wind is going to win the battle and scissor them off at the knees. But I'm able to get both feet on the ground, turn and plant my butt against the door and push against the car body with my hands. I shout, "Okay, go!" and Wayne slides passed me. He drops to the ground, grabs the outside handle and pulls for all he's worth, giving me a chance to sidestep to the left.

"I'm clear!" I scream. Salladé releases the handle and the door blows shut with explosive force. We both turn to make a run for the building. With my first step, I end up in a heap on the ground. "Mannaggia!" I yell.

Salladé reaches down to haul me up.

"I can't see!" I shout into the wind. My glasses are dripping wet.

Wayne grabs my arm and drags me up the curb, over the grass, and to the door, where arms reach out and pull the two of us up into the building.

"Having fun yet?" asks one of the deputies.

"I need a Diet Dr. Pepper," I croak. The deputy doesn't notice that I'm shaking.

chapter 1
jinx

Did I tell youse about the blood pouring through the ceiling and how I discovered the body?" Fly asked, giving a clue to his North Jersey roots with one word.

"Stop! Halt! Not another word" I shouted not only for emphasis, but to make certain he heard me over the noise of the boat's engines.

"Why should I stop? I wanna tell them the story. What—I'm not allowed to tell it?" he came back, acting like an indignant four-year-old.

"It's not that you're not allowed to tell the story, it's that you can't. You'll screw it up," I said while opening another beer.

I knew Fly would take that as a challenge, especially since we were out on *his* yacht with a captive audience—two couples new to our little corner of paradise in southwest Florida. Whenever he puts on that captain's hat he becomes even more full of himself, but I figured we've got time to kill, might as well give the newbies a show. Fly took the bait like a starving bass rising to suck down a popper.

"Wait a minute, Jinx, *I* found the body. *I* solved the crime. So why will *I* screw it up? You're the only *giamoke* on this boat with a Medicare card in his pocket. Your short term memory is shot, and your long term is nothing to write home about—if you could even remember the address," Fly responded loudly, and then popped the top on his ninth Diet Dr. Pepper of the day.

For some reason, his DDP consumption was really annoying me today. When restaurants tell him—for the millionth time—that they don't or won't carry it because it tastes like carbonated cough syrup and only weirdos drink it, it's like he's hearing it for the first time.

I shot a glance at Fly's wife, Sophia, who was ignoring us, which is what she usually does when the two of us get into mutual ball-busting. When I finally caught her eye I gestured to the can of DDP and said, "Does he gargle with that swill, too?" She went right back to ignoring us.

Let me introduce you to my target, I mean my friend, retiree and Charlotte County Volunteer Reserve Sheriff's Deputy Paul "Fly" Moscone. Why Fly? He's Italian, from Newark. Yeah, *that* Newark. New Jersey. *Moscone* comes from *mosca*, for fly. In the old country, that's what they called small, annoying people. Fly's five-six, maybe five-seven, five-nine in heels which he only wears on special occasions. You be the judge.

Fly is sixty. I'm sixty-five. But if you stand the two of us side by side, with his white hair, he's the one who looks like the codger. Fly grew up wanting to be a homicide detective, but his parents said no. Smart move, Mr. and Mrs. Moscone. Fly made a pile of money, retired early from his job selling mainframe computers for AT&T and moved here. Here being Punta Gorda, Florida. Don't be too quick to judge him for the occasional *youse guys*. He actually has a college degree and a ton of street smarts—but that Jersey accent doesn't go away. After a while it stops being annoying.

When he got here, Fly checked into volunteering with the sheriff's department. Ten months later, after passing the background check, a lie detector test, a physical agility test, and being scoped oto, stetho and procto, he got sent to the police academy in Lee County. Came through it near the head of his class, and now he volunteers a couple days a week. The best part for him is that they pretty much let him do what he wants. He's an extra body out on the street in a patrol car. And right after Hurricane Charley hit us, every little bit helped a lot. I think it might have gone to his head. But I digress. Back to our argument.

"Yes, Fly, you found the body. And every night while you worked the case, we talked. Or have you forgotten all those phone calls you made to me while I was trying to watch Jon Stewart or M*A*S*H reruns? I've got thirty-five years in as a journalist and a writer. Telling stories is what I do. Yes, even your story."

"Wait a minute!" hollered Fly. When he shouts his voice rises into a register that reminds me of a five-year-old scratching out "Twinkle Twinkle" on a quarter-sized Suzuki violin. "Telling stories is what you *used* to do," he continued. "You're the guy who introduces himself as a recovering journalist. Didn't I attend your press card burning ceremony when you arrived here from LA?"

"You know who he sounds like?" I said, turning to our ship-mates for the day. "He's just like that guy on CNN. The one who shouts like he doesn't realize the microphone has been invented even though he's wearing two of them." I raised my eyebrows and nodded at Fly, who was seated next to me on the flying bridge, adjusting the twin throttles of his not-so-secret lover, *Inamorata*.

There were six other passengers on the forty-two foot vessel. The two who were adeptly ignoring us were the aforementioned Sophia, Mrs. Paul "Fly" Moscone, and my long-suffering wife, Laura—aka Mrs. Bill Shiffman. Fly's nickname for me is Jinx. Mr. Jinx to be precise, but we usually aren't that formal. When we run aground or get struck by lightning out of a clear blue sky, they'll understand. The other four had just retired to Punta Gorda, and in a gesture of welcome which she was probably already regretting, Sophia had invited them to spend the day cruising on the boat with us from Punta Gorda to one of their favorite restaurants on the Gulf of Mexico for lunch, and back.

One of the husbands, Robbie Beiler, a white bread sort from somewhere in Ohio, turned toward Sophia and Laura, who were sipping Prosecco mimosas and nibbling on mini-danishes, and asked "Are they always like this?"

"Now you've done it," grumped Fly. "You've broken Man Rules. You never, *never*, side with the women. No matter what. Certainly not in front of them."

Beiler didn't know whether to take him seriously or not, so he looked at me. I leaned toward the confused guy, and stage-whispered, "Fly's heavy into that Man Rules stuff. Humor him, okay?"

Beiler's wife Kim, who'd taught third-graders for decades, seemed less disturbed with Fly's behavior. I guessed she was familiar with the type.

The other couple, Rich and Laurie Aronson, sat quietly, taking it all in without comment—if you don't count the raised eyebrows. I was already having doubts whether they were going to fit in. They'd come here from the Chicago suburbs, and had been introduced to us because we were part of a relatively small aggregation of Jews who were out of the closet. I don't mean gay out-of-the-closet, not that there's anything wrong with that, of course. I mean openly Jewish among a population dominated by upper-Midwest retirees whose notion of a great sandwich is a single slice of any Oscar Mayer meat and American cheese on Wonder bread. With mayo.

"For a trial lawyer, you're pretty quiet," I said to Rich, tossing him a softball just to see whether he could knock it out of the park.

"I'm just waiting to hear the story, whoever tells it." It was a weak comeback, and I was sorely disappointed. I'd been hoping for another major league ball buster, and so far, Rich wasn't even playing in the low minors. I looked at Fly, and I could see he had caught it, too. We both silently agreed: this guy was not going to be much fun to hang with. If he wanted to stick with us, we'd have to train him.

Just then, Aronson's wife Laurie, spoke up. "Oh, he'll talk a lot once he gets to know you. He talks too much, sometimes."

I waited. Nothing. Fly was waiting, too. Nothing. The wife gives him a shot and he doesn't respond? Just takes it like he didn't hear a thing. Huh. The engines weren't that loud. Another look passed between us; we were close to writing him off as untrainable.

Fly drained his DDP, then focused on Beiler. "Wait a second," he said, "didn't I hear you say you were an insurance guy?"

"Yeah. Pre-GEICO gekko." He held up his hands, his knobby knuckles toward me. "This is what happens after years of clients stomping on a pair of good hands."

"Geez. I just thought it was arthritis," I said, deadpan.

But Fly saw an opening and pounced. "You were an insurance guy? Then *I* gotta tell you the story."

"But you mentioned a body. I did mostly casualty stuff, not life," Beiler responded.

"This story has got it all, bodies, casualty, catastrophe, property, saints and sinners, cops and robbers, racists and rednecks. You gotta hear it. From me," shouted Fly.

"Wait a second," said Aronson. "Aren't racists and rednecks the same thing?"

I needed to regain control of the conversation, so I pushed back in before Fly could answer. "See, you just don't know what you don't know till someone tells you that you don't know. Rich, a redneck can be a racist, and a racist can be a redneck, but being one doesn't necessarily make you the other. Welcome to Charlotte County, our happy little corner of the South." I turned to Fly who was futzing with the GPS and plotter. "Fly, these folks are dying to hear the story. I have an idea. I'll do the play by play and you do the color. How 'bout it?"

Fly, the retired salesman, knew when to pressure and when to compromise. Annoying as he might be to his close friends, he was the kind of guy who could butter up the biggest jerk in the world and make the guy feel like he was truly special, or graciously lose by several strokes to a duffer –anything to close the deal. Using compromise as cover, Fly reached for another DDP. "All right, but I want to start with our last lunch at Dean's."

"I don't believe it," said Sophia. "Peace in our time."

"Hey, we're on the Peace River," I responded. "What did you expect?"

She shook her head. "I hope we have enough wine on board to get us through this."

chapter 2
jinx

Fly throttled *Inamorata* down so we wouldn't have to shout over the engines, set the auto-pilot to take her to Marker Five, about sixteen miles down the harbor, turned to his wife and said, "Sophia, take the helm. I need to concentrate on the story so Jinx here doesn't screw up his part." Fly stood up, ready to swap seats with his wife. That really surprised me. The look on his face betrayed inner turmoil. Fly had control issues, and even though he trusted Sophia at the wheel, he preferred to have his hands on the throttles. Suddenly, he blurted, "Never mind, honey, I'll drive." Then he looked at me and said. "You wanted to tell it. So tell it. I'll interrupt as often as necessary."

"No," I said, "you'll interrupt when I say you can—or that stash of DDP I have for you below decks is going over the side. And you'll be right behind it."

Surprisingly, he said nothing, so I took a breath and began.

Fly and I are sitting in our usual corner booth at Dean's South of the Border. Not the new one. The old one that got wiped out by the storm. There's heavy sun-reflective film on the windows and the lights are always kept a couple notches below dim. I'm not saying that the carpet looks like it might be moving, but dinner-time telephone solicitors should be forced to see it in bright light as karmic retribution. Frankly, the place looks like it should have been cleaned and burned a long time ago.

South of the Border occupies a couple of old, tattered buildings that over the years had been melded into a single unit. It sits in a prime location—just south of the bridge leading across the mile-wide Peace River to Port Charlotte. It's also on the east side of U.S. 41, the north-south thoroughfare down the West Coast that's known as the Tamiami Trail, since it runs from Tampa to Miami.

Fly is trying to interest me in a cop story, but instead of focusing on his first law enforcement triumph I'm fixated on watching the Weather Channel guys getting their jollies tracking Hurricane Charley through the Caribbean. Punta Gorda was already inside the absurdly named cone of probability, and it was troubling me. I'm a worrier; Fly, on the other hand, is not. He's beaten prostate cancer, and that's given him his outlook on life and death. He always says if you can't do anything about what's going to happen in the future, why worry about it. With respect to Charley, I'll admit that he wasn't being completely irresponsible—the National Hurricane Center's accuracy at predicting ground zero forty-eight hours out is plus or minus 150 miles. That means this storm could just as easily whack the trendy folks in South Beach or the casino players in Biloxi as it could Charlotte Harbor. So he's right when he says it's nothing to get excited about. Yet. But it takes a while for me to refocus, and when it happens, I'm annoyed with him.

"Paul, are you listening to them? There's a hurricane coming." I only call him by his given name when I'm a quart low on humor.

"Doesn't matter right now. You've gotta hear what happened to me. I took a radio call yesterday," Fly says.

"That's exciting. I'll bet you wet yourself the first time you turned on the lights and siren." Realizing that the time for surrender had come, I added two Sweet-and-Low to the tall iced tea that Maria had just refilled, settled back into the ripped-and-duct-taped dirty green Naugahyde and waved him on.

"Okay. You know most of the assignments they give auxiliary guys are boring. Traffic light out. Someone fills his gas tank and drives off without paying. Dull stuff. But I get this eighty-five year-old guy, takes his car into We Bee Tires and asks them to check the pressure for him. Next thing he knows, they're selling him four new tires, a muffler, a brake job and a blow job."

"A what?"

"Hah. Just wanted to make sure you're paying attention. I know how at your age, you can just drift off sometimes. I don't want to lose you."

I made a quick decision in the interest of progress to ignore the insult. Fly had taken a beat, expecting an interruption that didn't come. It threw his timing off. "Okay, where was I? Oh, yeah.

"An old guy down here takes his car into one of those chain stores, he's gonna get screwed. 'Oh, Mr. Geezer, your frazzinator and razzinator are ready to go, and you don't wanna be drivin' the car if that happens. And for sure you don't wanna know what it's gonna cost you, 'cause you couldn't afford it anyway. We need to do some preventive maintenance.' And then they got him. What should have been a twenty-dollar oil change turns into a two hundred dollar grease job. The old guy has to decide whether to fix his car—which isn't broken but he doesn't know that—or buy his heart medicine for the next month."

"How'd you handle the complaint?" I asked him not so much because I really wanted to find out, but because he knows that if I listen to him, sooner or later I'll get my turn. That's what friendship down here is really all about. Lunch in Punta Gorda is not like lunch in Los Angeles, where I came from. It's not about doing deals, gathering information, reveling in a friend's failure.

"Well," Fly says, visibly swelling with pride, "I pull in and park the cruiser right in front of the bays, lights flashing."

"They had cars on the lifts?"

"Of course they did. That's my point." I could see he was a little disappointed that I had to ask. He continued, smiling his crooked smile. "And they had customers in the waiting room. Senior citizens even older than you. So I ask for the manager, and this smartass good ol' boy comes out with attitude all over his face. It's a classic face off. The North Jersey Italian versus a

South Florida Cracker. But I'm wearing the badge. And I'm gonna bust his agates. He's got agita in his future, he just don't know it yet. It's no accident that I blocked not just one, but both bays."

Fly's breathless narrative is interrupted when a customer two tables away begins shouting into his cell phone. He was actually loud enough that folks turned away from the weather ghouls to see what was going on. "I don't give a shit what your problem is. I've told you not to call me. Ever!" And he snapped the phone shut with a vengeance.

Some people talk on cell phones unobtrusively; others act as though they've taken an oath to share their wireless conversations with everyone in the same ZIP code. Loudmouth was in the latter category. It was apparent watching him that he wasn't just another old guy with a hearing problem who thought shouting into the phone was the only way to be heard. This guy had "Obnoxious Asshole" written all over him. Or maybe it's just my petty prejudice against an overly-tanned loud guy in shorts and a yacht club polo shirt who wears a $15,000 gold Rolex Yacht-Master, an ostentatious gold crucifix on a heavy link chain around his neck, and a diamond pinky ring to the neighborhood bar and restaurant. Even at his age—maybe seventy-five or eighty—he didn't deserve the benefit of the doubt.

He was a schmuck, a word I've actually taught Fly and others here to use properly. Being one of the few bagel biters amid the sea of Wonder Bread eaters who've settled here, an educational campaign in basic Yiddish slang had been essential. Fly has reciprocated by teaching me eighty-five different ways to curse in Italian.

I turned back to Fly, asking, "You recognize the woman he's with?"

"Should I?" he responds with obvious annoyance.

"It's Lacey Dewers. She just buried her third husband a month ago. He was eighty-something." I'd seen her at several different club functions, and knew her reputation. Even the women called her *Lacey Drawers* behind her back. Her specialty was pump and hump: pump 'em for cash and hump 'em to death. Husbands two and three lasted less than a year each; died of heart attacks. Both had been rich widowers when she married 'em.

"Looks like she's working on number four. I wonder which one bought her the new tits? You don't see a rack like that on a sixty-year-old. Not around here, anyway," Fly says grumpily.

I suspected that, tits notwithstanding, Fly was annoyed at having the rhythm of his presentation interrupted again. He confirmed my suspicions when, in a voice dripping with sarcasm, he asked, "May I continue?"

"Go for it," I said.

"Where was I?" he asks, then remembers and continues with his true crime story. "Okay. I'm in the waiting room with the manager, and I notice that one of the cars on a lift is coming down and they're going to want to pull it out very soon. I can see the owner, pacing back and forth, looking between his old Buick gunboat and my squad. Not happy."

"So what do you say?" I ask, my voice conveying the vain hope that his telling of the tale will be shorter and induce less pain than the local community theater production of *Cats.* I should have saved my breath—or lent it to the ex-smokers at the nearby table who were sharing a pitcher of margaritas while inhaling medical oxygen through nasal cannulas from the porta-tanks strapped to their ample waists.

"I don't say anything, I wait. Just looking at all the old people sitting around, then at this cracker." By this point in the telling, Fly is actually in another dimension, reliving the entire happening as he tells it to me. *Insert time-warp fade-in here.*

"How can I help you, Officer?"

With his right hand caressing the 9mm in the fast draw holster on his belt, he swaggers up to the manager and strikes a pose. "I need you to pull your service records on—" He pauses for effect, flipping the pages in his little notebook, although he'd thoroughly rehearsed the speech and knew the details cold "—an '89 Dodge Dynasty, cream colored, owner is Jack Young."

The service manager, still trying to stave off what he's beginning to realize could be turning into a very bad day, volunteers that he remembers the car and the customer.

"Nice old guy. Not sure he should still be driving."

That was the wrong thing to say. "Did I get lost?" Fly shouts, dramatically spinning around to take in the tire-filled waiting room. He was channeling Joe Pesci in *Goodfellas*. "I thought I was at We Bee Tires, not the DMV. You gonna pull those records now, or are we just going to keep all your customers waiting?" he says, with a nod to the two cars in the service bay that are now ready to leave, but can't.

It's beginning to dawn on the manager that someone has blown the whistle on him. Following him to the counter, Fly notices a plaque on the wall from the company's regional headquarters giving the store the annual award for "Highest Incremental Revenue by Add-On Sales." Without missing a step, he snatches it off the wall as he passes by, holding it alongside his leg.

The manager starts poking through some folders in a rack on the desk, and then pulls one service order out, proclaiming as though he should be rewarded like a dog that has properly fetched a slipper, "Right here."

"Read it to me," Fly says.

"Brake reline. Turn rotors. Four Pirelli tires, mount, balance, new stems and valves. Alignment. New muffler and tailpipe. Oh. And a lube and oil change."

"What'd you charge 'im?"

"He got the top of the line Pirellis. Set of those usually goes for $600, but I slipped him a coupon to use so he only paid $549." He pauses, hoping that I picked up on the favor he'd done for the old guy. "With everything, the bill came to $855.89," choking a little as he says it. "But that includes tax," he adds with a hopeful grin. Beads of sweat have broken out on his upper lip and he wipes them away with his sleeve, leaving a grease mark like a scar across one cheek.

Fly is ready to go in for the kill. "On that form, you write down what people bring their car in for?" Now he's doing Dennis Franz. It's chilling.

"Of course."

Fly can see that the guy's hands are getting sweaty, and the grease embedded in his fingertips is beginning to rub off on the work order. Fly also notices that the manager is having a difficult time looking him in the eye. The guy keeps glancing up at the ceiling, and his blink-rate has skyrocketed. It's just like when Fly was selling. He could always tell when the customer was jerking him around; he was especially good at detecting lies. "What did Mr. Young bring his car in for?"

"He wanted us to check the air in his tires. Said the car was pulling to the left when he stepped on the brake."

"And did you check the air in his tires?"

"Me? Personally? Not me. I had Miguel do it."

"Was that before or after you scared the crap out of him? And where can we find Miguel?"

"Look, what's the problem here?"

Wrong thing to say. Again. Fly's a man on a mission. "Let's cut to the chase—what's your name?" Clearly, he was expecting to hear Bubba or Billy Bob. He was half right.

"Billy." The way the guy says it, Fly knows he's got him on the run. The attitude is significantly diminished. Does he let up? No way.

Fly pauses dramatically. "We got an eighty-five year old man who pays three hundred bucks a month for his meds so he can live a little longer and enjoy his grandchildren when they come down to visit from Indiana. His car doesn't feel right and he asks you to check the air in his tires, and you nick him for nine hundred bucks?"

"It was only eight-fifty-five."

"You just don't get it, do you?" Fly leans over the desk, bathing Billy in the residual garlic from Sophia's homemade ziti that he had for lunch. "Let me tell you what you were doing, 'cause I hate the thought that you're playing me for the fool."

Fly whips up the plastic award plaque and slaps it on the counter, causing Billy to exhibit a startle response that would do a combat vet with Post Traumatic Stress Disorder proud. "You were trying to win another one of these. Everybody up-sells. Customer comes in for your advertised 35,000-mile tires; you sell him 50,000-mile jobs. Get him to spend an extra fifty, seventy-five bucks. Doesn't hurt him and you're a hero with the district manager. But you went for the jugular when old Mr. Young came in. Did you think the way he drives his antique Dodge he really needed the Pirellis? He just wanted you to put air in the tires you sold him *last year*, tires that didn't have more than five thousand miles on them.

"What kind of bonus you get for up-selling, Billy? Or are you on straight commission? Never mind. Frankly, I don't give a crap, because what you did sickens me. How would you feel if someone did it to your daddy or grandpa?"

"Folks," Fly says, turning to the half-dozen elderly customers who had been watching and listening with more than passing interest, "if I were you, I'd take my car somewhere else. Billy here has a little problem with how he treats good retired people like you."

I realized that Fly was in a zone and could go on in painful detail for the next two hours with the story, so I tried to interrupt him. "Fly, you want more chips, or should we order? Maria's been over here three times and you never even noticed."

"Wait a second," he protested, "I'm just getting to the good part."

"Why didn't you start with the good part?" I don't wait for a response. "Just tell me what happened in the end."

"What happened? Whattaya think happened? When I showed him the paperwork that proved they'd sold the old man new tires a year-and-a-half ago, and did a brake job with a lifetime guarantee six months ago, my friend Billy crumbled like your house in the Northridge quake. He refunded the cost of the tires and the brakes. That left old Mr. Young paying for the alignment, the lube job and the muffler, which he says he thinks he really did need. It was bee-you-tee-full," he summed up, reverting to the Jersey pronunciation that turns a three-syllable word into four. He paused to take a dramatic swig from the last of the Diet Dr. Pepper six-pack he'd brought with him to Dean's—he's a good customer, so they cut him some slack on the BYO—signaling that the end was nigh. Setting the can down on the table with an air of finality he says, "People who take advantage of old folks down here make me sick."

"But Fly, old people are the only ones down here. Who else *can* they take advantage of?"

chapter 3
jinx

Seeing that Fly had come up for air, Maria rushed back to our
table, a hopeful smile on her face. She has long, jet-black
hair and deep brown eyes that glow like hot coals when she
smiles. Not even the crow's feet that hinted she might not be as
young as she appeared at first glance diminished the impact of
that smile. There are guys who come to this place just to see her
smile, present company included. Like many who work in Charlotte County's minimum wage, service-based economy, Maria
held down two jobs, one here, and another at a real estate office.
Even through the smiles you could tell she was clearly under a
lot of stress. Three kids, a husband who was home when she was
working and working when she was home, a mortgage, and not
enough money will do that to you.

We ordered quickly, with Fly's meal matching his personality—plain burger, medium, ketchup only, fries. Four pages of
menu plus lunch specials, and he never deviates. As Maria
rushed off, Fly started his usual rant about how they refuse to
serve DDP, forcing him to settle for Coke. This time, I don't
want to hear it. "Have you noticed that something unusual might
be going on?" I said, gesturing toward the TV with the Weather
Channel guy working hard to look simultaneously sincere and
borderline catastrophic.

"What? You think I'm oblivious?" responded Fly. "I checked the computer just before I came over here. Charley's south of Havana, heading north. But you know how the Hurricane Center puts out the advisories and the discussions and the probabilities? A smart politician would call it 'nuanced.' Why can't they just say, 'based on everything we know, there's a possibility you're all going to die on Friday'?"

I reached into my pocket and pulled out a sheet of paper. "Don't say I show up unprepared. Here's the line in the 11 a.m. discussion that tells the tale. Ready? 'Charley should continue to intensify and could possibly reach major hurricane strength before impacting western Cuba. After passing over Cuba, the intensity may drop slightly, but'—are you paying attention?—'but re-strengthening appears likely. There is a distinct possibility that Charley could be near major hurricane strength when it makes landfall along Florida's West Coast, especially if it makes landfall from the Tampa Bay area and southward.'

"Tampa Bay area and southward," I repeat for emphasis. "You know where we are, don't you? 'Southward' is us."

"Yeah, but there's a lot of margin for error," Fly responds, "You know that as well as I do."

"Better. It could pass fifty or sixty miles offshore on the way to Tampa. They're already evacuating parts of Pinellas County and say they're making plans to turn the power off in downtown Tampa. But you should be looking at the cone of stupidity, 'cause we could get smacked." It's really called the *cone of probability*, but we hurricane aficionados call it the *cone of stupidity*, because a day out, if you're still in the cone and you haven't left yet--well, you're bright enough see where I'm going with this.

"Fly, you've been in Florida how long?"

"AT&T moved me to Orlando from Jersey sixteen years ago. Been through three hurricanes. Nothing that serious."

"So with that reservoir of severe meteorological experience, do you look at the line in the center or the entire cone?"

"Mock me at your peril, Be-Bop. But it depends. Are you a glass half full or a glass half empty kind of guy? If you're an optimist, watch the line and if it isn't pointing at your head, you can be happy. If you're a pessimist, you gotta keep your focus on the cone. The National Hurricane Center says their margin of error five days out is 350 miles. Three days out it's down to a couple hundred miles. Twenty-four hours away and they're accurate to within ninety miles. So as Charley says adios to Fidel on a line that's climbing right up our asses, the storm could pass by ninety miles to the east or west and we'd get some wind that'll ruin fishing for a few days, or it could kill us. Either way, their prediction would have been right. Gotta love government bureaucrats."

When Fly has the facts on his side, he can be really smug. His own wife says it's not very attractive, and she's right. But he can't help it.

"So let me ask you a question," Fly says, "You spent twenty years in Los Angeles. How did you deal with the earthquakes?"

I dipped another chip into the three-alarm salsa, and then responded, "The small ones, the two-point-fives, even up to four or five, were no big deal. The Northridge quake in '94? It was somewhere between 6.8 and imminent death on the Richter Scale. One minute we're sound asleep. Next second I'm hearing the voice of God saying, "Hope all your affairs are in order."

"How long did it last?" Fly asked me. The fact that he was actually interested shocked me.

"Is that a *perception* question or are you asking if I timed it?"

"Yes."

The answer was momentarily delayed as Maria arrived with lunch. This was a switch. Usually, I was the one asking the questions, a habit from my past life as a journalist, which, despite my protestations to the contrary, I'm emotionally unable to give up. Long ago I'd observed that if you ask good questions that don't lend themselves to yes or no answers, you have plenty of time to eat. Now, the shoe was on the other foot. To really give Fly an answer, I'm looking at congealed quesadilla. Such, however, is the price of friendship.

"Officially, it lasted fifteen seconds. But when you're lying there and wondering if the ceiling is about to come down on you, or if the entire bed is going to crash through to the first floor, it feels like forever. The jokes—'Honey, did the earth move for you this time?'—don't come to mind until much, much later. That was a rough quake that scared the piss out of me. No prostate jokes, please. It was an up-and-down shaker, not one of those slow rollers that make you think your house was built on a slab of Jell-O. And it was loud. I don't know if you know it, but when they finally did GPS measurements, they found that the San Fernando Valley lifted like a dome, and the highest parts ended up twenty inches higher than before the quake."

"Wait a second, wait a second," Fly says, putting down his hamburger and dabbing at a spot of ketchup he could sense was slowly dribbling onto his chin, "You're telling me an earthquake lifted the valley and everything in it almost two feet up? C'mon."

"You ever fly over Mt. St. Helens?"

Fly paused before answering, "No, but I seen the photos. Top was blown clean off. Okay. I take your point. Mother Nature is a bitch."

I let the Jersey grammar go without commenting. "She can be. The aftershocks began almost immediately. I mean a minute after the big jolt. Laura and I are standing outside in the dark, all the neighbors are out, and the ground starts shaking again. Fly, there's nowhere to run to get away from it. Your whole world is shaking. You grab onto the car, but it's shaking too. That went on for six months at least, slowly tapering off. You could be in bed and all of a sudden, the shaking starts and you don't know whether to run or just lie there and wait 'cause it'll be over in a few seconds. No warning before it starts; no idea how long it'll last. You have any idea what that does to my gut?"

He scowled, shoving another French fry into his mouth. "Some things I don't need to know. Especially while I'm eating."

"I'm telling you now," I said, "having lived through one natural disaster, I'm not anxious to try my luck again. If that hurricane really looks like it's coming, we're outta here."

Before Fly could respond, Mr. Rolex Man has taken center stage again; only this time his victim is Maria. Grabbing her wrist and using it to twist her around as she passed by his table, he shouts into her face, spittle flying, "I said 'rare.' Can't you stupid people get anything right? Get this shoe leather out of my sight." Releasing her wrist, he shoves the colorful plate with the offending rib eye at her so hard, it flies off the edge of the table, bounces on the carpet, and scatters mixed grilled vegetables and Mexican rice over her shoes and socks. Lacey Drawers has stopped in mid-chew, and is staring wide-eyed as potential hubby number four goes nuts.

In half a second, Fly is on his feet, moving toward Maria, who has broken down in tears. He put his hands on both her shoulders, and with a Baryshnikov-like move that shocked the crap out of me, he spins her away, trading places with Maria so that he is now standing over Rolex Man. "I think it'd be best if you paid for your lunch and left. Now," he orders in a voice I didn't know he had.

Some people feel that since they've made a lot of money while bullying people in the process, it must be acceptable behavior, and they use the tactic even after they've retired. This guy fit that description perfectly. Rising to his feet, which gave him a good 10-inch height advantage over Fly, he snarled, "You and what army is going to make me?" For a second, I had to wonder if the guy had had too much to drink, but there was nothing but a pitcher of iced tea on his table.

Fly didn't hesitate. With his left hand, he reached into his back pocket and came out with a leather case, flipped it open to reveal a badge. Simultaneously, with his right hand he took what at first glance appeared to be a black mini-Maglite flashlight from his belt. But with a flick of the wrist, he was suddenly—and surprisingly—armed with a sixteen-inch long tactical steel baton and giving every impression that he knows how to use it.

"You assaulted this woman when you put your hands on her. I'm only going to say it one more time. Please pay for your lunch and leave quietly. I want you out of here in the next sixty seconds."

Terrified that someone was going to get hurt and she'd be blamed, Maria was already picking up the plate and food, protesting that everything was all right. Fly looked down at her momentarily and said, "Everything's going to be just fine, Maria.

Just step aside so this gentleman can leave." I think I also saw Fly checking out Lacey's rack, but I couldn't swear to it.

I was shocked when Rolex Man dropped two twenties on the table, motioned to Lacey to follow him, and the pair made their way out the door. Now I had a fresh worry: The incident might leave me with a newfound respect for my friend. Hell, respect could really screw up a relationship built on mutual ball busting.

Returning to our booth, Fly tucked the badge back in his pocket, and then bent over and used the floor to compress the baton before putting it back on his belt.

"What the hell was that?" I asked, pointing to the weapon.

"Hey, I went through the police academy. You think the only thing they teach us is how to harass teenagers trying to get laid at Gilchrist Park?"

"I had no idea."

"And you thought I was just another pretty face." Nodding at the door through which the loudmouth had exited, Fly said, "I think I know who that guy is."

"You know him?"

"No, I don't *know* him. But the *Sun* did a story on him with a bunch of photos. Rich retired guy; paper said he made his money renting subsidized apartments to poor people up north. Probably means he was a slumlord. He owns a big cruiser he keeps at the yacht club and has some high-priced art in his condo on the harbor. The article didn't mention that he was an asshole."

"Must've been an oversight. Write a letter to the editor. Use bad grammar and don't bother to spell-check it. They'll print it. They print anything, and they're proud to do it."

Fly ignored me and picked up our conversation as though nothing had happened. "You were saying that if Charley comes this way, you and Laura are going to evacuate."

I was about to answer, but out of the corner of my eye I saw a couple I recognized making a bee-line right for our booth. "Fly," I said sotto-voce, "someone's heading our way. They look familiar, but..." He looked up quickly, and mumbled that he can't remember their names either just as they reached us.

"You were wonderful," the woman gushed to Fly. Then she turned to me for verification. "Wasn't he wonderful?"

"He was," I respond reluctantly. "It's still taking him two bounds to leap tall buildings, but he'll improve."

She looked at me quizzically as though the Superman reference was obscure, and then turned back to Fly. "We don't need rude, nasty people like that in our community. Tell Sophia and Laura I said hello, and that you were wonderful."

As she moved on, her husband followed, mimicking his wife in falsetto loud enough for both of us to hear. "My freakin' hero. You were wonderful."

As they moved to the door, I looked at Fly. "What's his problem? And who the hell are they?"

He nodded. "Jerry and Lucie Renfroe. Sophia's on half a dozen church committees with her. You met them at a dine-around dinner at our house. He's a retired attorney, an obnoxious prick who thinks he's fooling everyone with that red dye job. Screw him. Now where were we? Oh, yeah. I had asked if you and Laura are planning to evacuate if it looks like the storm is coming this way?"

"Absolutely. We both remember way too much about going through the earthquake in LA." Putting down my fork, I took another swig of iced tea, and got that intense look on my face that Fly has learned to recognize as a tip-off that what comes next will be serious. "Fly, we've never been through a serious hurricane warning cycle. When Charley got upgraded to a hurricane, it was way out in the Atlantic and no one here paid it much attention. Now it has sustained winds up to 85 MPH, predicted to get stronger, and we're in the cone of stupidity. We're not staying. And neither should you, no matter how bad you want to play Deputy Moscone.

chapter 4
jinx

At seven the next morning, my phone rang. I didn't need caller ID to know it was Fly. I grabbed the cordless phone on the dresser. Out of juice. What I'd heard was the phone in the kitchen. Mumbling words that would get my granddaughter's mouth washed out with soap, I quick-walked toward the kitchen, picking it up just before the call shunted to voicemail.

"You rang?" I asked.

"You awake?" Fly responded.

"Do you care?"

"Why'd it take you so long to answer?

"Battery was dead; had to grab it in the kitchen. What's going on?" I said, rubbing the morning gunk out of my eyes.

"What's going on is that it's bee-you-tee-full outside." Looking out the window onto the canal, I could see that the sky was bright and true blue, just the way a little child would draw it if she had the really big box of Crayolas. And the water in the canal was so mirror flat I could use it to shave. The perfection of this morning was nothing less than diabolical, perhaps God's way of sandbagging us. Were it not for weather satellites, we'd be scoffing at any notion that a hurricane was little more than a day away. I couldn't help but imagine how people centuries earlier would have been blithely ignorant of what was coming at them from the south until it was too late.

"You're sure there's a hurricane coming?" I queried.

"Sure? I'm too smart to be sure," Fly answered. "The last time I was sure of anything I was sixteen, and was sure I'd wake up with a hard-on that could pound nails into a concrete block. I have a question," Fly said abruptly. "Why do you hang with me?"

"I don't know. I like your company?" I was still not awake enough to engage in serious repartee and introspection.

"Then I have no respect for you. You're a loser!" Without waiting for a comeback, he continued, "Have you seen the latest forecast? Of course you haven't. What time can you get over here? I need your help with the boat."

"The forecast get worse?"

"Actually, no. But we're still in the cone and who knows what might happen, so get your ass over here."

Half an hour later, I walked around the back of his house in the super-fashionable bird section of Punta Gorda Isles. Every street was a bird's name. Towhee. Whippoorwill. Osprey. To live here they make you join the Audubon Society. He and Sophia live on Blue Heron Lane.

When I arrived Fly was on the fly bridge of *Inamorata*, his forty-two foot Viking convertible cruiser. He'd already removed the depth finder, plotter, GPS and VHF radio and was starting on the curtains. He stopped me before I could even set foot on the boat.

"Hey, you *stunad*, you didn't really think I'd let you touch the zippers on these curtains, did you?" The boat had isinglass curtains enclosing the upper deck. They had to be unzipped carefully and precisely folded.

"Aye aye, captain. I'll just wait down here till you need me."

"When I hand these curtains to you, take them below and lay them on the bunk in the forward cabin." He turned back to get the next curtain, but decided that perhaps he should soften his approach, so he yelled "Please" over his shoulder. I took it as a sign of weakness and climbed aboard.

Let's talk about the boat for a second. It's crucial to understanding him. It's not that he isn't in love with Sophia, but for a guy who just hit sixty, there's something incredibly seductive about a boat. That explains her name. *Inamorata.* Maybe it's one of those things that are impossible to explain. Some guys here have a thing for golf and thousand dollar titanium drivers. Fly loves boats. As a kid, he used to ride his bike down to the Port of Newark just to watch the ships. And he enlisted in the navy to cruise the high seas, but ended up as part of the brown water fleet in Nam.

I don't get it, but he loves the boat and doesn't mind all the high maintenance she takes. Sophia says she wishes he were as anal about keeping the house clean as he is about *Inamorata.* I still give him crap about his announcement one day that "if you judge a man by the cleanliness of his bilge, I am a great person." At the time, he was on his knees in the engine compartment, spit-shining the steering hydraulics.

We spent the next half hour taking the canvas down. Then at least another hour arguing over the best way to secure the boat in a storm. He finally opted to triple up all the lines and tie her to the dock and the offshore pilings he'd had installed just for this eventuality. But even with rubber fenders, odds are that high winds or a storm surge could still knock her into the dock.

It was only when we were fully involved in tripling the lines that he acknowledged the potential futility of what we were doing. "It's a joke, really. We could get 140, 150 mile an hour winds that will be turning roof tiles and coconuts into missiles. A couple of direct hits, and she could go down. We could tie her to the dock with chain that would hold the *Queen Mary 2*, and if just one of my neighbors' boats breaks loose and hits her, she could go down. If my lines break, or the cleats rip out, or the pilings she's tied to pull out of the bottom, she could slam into the canal wall and go down."

"Fly," I responded, "You realize that in two years in PGI, I haven't heard the words 'she' and 'go down' in the same sentence as much as I heard them in the last thirty seconds?"

"That may be true, but it don't change the facts," he said, "And I didn't even mention that a moderate storm surge—say fourteen or fifteen feet at high tide—could put her on the lawn or into the living room." As soon as we finished, Fly said, "We need to see what the 11 o'clock says," and he headed toward the guest room.

After checking the computer and getting the report from WINK-TV, Fly said, "The consensus looks like maybe thirty-five, forty miles offshore as it passes the mouth of the harbor. We're another twenty miles inland from the Gulf, so that gives us maybe sixty miles of cushion."

"They saying how big the storm is going to be?" I asked.

"Not yet. But I've been watching hurricanes since I moved to Florida from Jersey, and even in small ones the hurricane force winds extend out at least sixty or seventy miles from the eye."

"So what do we do?" I asked.

"We wait and see what they say at five o'clock," said Fly.

"And if they say it's coming here?" I said, trying to hide the anxiety that I felt building.

"Geez. You're a real pain in the ass. You should've stayed in California. You're definitely not doing well with the stress. You know, they say agita can shorten your life.

"Thank you Dr. Phil. You still haven't answered the question."

"If the storm comes off the Gulf north of us, we're on the bad side. Elevation of most houses here is nine to thirteen feet above sea level."

"Fly, come clean. You're planning on staying, aren't you?"

"What makes you say that?"

"Because you've been avoiding the whole subject of getting the hell out of here. And when we first met you, you gave me this big lecture about not waiting till the last minute to make a decision to leave if a hurricane is coming."

Fly just sat there, quietly listening to me, a reaction so out of character that it unnerved me. So I asked him again, "What's going through your head?"

"I'm going to stay," he said quietly. "I joined the cops because I wanted to do something useful. It's what I need to do. People are going to need help. And you know what really intrigues me?"

"I'm afraid to ask."

"Insurance fraud. Nice, law-abiding, God-fearing *giamokes* who wouldn't steal a Snickers bar won't think anything of trying to rip off their insurance companies for thousands, hell, tens of thousands. Guaranteed to happen. The opportunity to lock up some of these self-righteous bastards is too good to pass up. When the fraud investigators come in, it'll help to have a local liaison. I already talked with the sheriff."

"And you've discussed this with Sophia?"

"Not exactly."

"What's that mean?"

"It means not exactly. She was okay with me doing the police thing, going through the academy. She wasn't happy seeing me with a gun on my hip, but she understood. Or at least I think she understood."

"Understood what? That you need to be a hero?"

"Jinx, that's not it."

"Of course it is."

"No, you're wrong. You know what I did for most of my adult life? I helped a giant corporation make money for its stockholders."

"And your point is what?"

"It's not that it's dishonorable. I supported my family. Gave them nice things. It's just that in the big picture, it don't mean squat. I mean—what did I do to make things better? What did I really contribute? What kind of a difference did I make in the world? I think that's why I wanted to be a cop when I was a kid. I had this need to do something important, something good. I really wanted to put bad guys in jail. And now, who knows how many years I have left. I don't want to die with regrets. I might have an opportunity in the next few days to fix something that's been wrong with my life for years."

"But Fly, it's a hurricane. Let's be real. People *are* going to die."

"I don't think it's my time yet."

"Sophia's going to buy that? And what about your son?"

"Rob knows. When we brought the boat down from up north, it gave us a lot of time to talk about things that matter. I've never discussed it with Sophia, but we've been married thirty-two years. You don't think she's got me figured out by now? But I need a favor from you. A big favor."

"What?"

"If you and Laura evacuate, I want you to take Sophia and the mutt with you. Will you do it?"

"You're asking me to enable your craziness. If I say no, you have to take your wife and dog away from here yourself."

"But you won't say no."

"How do you know that?"

"Because you're just like me. That's why we get along. You already did your thing to change the world, Mr. Investigative Reporter-Slash-Columnist-Slash-Producer. I was a friggin' computer salesman. You've got to help me here. When I go, I don't want any regrets."

He dug around in the desk drawer and pulled out a small, worn, leather bound volume. "You ever read *Little Foxes* by Harriet Beecher Stowe?" Without waiting for an answer, he opened the book to the page marked by a burgundy colored ribbon, and read, "The bitterest tears shed over graves are for words left unsaid and deeds left undone." He closed the book.

"Jinx, this might be my one last chance to do something important. Please help me do it."

chapter 5
jinx

It was during the 11 p.m. local news that Fly called. "I'm about to save your life," he whispered into the phone.

"Why are you whispering?" I asked, since he was speaking in a very un-Fly like mode.

"Because I don't want Soph to hear me. The Hurricane Center just rerouted Charley. Instead of Tampa, they got him goin' to Sarasota—or south. You need to get going. I'll be over with Sophia and the mutt in about an hour. Pack the car. And no drama about me staying here. Got it?" He hung up before I could respond.

The moon cut through broken clouds, and it was getting a little squally as we all stood in front of my house just before one. Fly's mutt and Alfie the Aussie had gotten reacquainted, and were now settling onto some blankets Laura had put down on the floor of the mini-van. The rear of the van held a couple of suitcases, our plastic getaway box of important papers, and the antique metal table from the 1893 Columbian Exposition in Chicago that had once belonged to Laura's grandmother. I'd also taken my desktop computer and most of my camera equipment.

We were all in full stall mode. Laura was afraid she'd never see her house again. Sophia was trying hard not to cry as she pleaded with Fly to evacuate with us. He gave me the high sign, and I told the women it was time to get in the car. Laura took the passenger's seat, and Sophia got in back. Fly leaned in for a quick kiss, then handed her a small, gift-wrapped box containing a bauble he'd picked up earlier in the day at Westchester Gold and made her promise not to open the box till they'd gotten across the state to our cousins' condo in Weston, just east of Alligator Alley. Marvin and Bernyce Zimmerman were snowbirds from Chicago and they'd given us a key just for a mid-summer eventuality like this one.

After extracting some last second promises from Fly not to do anything dangerous, I put the van in gear and we drove off.

I stood up and tapped Fly on his shoulder. "Captain, you want to keep driving the boat, or you want to tell your passengers what happened during the hurricane? I wasn't there, so it's only fair."

Without throttling back, Fly rose, poked a finger into my chest, and said, "Jinx, you can drive. But be careful. I could get so wrapped up in the story that I might forget I've turned the helm over to a *stunad.*"

That's when Rich Aronson piped up. "I didn't want to interrupt, but I've got a couple of questions."

"Just a couple?" Fly said. "By now I would have thought you'd have a legal-pad full, counselor. You didn't really buy that whole no-regrets-life-fulfillment run that he shoveled? Tell me you didn't."

"Actually, I thought it was pretty good. I've used the same sort of bullshit on a jury."

"Did you win the case?" Fly asked.

"No, but it sounded good," Aronson said, dead pan. "I want to hear your version of things. Go ahead. My questions can wait."

I had slipped into the captain's seat, checked the course we were on, and said, "I've got the con. Anyone need to use the head?" I paused briefly, looked around. "Nobody. Then on with the tale."

Fly popped open a fresh DDP, and picked up the story.

fly

As soon as Jinx drove off, I went back home and took a look at the weather radar online. They were going to be passing right through the early bands of thunderstorms down near Naples, and they might be in the thick of it halfway across the state. But contrary to local common wisdom that you always run north from a hurricane, with Charley, it seemed that getting to the east coast was the safest bet, even if getting there wasn't going to be half the fun.

I tried to get a few hours sleep, but it wasn't working. So I put on the forest green deputy's uniform, packed three days worth of underwear, socks and a couple of cases of DDP into the back of our SUV, and with one final over-the-shoulder Bogey-like glance at *Inamorata*, headed to the sheriff's office near the Charlotte County Airport.

Shortly after checking in I found myself accompanying the department's community service officer on a mission to motivate the trailer park residents who were defying a mandatory evacuation order.

Deputy First Class Maggie MacNeil is an eighteen year department veteran. She looks and sounds like my grandmother would have if she'd been born in Glasgow instead of Napoli. Maggie managed a chuckle when I suggested that *diehard* might be both a description of attitude and physical condition of the folks we were about to see. "Try being gentle," she said to me as we rolled to a stop in front of acres of soon-to-be aluminum scrap. I didn't respond. Just sat there, staring at the residents of the Windmill Village Trailer Park. "What's wrong?" she asked me.

"I see dead people," waiting a beat for her reaction. She didn't bite.

"Just follow my lead," Maggie replied, shaking her head at my irreverence as she exited the car and headed for the nearest trailer. We went door to door, and when we found residents who said they had no plans to leave, she explained what a hurricane's wind and surge could do to a house trailer.

The usual response was that since no one was saying that the hurricane was definitely going to hit Punta Gorda, there was no reason for them to leave. Maggie was patient, but it made me crazy. I didn't have time for the good cop-bad cop waiting game. My law enforcement paradigm was the Newark of my youth, where bad cop-worse cop was the way they dealt with neighborhood kids. Or maybe it's just that I don't do subtle very well. I told Maggie that at the next trailer, I wanted to take the lead. In a moment of weakness she agreed.

I knocked on the door, and when the octogenarian resident responded, I began talking. "There's a hurricane coming and you need to evacuate. You got a car?" I didn't wait for an answer. "Get in it now; haul yourself over to the Interstate, get up to 75 miles an hour. Got it? Now roll down the window and I want you to stick your arm all the way out and hold it there. That's a weak Category 1 hurricane. Right now Charley is a Category 2, and he's predicted to hit Category 3. You know how fast the wind is in a three? I'll tell you. Try 112 miles an hour. You think that thing"—I jerked my head toward what was obviously a mobile home that had been rolled into the park when Jimmy Carter was shelling peanuts in the Oval Office—"will still be there after the storm?" I got nowhere.

Maggie tried once again, with the subtle approach. "Darlin', the county supervisors are the ones who signed off on the evacuation order for every trailer and RV park in the county. They're trying to save your life." But it was apparent that logic, even in the face of potential sudden but unseen death, wasn't going to get these oldsters to abandon their homes and everything in them. So she threw in the towel and nodded to me. I whipped out the Next of Kin Information Card, handed it to the trailer park resident with a pen, and ask him to fill it out. The usual reaction was, "Why should I?"

"So when your kids call and ask us why we didn't make you evacuate, we can show them that we tried, and you were too stubborn to leave." I'd say it without any hint of compassion.

After he signed, I'd give them my best Columbo imitation. "Just one more thing." Then I'd bring out the inkpad and tell them I needed to take their thumbprint.

"Why do you want to do that?" they'd ask.

"So it'll be easier to identify what's left of your body after the storm."

In all but the most extreme cases, we would usually see a light bulb go off over the individual's head, as they seemed to suddenly get it. This isn't a game. This isn't about the cops being in control. This is really about life and death—and it's one of those rare instances where the individual might actually have a say on which side of the ledger his name ultimately appears.

Of course me being me, I had one, final, over-the-shoulder line to toss at a resident we weren't sure would really pack up and go. "You know, you're lucky we're not in Clearwater or St. Pete."

"Why is that?"

"Because if you were up there, I'd be handing you a toe tag and a grease pencil, telling you to fill it out and tie it on your foot just before the storm hits. Some jurisdictions have you write your social security number on your arm with a Sharpie. Have a nice day." I'd picked up that piece of information at lunch one day with Wayne Salladé, Charlotte County's Director of Emergency Management, who said that when the firemen handed out the toe tags it usually did the trick. They'd always end up with a convoy of evacuees following behind their truck.

Having failed miserably at convincing more than a handful of folks that a forty year hurricane drought might be ending soon, we returned to headquarters. Plans had been in the works for half a dozen years to build a new all-in-one emergency operations center, county fire headquarters, and 911 call center, but, like plans for world peace, there'd been a few delays. That's why, with a hurricane approaching, we found ourselves inside a structure whose ability to stop a runaway tricycle was questionable.

I spent some time listening into the incoming 911 calls— people finally getting the hint that something bad was coming and wanting to know what they should do. If the callers lived in the areas under a mandatory evacuation order, they were told to leave. Beyond that, the operators could only say that once the winds hit 45 MPH, no deputies or EMS people would be able to help them.

"But does that mean I have to leave?" the callers would ask. I couldn't take any more stupidity, so I grabbed some homemade ziti that one of the women had brought in and wandered into Salladé's office.

"What's going on?" I asked. Apparently, the question wasn't precise enough for him.

"You're kidding, right?"

"I mean with everyone getting ready to bail."

"It's time to pull the plug."

Salladé had ordered everyone to relocate to the county jail, about a mile away. In a rare exercise of governmental foresight, he and the sheriff had built a backup emergency center into the jail's infrastructure. All the first-in team had to do was remove the ceiling panels in a central corridor locked off from the prisoners, and lower phones and computer cables stored up there. They'd tested the system, and knew it could be operational in under an hour.

The various departments represented in the EOC—emergency support functions such as public works, utilities, human services, fire, law, animal rescue and animal control, and PIO—had sent a staffer or two over to the jail as soon as it became apparent that Punta Gorda was riding the center rail inside the cone. Now, everyone was moving to the jail, including the 911 operators I'd just left.

"They give you an assignment?" Salladé asked, not looking up from the weather radar on his desktop computer.

"Nothing in particular. Just make myself useful. And try not to shoot anyone."

"Or yourself," he responded, a smirk on his face.

"You want the pleasure of my company?"

"Why not? I want to keep an eye on the radar for as long as I can. Then we'll head for the jail."

It sounded like a reasonable idea. Besides, I'd be able to tell Sophia that I opted to stay with the guy who had his finger on the pulse of the storm. If the boss wasn't going to be safe, who was?

Of course I hadn't taken into consideration the possibility that after seventeen years contemplating the storm that could destroy his county, he now had an overwhelming need to experience it firsthand.

Two hours later, with the building being dismantled around us, I tapped Wayne on the shoulder to draw his attention from the radar screen. The noise of the storm and the creaking of the building were so loud that calling his name was futile. "Don't you think now would be a good time to exit stage left?" I asked.

"I think a couple hours ago would have been a good time. But we better give it a shot."

An hour earlier, I'd stuck my head outside to see what was going on. The promised tropical storm force winds had already arrived and rain was falling sideways. Palm trees were leaning, loose debris was blowing around, and dozens of small aircraft at the adjacent county airport were fighting their tie-downs in an attempt to become a squadron of pilotless kamikazes. Only the ancient DC-3 parked near one of the corrugated steel hangars seemed capable of handling the winds.

"I think it's time we go for a ride," Salladé shouted. At least that's what I think he said, because just then another piece of the roof peeled away with the most ear-piercing sound you can imagine.

Just opening the glass door from the sheriff's office to the parking lot was a struggle. The second we stepped outside, we were both soaked to the skin. As we fought our way to Wayne's two-and-a-half ton, four-wheel drive behemoth, it never dawned on me that a Ford Expedition would have difficulty moving forward in a seventy-mile-an-hour headwind. But from the moment Salladé turned the car south on Golf Course Boulevard, it was apparent we were going to have a problem.

"Wayne, you might want to give it more gas," I shouted over the roar of the wind and the sound of rain pounding the car. Wayne is Charlotte County's Emergency Management Director. I thought he would have had this all figured out.

His response wasn't comforting. "I got it floored and we're going nowhere." As he said it, something slammed into the windshield on my side, caromed off the glass, and blew past us, leaving a spider-web pattern and cracks in front of me. We both cringed at the impact. I reached out and put my hand flat on the center of the web.

"It'll hold. How much farther we got to go?"

"Farther isn't the problem. We've got two choices, both bad. When we get to the stop sign, we either go right and drive a mile to the jail, or turn left and head for the airport terminal. Either way, we end up broadside to the wind."

"You think you can keep us on the road?"

"I'm going to try."

"Try is not what I want to hear from you. Try is what I ask my grandkid to do when I put her on the potty."

"Look, the airport is closer, but the jail is probably going to do better in the storm. Besides, all my people are there and they've got generators. What do you think?"

"They're paying you the big bucks to be the manager. So manage."

"Then hang on. Things are about to get interesting."

Out of force of habit, Salladé signaled for a right turn, which caused me to snort. It would prove to be my last laugh for nearly an hour. The wind caught us broadside as we came around the corner and the 5,000 pound SUV leaned so far over to the right that the two left tires were way off the pavement. If he hadn't been strapped in tight, Wayne would have ended up in my lap. For an eternity, it felt like we were going to be tossed on our side. Not that big a deal inside this beast, until I saw that we were sliding toward the swale which was now a fast-flowing creek maybe five feet deep. Drowning was now a distinct possibility.

"*Bafongool!* Do something, Wayne," I yelled, over the roar of the wind.

He didn't answer; just kept wrestling the wheel. The look on his face scared me—'cause I can tell he's as terrified as I am. For a second the wind slacked off, and the Expedition bounced back onto all four tires. And then it felt like afterburners kicked in. He still had it floored and we shot ahead till another blast of wind hit us. It was like we slammed into a brick wall. Once again, we were barely inching along, occasionally getting pushed toward the shoulder and the swale, but somehow, he managed to keep us on the pavement.

After what seemed like enough time to watch the Godfather Trilogy with commercials, he threw the wheel to the left and we shimmied into the road that would lead to the county jail parking lot.

Thinking the adventure was over, I took a chance and started to exhale. Big mistake. Another missile crashed into the windshield, this time creating a spider web on the driver's side. If I hadn't been strapped in, my Vietnam legacy startle response would have had me hitting the floor. Between the cracked glass and blinding rain, the only parking technique that would work was one taught by the Braille Institute. We slammed into the concrete barriers strategically placed around the jail.

"We're here," my chauffeur announced. He then laid on the horn for several seconds, hoping the people inside would respond by opening the lobby door. The thought of standing there, pounding on the locked door while getting blasted by wind, rain and seashell fragments from the unpaved parking lot was not comforting. But getting the jail door open was not our immediate problem. It hadn't dawned on either of us that just getting out of the car was going to be a test of strength. The Expedition's large front doors were like sails and the wind slammed them shut every time we tried to crack them open.

Finally, I came up with a plan to get us out of the car. I put my shoulder against the inside of the door and muscled it open, and then I turned sideways and jammed my legs down to the ground. For a second it seemed as though the wind was going to win the battle and scissor them off at the knees. But I was able to get both feet on the ground, turn and plant my butt against the door and push against the car body with my hands. I shouted "Okay, go," and Wayne slid passed me. He dropped to the ground, grabbed the outside handle and pulled for all he was worth, giving me a chance to sidestep to the left.

"I'm clear!" I screamed. Salladé released the handle and the door blew shut with explosive force. We both turned to make a run for the building. With my first step, I ended up in a heap on the ground. "*Mannaggia!*" I yelled.

Salladé reached down to haul me up.

"I can't see!" I shouted into the wind. My glasses were dripping wet.

Wayne grabbed my arm and dragged me up the curb, over the grass, and to the door, where arms reached out and pulled the two of us up into the building.

"Having fun yet?" asked one of the deputies.

"I need a Diet Dr. Pepper," I croaked. The deputy didn't notice that I was shaking.

chapter 6
fly

At 4 p.m. on Friday the thirteenth of August, someone shoved a towel into my hands as I stumbled into the jail. I was soaked to the bone and even though I'd managed not to lose my glasses in the battle to get from the car to the door, going from 95 degree heat to 78 degree air conditioning, they'd become completely fogged over and useless. I took more time than necessary to wipe them off. It kept me from having to engage in conversation before I'd recovered. Wayne and I could have easily died. For a couple of minutes I had flashbacks to the moment we turned broadside to the wind and two wheels lifted completely off the pavement. What stuck in my head was the noise. It was so loud I didn't realize that one of the deputies was talking to me until he punched me in the shoulder.

"Fly, you wanna get out of those wet clothes?"

He was right in my face so without my glasses on I could see him clearly, but I really had to focus on what he was saying in order to drive the sound of the storm out of my head. All I could muster was, "Huh?"

He tried again. "You want a dry shirt? I've got one that should fit you."

For the first time in recent memory, I didn't respond with a self-deprecating or agate-busting wisecrack. There was nothing amusing about what Salladé and I had just been through, and the realization that this was just the beginning, and that the people I had made fun of that morning could be dead within hours, was sobering.

I managed to wipe the glasses clear and put them back on, and hoping that my voice wouldn't break said, "No thanks. This'll dry soon enough."

I followed my rescuers up to the second floor corridor where everything had been set up, and then just leaned against a wall, trying to stay out of the way while catching my breath. I'd come to rest near the bank of 911 operators who were now fielding calls from people having second thoughts about riding out the storm at home.

With nothing better to do, and beginning to feel somewhat smug because I'd sent my wife out of harm's way and I was now safe in the bosom of seven hundred or so accused or convicted thugs, druggies, robbers, rapists and murderers, I picked up an extra headset and listened in. The calls fell into two distinct categories: those reporting injuries, and those asking to be rescued. It didn't matter; they were all S.O.L.

"Nine-one-one emergency. This call is being recorded. What's the nature of your emergency?"

"We're scared. Can someone come get us? We need to go to a shelter."

"I'm sorry, ma'am, once the wind hit forty-five miles an hour, all the deputies' cars were taken off the street. There's no one who can come get you now."

Some callers just resigned themselves to their fate and hung up. Others asked what they should do and were told to drag a mattress into a closet or room without windows, get under it to protect themselves from flying glass or debris, and wait out the storm. Still others chose to argue.

"You need to send someone to get me now. I pay my taxes. I know my rights."

The operators—who'd all left families at home in order to work through the hurricane—managed not to respond. They had more self control than I would have had. When one of the women took off her headset and stood up to take a break, I told her as much.

"I really admire you. I couldn't do your job. I would've told them that they should have paid attention last night when they could have taken care of their families by getting them the hell out. How stupid are these *giamokes*? They want us to come get 'em now? Are they nuts?"

Clearly, I was getting over my recent brush with a wind-driven death and was returning to form. As you've noticed, empathy is not high on my inventory of core values. The operator looked at me with disdain, "No, they're just scared shitless with nowhere to run."

"And whose fault is that?" I countered.

"You're right," she said, smiling at me, "you couldn't do my job."

"Well, I could—but I shouldn't," I countered, trying to save face.

About half an hour later, Hurricane Charley struck with full force. The jail building was relatively new, built to the latest codes, and understandably, designed to withstand attack by man or nature in much the same way as an old English castle could. All that was missing was the moat. Nevertheless, the sound of debris striking the walls—and occasionally the shatterproof windows—was unnerving. No matter how hard I tried to bring my startle response under control, I still twitched with every impact.

The same 911 operator I'd been kidding with earlier now had tears running down her face as she listened to the callers. I decided to listen in again, joining the call in mid-scream.

"You've got to get us out of here!" By itself, that sentence is pretty benign. But give it a line reading like it's from a horror film, and the guy with the big knives is almost on top of the damsel in distress. Imagine someone screaming it so hard that it peels vocal cords like a banana. Now you've got it.

"We're all going to die," shouted a woman whose voice kept getting drowned out by the sound of what I figured was her house being ripped apart by Charley.

The operator did her best to sound reassuring, but her husband was at home with their three kids, and she could only imagine their own house was getting torn apart around them just like the one belonging to the woman on the phone. "Do you have your family all together?"

"Yes, yes, we're in a closet, but the roof is gone and the ceiling is breaking apart. Can't you send someone for us? Please!"

How does one mother tell another that there's nothing you can do to help save her or her family.

"Ma'am, we've got your address. As soon as the storm passes, we'll send deputies to help you. Until then, stay where you are, okay?"

There was no response. Just more of the sound of the woman's house being torn apart. The 911 operator looked at me, tears in her eyes, and broke the connection. She put her head down on the table, closed her eyes, and I could see her lips moving in prayer. I put my hand on her shoulder, and said, "That's all you can do. For all of them."

It was one of those moments where I find it easy to believe that prayer helps. When I was first diagnosed with prostate cancer, I know it helped Sophia to pray for me, and it helped me knowing she was praying. And I even believe it helped me to pray. I'm not saying I'm a religious man, but I believe in an afterlife. We put up with too much in this world for it not to be better in the next one. Jinx doesn't believe in it. When we got nothing better to argue about, we beat that one to death.

I moved down the line of 911 operators and plugged in again. This time it was a man's voice. "We need help. My son's bleeding and I can't get it to stop." He was working hard to control his emotions, but he was still on the edge.

"Where is your son now?" asked the operator.

"I dragged him back in the closet with us. He was trying to keep our front door from blowing in, but something hit the glass and it exploded. There's blood pouring out of one arm. Can you send an ambulance?

"I'm sorry, sir. All emergency vehicles have been pulled off the road till the storm passes. Are you applying pressure to the cut—or have you tried a tourniquet?

"My wife is pressing on it with a towel, but it's still bleeding."

"Is there a belt in the closet you can use? You need to try and wrap it around his arm above the cut, and keep tightening it until the bleeding stops—or at least slows down."

"But won't that kill his arm if I cut all the blood flow to it?"

"Sir, let's worry about making sure your son doesn't bleed to death. Get a tourniquet on that arm now. In fifteen minutes, loosen it a bit and see if the bleeding has stopped."

"But can't you send an ambulance?"

"I've put your address on the list. As soon as the storm passes, we'll get help to you as quickly as possible."

That's the way it went for the next fifteen or twenty hours. Well, it only seemed that long. The good news about Charley—the only good news—is that he was small, tightly wrapped, and moving very fast. Kind of like me when I ran track in high school, or got chased through Newark by the cops. The highest winds were over us for no more than an hour, with a twenty minute break halfway through as the tiny eye passed by. I stepped outside during the eye of the storm. The sky directly above was a beautiful robin's egg blue, but it was as though we were at the bottom of a barrel looking up. All around us was a wall of dark ugly cloud.

"It's only half over, the sheriff said, looking at me. "Where's your wife?"

"On the East Coast. She's probably going nuts right now."

Just then we got hit with a fresh gust. "Coming from the other direction," the sheriff said, "we'd better get back inside."

The next hour was hell revisited. Even at the height of the storm, the 911 phones continued to ring, and people continued to scream in agony—some physical, all of it emotional.

We'd learn later on that winds at the airport were clocked as high as 175 MPH, which means that for a few minutes Charley had hit Category 5 status. The best hurricane construction codes in the state, in Miami-Dade County, were designed to keep buildings intact in winds up to 140 MPH—the low end of a Category 4 storm. There were maybe a hundred buildings in all of Charlotte County built to Miami-Dade code. My house wasn't one of them.

With all the distractions it hadn't dawned on me that since the phones were still working, I could call Sophia. Because I had no idea what shape she was in, I figured I'd try Jinx's cell phone first. He answered on the first ring.

"You're still alive?"

"It's not over yet, you *gavone*," I said, probably sounding a bit harsh, but considering that a cat four-plus hurricane was raging outside the building, harsh is appropriate. "The eye just went by. We should be out of it in less than an hour. Thank God it's moving fast."

"Seriously," said Jinx, "you're okay?"

"I'm at the jail. Salladé and I had a few interesting moments on the ride over here from the EOC, but aside from getting soaked, I'm fine." I really wasn't interested in going into the details right now, so I changed the subject. "How was the trip?"

"There were a couple of rough spots, but we made it?"

"What's a rough spot?"

"It's when you're doing seventy southbound and forty westbound at the same time. There were wind gusts that nearly blew us off the road. It was ugly."

"How were the women?"

"Sophia never said a word. And Laura was Laura. She's got advisory driving down to a science. 'Slow down. Be careful. What's that car doing? Why are you in this lane? Are you going too fast? Can you see? Won't the wipers go faster?' You want me to continue or have you got the picture?"

"Got it? I've lived it. What else?"

"I'm done with local radio. Soon as I can, I'm getting satellite radio."

"Where'd that come from?"

"You'd think that our so-called radio news source for southwest Florida would have kept a light on with a hurricane coming, just to let us know what we might be driving into. Thirty thousand people in Charlotte County are ordered to evacuate. We could use a little guidance. But no. Instead, they stuck with classical music. Perlman fiddled while Charley churned. Radio down here is a half-vast wasteland. The closest we got to news was audio being simulcast from a Fort Myers TV station. Do you have any idea how annoying it is to hear some newbie kid reporter at the beach telling us that nothing was happening while we're getting blown off the highway?"

"Yeah, but you must have got the weather forecasts."

"Sure we did. Try listening on radio to a TV weatherman say that those 'bands of heavy rain spawning tornadoes are here, here and here.' Television news without pictures does not equal radio news."

"We can discuss this when you come back—if I live that long. Meantime, can I please talk to my wife?—and don't tell her I said that!"

I heard Jinx calling for Sophia. A few seconds later, he handed her his cell phone.

"Honey, are you okay?" After thirty-some years of marriage, I can tell when Sophia is stressed out. She was off the chart.

"Yes, honey, I'm fine. I'm at the jail with Wayne and the sheriff and a few dozen deputies and seven hundred of Charlotte County's finest citizens. This building isn't going anywhere."

"And what about storm surge? You're not going to get flooded?"

"The word we have is that instead of flooding, Charley is actually sucking the water out of the harbor to the Gulf. I'm not going to drown. I promise."

"You're sure?"

See, that's the trouble with women. They can ignore the fact that you're in a completely uncontrollable situation, and they want guarantees. Maybe it's our fault. Men spend years convincing them that we can handle anything, and when the shit hits the fan, we discover that they believed us.

"Yes, Sophia, I'm sure. I wanted to call you while the phones were still working, and tell you that I'm okay. As soon as the storm passes, I'm going to check out our house. If the phones work, I'll call and let you know how things are. Meantime, go rent *An Affair to Remember*. The old one. That'll keep you and Laura busy and out of Jinx's hair."

"Honey, thank you for the cameo. It's beautiful. I love you."

"I love you, too, dear. I'll see you soon. Put Jinx back on."

A few seconds passed, and then I heard a whispered, "How'd that go?" from Jinx.

"Didn't seem to be a problem. Although it sounds like she was getting a little weepy."

"Send 'em shopping at the outlet mall or rent them a couple of DVDs. It'll take their minds off what's going on. I'll try and call from the house if I can. I'll check your place out, too. Just don't come back here until I give you the green light. I have a feeling it's going to be really ugly out there."

"Got it. Fly, don't do anything stupid. Well, stupid for you."

"Too late." I quickly snapped the flip phone closed, then threw my shoulders back and wandered down to Salladé's end of the corridor as though nothing was bothering me.

Truth is, what was playing through my head were the screams I'd heard on the phone from people who thought they were going to die. Mark my words, when this is over, officially they'll keep score by the number of people killed. But it's the number who got mentally screwed up by the storm that's really going to matter. There'll be people who won't stay here because they're afraid it'll happen again. And people who won't stay here because of bad memories. And people who'll leave because their kids up north insist they get out of here. You watch. It'll be the walking wounded we need to worry about. The dead ones aren't the problem. They're gone. It's the survivors. Just watch.

A blind man would have known that the storm had moved on just by the sound of the wind. What had been a steady roar was now down to an occasional gust that blew debris around. And as the sound outside abated, it was sort of funny to notice that people were still shouting to be heard. I watched the sheriff issuing orders to the troops and about two minutes into his spiel he just stopped cold. Looked around, grinned sheepishly, and said, "I guess there's no need to yell any more. Why didn't one of you comedians tell me? Or were you just having fun watching me scream?" Everybody laughed. We needed to.

While the sheriff and I had been admiring the eye of the storm, he'd told me to go home when it was over, check the house, and then ride around the Isles to report on damage. But as he ended the meeting with the deputies, he flagged me down.

"Fly, one of the operators got a call from the old multi-story condos out at the end of Marion in the Isles. Caller said blood was pouring through their ceiling from the floor above. You up to checking it out?" He riffled through a stack of emergency calls, adding, "We're full up."

"But isn't that Punta Gorda PD territory?" I asked. When I'd been given my orientation, they'd been very emphatic about where the county sheriff's jurisdiction ends and PGPD begins. It didn't sound like people would be too happy with me if I crossed it.

"Don't worry about the fine points of jurisdiction now," he said. "We're all in this together."

Five minutes later I was in a squad car catching a ride to what was left of the emergency operations center. When we got there, I found that the only damage to my Toyota 4Runner was a couple of cracked windows on the right side of the vehicle. The deputy who brought me over waited until I started the car, and then took off. I grabbed a cold DDP out of the ice chest, then said to myself, "Moscone, you *gavone*, mama always said 'be careful what you wish for.'" I put the car in gear and headed west.

chapter 7
fly

On a normal day I can make it from the sheriff's office to Punta Gorda Isles in about fifteen minutes. Today, the trip took me almost an hour. Stoplights weren't an issue because they were gone. I don't mean out because the electricity had failed. I mean physically gone. Actually, so were the railroad crossing arms and warning signs along the Seminole Gulf Railroad tracks. I tuned the car radio to WCCF, the local AM talk station, not even sure they'd be on the air. But there they were trying to be reassuring while saying most of the roof was off the studio and asking anyone with a tank full of diesel fuel to drive over and refuel their generator so they can keep transmitting. One of the guys on the air said that a couple of carpenters and a roofing guy had volunteered to come over to rig something to keep the studio dry so they could stay on the air with emergency information. Odd, but I got a little teary-eyed when I heard that. People helping people in my little corner of the world. What a friggin' concept. Maybe I need to reevaluate my feelings about local radio down here.

The cow pasture on my route home was now a lake. I'm not sure where the cows went, but they were MIA. There wasn't a single power line that hadn't been ripped from the poles, and only a few of the poles were still standing straight up. Without four-wheel drive, I'm not sure that I could have even made it home. The trip was more an up and down and side to side undulation in a general direction than a series of straight lines, sort of the way a rattlesnake moves across the desert. With trees and wires down all over the place, the route home required using four-wheel drive to cut across swales and lawns.

Even though I've been driving here for years, now that the street signs had disappeared, I found myself hesitating at intersections that no longer looked familiar. The landmarks weren't all gone—just modified. The tall pine tree where I'd occasionally seen a bald eagle surveying the scene no longer had any branches. Not one. It was pine pole. Nearly all the tiles had blown off the red-roofed house on the corner where I usually turn.

When I first came down here, people called Punta Gorda paradise. Looking around, it suddenly dawned on me that this was now paradise lost. And then I remembered *Inamorata*. What struck me is that this was the first time I'd thought about the boat since before the storm. I guess there's nothing like a hurricane to give a guy some perspective. Out of nowhere, a chill went through me. I had visions of the boat perforated like Swiss cheese. I wanted to floor it and go check on her, but duty called. Talk about being torn.

I drove toward Marion Avenue, gingerly picking my way around power lines and fallen palm trees. Everyone I saw looked shell-shocked. Some just stood on their driveways, staring at the devastation, unable to figure out their next move. Once I actually stopped to gawk at a house bisected by a fallen pine.

Halfway to the first of the two bridges I'd have to cross, the street was blocked by a large palm, but I put the car into four wheel drive, went up and over the center median, and drove west in the eastbound lanes. It's not as though there was any other traffic to worry about.

Going over the bridge, I had my first view of the western edge of Punta Gorda Isles. I stopped briefly at the top to look at the condos I was heading to, and even from this distance, it wasn't a pretty sight. Looking in both directions down the canal I could see boats hanging from their lifts, and more than a few half submerged. On the northern side of the bridge—the sailboat water—

I was able to spot the remains of a large boat, I'm guessing a for-ty footer, lying on its side across the canal.

As I started down the bridge, I was surprised to see an old gray pickup truck crest the second bridge, heading toward me. In less than a minute we picked our way past each other. The driver had a baseball cap pulled low over his eyes and he didn't slow up or indicate that he wanted to talk. I waved and he did the same.

Climbing the second bridge, I could see tracks showing that he'd had to take to the swale in order to get around a couple of trees and assorted debris, and I just followed his path in reverse, staying in the swale for nearly a hundred yards before turning back onto Marion. I tried to prepare myself mentally for the task ahead. Was the victim dead or barely alive? Odds are it was an arterial bleeder. I had a small first aid kit in the back of the car. I know it had sterile gauze bandages, but I wasn't sure if it includ-ed a tourniquet. Instinctively I brushed my waist to make sure I had a belt holding up my pants. I was excited about the assign-ment, but I was fairly calm. Pulse wasn't racing, palms weren't sweaty, even though I realized that I might be alone on this one for quite some time.

There were several people standing in the driveway, watching me as I got out of the car. A painfully thin woman looked at me and reacted to the uniform, "Thank God you're here." I'd always wanted to hear those words from a woman; if only we were both forty years younger.

"Are you the one who called?" I asked. Maybe I need to brush up on my curbside manner, because she immediately broke down. I couldn't believe such huge sobs could come out of such a tiny body.

"Yes, I'm Mrs. Forrester from 3-C. There's blood dripping through a ceiling vent into our unit."

She said *our*. "Is someone in your unit now?

"My husband Walter is there."

"Is he okay? Is he hurt?"

"No. It was terrible. We hid in the bathtub with a mattress over us the whole time. When the wind stopped, we got out. There was broken glass all around. Everything is soaking wet. And when we got to the bedroom, that's when we saw the blood."

I was beginning to understand the subtext of Joe Friday's *just the facts, ma'am.* I really wasn't looking for the unabridged version of her story. I just needed the basics. My inclination was to race up the stairs to see what was going on, but my training slowed me down, compelled me to ask questions first.

"How many people live in the unit above you?"

"Just one in 4-C."

I thought I detected a whiff of something unpleasant as she said it. "Did you or your husband go up to check on him?"

"No. Absolutely not. As soon as we saw the blood I called 911."

I told her to wait there and ran into the building.

Using the elevator was out of the question. Good thing the sheriff's volunteer training program at the police academy in Fort Myers included plenty of PT, otherwise I'd be in a big hurt climbing four flights of stairs, two at a time.

The interior stairway had a lot of water damage, but there was no debris. As I passed the door leading to the first floor apartments I could see that the building had been slammed hard. Doors were wide open, some off their hinges. The second floor hallway was the same. As I climbed to the third, I noticed a trail of white ceiling insulation coming down the stairs. It got a bit heavier as I began huffing and puffing my way up to the top floor.

When I came out of the stairwell, it looked as though it had snowed all the way down the hall. The ceiling had been breached and blown-in insulation was everywhere, a couple of inches deep. As I moved down the hall, I detected a trail of footprints in the soggy mess.

The door to 4-C had been blown open so hard that the doorknob had slammed a hole in the wall. I walked into the apartment, and just because we'd been trained to do it, I announced my presence. "Hello? Sheriff's department. Is anyone home?"

I wasn't surprised that there was no answer. That's when I realized that the sliding glass doors to a tiny balcony overlooking the harbor—a million dollar view—were missing. Actually, they weren't missing, just shattered into dozens of shards of nasty looking glass scattered all over the living room. All the ceiling insulation on the floor was soaking wet, but as I approached the balcony, I noticed that the stuff near the doorframe was pinkish-red, as though it had blotted up a colored liquid. It wasn't difficult to follow the tinted insulation. It led directly toward the door to what I presumed would be one of the bedrooms.

I had a bad feeling about what I was about to see, and as soon as I walked into the room, my premonition was confirmed. The apartment's occupant was lying on the bed, on linens completely soaked through with blood. The sight of so much blood caused me to stop, which was good, because had I kept going, I would have obliterated what I could now clearly see were non-bloody footprints in the insulation leading from the bed to the bedroom doorway, and continuing to the apartment doorway leading to the hallway. I wanted to kick myself, because I hadn't noticed them when I entered the apartment. All I'd focused on then was the broken glass from the slider to the balcony.

At that point, I probably should have strung up the yellow crime scene tape, backed off, and waited for the boys from homicide. But I didn't have any tape and I knew that the detectives were not likely to be available anytime soon. I flashed back on what they'd taught me at the academy. Don't disturb the crime scene, but if there's a possibility that the victim is alive, do what's necessary to save him. Gingerly, I walked to the bed, taking a circuitous route that kept me from stepping in the footprints.

The man laying there was clearly beyond help. Nevertheless, I felt for a pulse in his neck, pushing aside several gold chains in an attempt to locate the carotid. He was turned so that he faced away from the door, and I could see a bloody towel tied around his right thigh close to his groin. I got the sense that he was tall, and that had he not bled out, he would have been displaying a rather nice tan. I touched his uppermost shoulder, causing him to roll onto his back. That's when it struck me: I know this guy. Around his neck was a fairly ostentatious gold cross that looked familiar. And on his left wrist was a Rolex Yacht-Master. It was the asshole I'd encountered at South of the Border with Jinx. "*Ba fongool!* Maybe there is a God," I muttered aloud. If Sophia knew I'd thought that—much less said it—she'd have dragged me to see Father Tim, and then she would have tripled whatever penance he gave me at confession.

There was a cordless phone base station on the nightstand, but when I picked up the handset, there was no dial tone. I already knew that cell phone service was out; the towers had been blown down. It's just a good thing I didn't need to call an ambulance.

Once I realized that this was no longer an emergency, I found my pulse slowing, and I was beginning to analyze what I'd seen. And that analysis led me to the inescapable conclusion that someone had been in this apartment before I got here, someone had entered the apartment and stood next to the bed, right where I was now standing.

The cause of death was evident. The guy had bled out. Exsanguinated would be the word used by the medical examiner on his autopsy report. There in Rolex Man's thigh, just below the towel that didn't do much of a job as a tourniquet, was a shard of glass that probably came from one of the sliding glass doors in the living room.

My mind began to race through the scene, trying to reconstruct what had happened. First of all, the guy opted to stay in his condo with a Category 4 hurricane coming. Not only that, his condo is on the top floor of the building—he probably paid extra for the penthouse label, and the building fronts on Charlotte Harbor. There's nothing to protect it. Also, this is one of the older condo buildings in Punta Gorda—probably constructed in the early 1990s, which means it didn't meet the post-Hurricane Andrew building codes that went into effect in South Florida after the Miami area got clobbered.

So here's what I'm guessing happened. The guy is single, maybe a widower or divorced, and he's got an apartment filled with stuff—antiques, paintings, objet d'art. And he doesn't want to leave his stuff. So he stays. Charley jogs to the right and comes up Charlotte Harbor, and Rolex Man has a primo view of the action—it's like he has the best suite in the Garden to watch the game. The way things look he was stupid enough to stand in front of a floor to ceiling glass door with a 140 mile an hour hurricane blowing outside. Early in the storm, it was probably just raining sideways. Then debris began flying through the air. At first, it was small stuff—pieces of aluminum and screening ripped from hundreds of pool cages. And then the heavy stuff began flying through the air. Branches. Concrete roof tiles. Mailboxes on their posts. Sooner or later it was inevitable that something was going to slam into the glass door. Whatever hit it must have shattered the glass and bounced off.

I would have thought that the doors were made of tempered glass, like car windshields. But judging from the chunk of glass in his thigh, I guess not. The glass shattered and a shard slices into him. Based on all the blood, it hit the femoral artery. Can't tell whether he was knocked down, but he managed to get a towel, get back to his bed, and tie it around his leg. And then he lay down—and bled to death. From the puddling on the floor and his pasty color, I'm guessing the tourniquet didn't do a damn thing. He's six quarts low.

What I need to find out is who came into the apartment, walked over to the bed, took a look, and then left? And why? Mrs. Forrester said neither she nor her husband came upstairs after the blood began pouring from the ceiling. Time to play detective.

chapter 8
fly

I stepped away from the bed and retraced my steps to the doorway, trying not to obliterate any of the tracks in the ceiling insulation that carpeted the tile floor like new fallen snow. Considering that I was in the room with a stiff who I'd met for the first time just two days earlier, I seemed to be taking it all in stride—especially the notion that I was on my own and would likely be flying solo for the next several hours. And that's if things went well.

While in the EOC, I'd overheard a conversation between Salladé and someone at the state emergency headquarters about the number of body bags being sent to Charlotte County along with a refrigerated eighteen-wheeler to serve as a temporary morgue. I was shocked when Wayne asked for seventy-five bags. I wondered whether any of those people who were giving me the "we'll ride it out here" speech were going to be bagged, tagged and slabbed in a reefer truck parked outside whatever was left of our riverfront Holiday Inn.

I'd hoped that by standing across the room and looking back at the body I'd get an inspiration about the mystery visitor. But nothing clicked. The stiff—whose name, John Catlett, I cleverly figured out by looking at a letter addressed to him that was, amazingly, sitting on the dresser—was still wearing the $15,000 Rolex. That would seem to rule out robbery or theft as a motive for the visit. It's possible that something else might have been taken—hell, the place was filled with antiques and artwork and there was no way for me to figure if anything was missing what with the wind having knocked things off the walls and blown everything around the place. But the wristwatch would have been the easiest thing to pocket, and, probably, to fence.

What I needed to do was go downstairs and talk to the guy who made the 911 call, but for some reason, I was stalling. Maybe I was facing the reality that it's one thing to be a smartass and bust some redneck's balls for screwing a senior citizen at a tire store, but another thing entirely to question people who might be involved with a death that may or may not be accidental.

I retraced my steps down the stairs, figuring I'd look for the husband of the lady I'd met. Then it struck me that since I wasn't in an emergency situation any more, maybe I should be writing things down. It would make my lieutenant happy. So I stepped out of the dark stairwell and sat down in the third floor hallway and began jotting down everything I could remember from the time I pulled up to the building. It took me almost ten minutes, because I kept going over and over the scene in my mind, trying to make sure I didn't forget anything. At the academy they'd knocked into our heads that crime scenes needed to be documented and protected. So here I was on my first big case and there's no way to do either short of me camping out with a ripening stiff in an apartment with no air conditioning. Outside temp, mid-nineties; humidity about the same. Like a nice fall day in Vietnam, only no one was shooting at me. Yet.

Shoving the little spiral notebook into the breast pocket of my uniform shirt, I stood up and stared down the hall. "*Mannaggia! What a fuckin' mess,*" I muttered.

I was about to walk down the hall toward the Forrester's apartment when I noticed something that seemed out of place, even in this mess. There was a broken trail of ceiling insulation leading from the stairwell to an apartment door, sort of like breadcrumbs scattered by Goldilocks to track her trail through the forest. I knew the only floor with ceiling insulation in these buildings was the top floor where Catlett lived. The stuff was clearly out of place here.

I followed the trail to the open apartment door, knocked on the doorframe, and waited a second. A man's voice called from somewhere in the apartment, "Back here."

I took that as an okay to enter, and did so. Once I had taken a few steps, I stopped and looked around for more insulation on the floor, but there either wasn't any, or it was hiding amid the soaked crud covering what had been a fairly expensive Berber carpet. These sliding glass doors had survived the storm, but the windows had been blown out. What's wrong with these people? Don't they believe in storm shutters?

As I was silently denigrating them for what appears to have become terminal stupidity, a guy wearing faded gray fishing shorts, a navy blue Deep Creek Golf Club golf shirt, and Reebok walking shoes that are part of the retiree uniform here came into the living room and mumbled a greeting.

"Hello, I'm Deputy Moscone. Sorry I couldn't get out here sooner." Okay, so as icebreakers go, it was pretty lame. If you have better suggestions for the next time, email 'em to me.

He stuck out his hand and gave me a reasonably strong hand-shake. "I'm Al Forrester."

"You're the one who called about the blood?"

"Yeah," he said, turning and walking back to the bedroom with a follow-me gesture. "It's terrible."

I followed him, assuming that with his back to me he couldn't see me checking out the floor, looking in vain for any trace of Goldilocks's trail of breadcrumbs.

We walked through a short entryway, on either side of which were his and her walk-in closets. The bedroom was large, with Florida modern furniture. The bed was king sized, featuring wicker head and footboards that probably wouldn't recover from the dousing they'd received from the water that came through the now-missing windows.

Just above the foot of the bed was an air conditioning vent that was stained with dried blood, the source of which I'm sure the coroner would say was the dead guy's thigh.

Forrester must have seen the look on my face. "It was worse when it was dripping."

I began to say, "Probably a good thing the power was out…" and then mumbled something.

The guy looked at me, "What?"

"Nothing." I'd caught myself just in time. The rest of the sentence was …*and the fan was off or it would have sprayed around the whole room and looked like a Jamba Juice smoothie maker gone wild*. With strawberries.

"What'd you do when you first saw the blood coming down?"

"Actually, it was Marge who saw it first. We'd hidden in the bathtub during the storm. Pulled a mattress from one of the twin beds in the guest room over us like they said to do. The noise just about scared the crap out of both of us."

My interviewing instructor probably would have said to let the geezer talk, but it was hotter'n hell in the apartment and I really wanted to get outside, so I tried to push him along. "And when the noise stopped you came into the bedroom…?"

"Yeah, I think we both broke down and cried. Not because of the stuff"—he gestured around the place. "Stuff can be replaced. We just didn't think we were going to live through it."

"And the blood…?"

"Oh, right. We both walked out of the guest bathroom—it's smaller and just has a tiny window, so I thought we'd be safer in there—into the living room. Then Marge was the first to walk into the bedroom. I heard her yell, 'Alfonse!' She only calls me that when something's wrong or she's pissed off at me."

"I understand. Trust me on that one."

He smiled, and then continued. "I came into the bedroom and she was pointing up at the ceiling. At first, I couldn't figure out what it was. But then I smelled that coppery smell that blood has, and I knew. Luckily, the phones were still working, and I only had to dial three or four times before 911 rang and I got through. And that's it."

"What's directly above this room?"

"A bedroom in the penthouse."

"You know who lives up there?" I asked, jerking my head the equivalent of one flight up.

"John Catlett. He's dead isn't he?" He sort of spit out the name before asking the question.

"You took a look around up there?"

"Oh no. I wanted to go up there after I called 911, but Marge wouldn't hear of it. She wasn't doin' too well just with the storm; the blood pushed her over the top. You met Marge outside?"

"I did."

"I suppose you can see she's not well and she didn't want me going up there, so I didn't."

Three denials in under ten seconds. My instinct was to call the *stunad* a lying sack of shit. Either that or a heartless son-of-a-bitch. You know that a neighbor is bleeding badly, and you don't see if you can maybe save the poor bastard's life? I didn't know which pissed me off more—the fact that he's asking me to believe that he didn't have the human decency to go up and see if he can help, or that he went up there, left a trail of ceiling insulation on the way back down, and for some reason doesn't want me to know that he took a look, so he's lying.

"You think anyone else in the building may have gone up there?" I asked.

"No. Most of the units here are owned by snowbirds. In August, there may only be five or six occupied apartments. Actually, I think only us, the Marciniaks, the Faucis, the Wecers, and the Verhagens stayed. Everyone else left last night or this morning, when they heard the warnings."

"What made you decide to stay? I mean, this place is pretty exposed, sitting right on the harbor."

"We've been down here in Punta Gorda for ten years, and everyone is always saying that a hurricane could never hit here. Last one was Donna way back in the Sixties. Something about the air pressure that kept storms from coming in here from the Gulf."

"Ah, the Bermuda High."

"I just assumed people knew what they were talking about. When the warnings got issued, I thought it was some government guy covering his ass, you know, after what happened with Andrew. I guess he knew what he was talking about."

"I guess he did." I believe sardonic is the appropriate description of my tone of voice, but I don't think Forrester caught it.
"I'm going to go downstairs and speak with your wife. Have you
checked your car? Do you know if it's okay, and if you can get it
out of the garage?"

"When I went downstairs with Marge right after—he twitched
toward the ceiling vent—we took a look at the car. It starts, and
if we can get around the downed trees, we'll be able to get out. I
just don't know where we'll go."

"My suggestion would be to head toward Englewood, Venice
or even Sarasota. They were supposed to get hit, but we became
the chosen people. They should still have power, so you might
be able to find a hotel room for a couple of nights. That'll give
you time to figure out what you need to do. By the way, I see
you're walking around barefoot. Not a good thing to do with all
the debris."

"I had shoes on until just before you got here. Took 'em off
because they got wet. I'll put some on and meet you downstairs."
It was killing me that I couldn't ask to see the shoes. I figured
maybe I could get lucky and find chunks of ceiling insulation
stuck to the soles.

I turned and left the apartment, not bothering to wait for Lyin'
Al. At the academy, we'd go out for coffee after class, and some
of the veterans they brought in to lecture would tell us about getting an attitude toward civilians. I was beginning to understand
what they were talking about.

There were half a dozen people including Mrs. Forrester gathered in a little knot when I came out of the building. They all had
what in Nam we used to call the thousand yard stare. They were
coming to the realization that they might have been killed.

I added a few scribbles to my notebook, and when I looked up,
one of the men asked me if Catlett was dead. "I'm sorry, yes. I
don't know if you folks are planning on going back into the
building, but I'd ask you to stay out of Mr. Catlett's apartment.
For now, it's a crime scene."

"A crime scene? What do you mean?" It was Mrs. Forrester,

clearly upset—probably because she knew her husband had been up there poking around.

"We have a man who's died, presumably from accidental causes, but until the medical examiner gets out here, we can't make any assumptions."

That's when Mrs. Forrester discovered her voice. "You don't think any of us had anything to do with his death, do you?"

Now that was an unexpected question. "Do you think that's what I should be thinking?"

The woman got all flustered, "No, of course not. I was just surprised." Then she seemed to compose herself, and sounding indignant sliding toward angry, said, "You should consider what we've been through."

I wasn't in a charitable mood and couldn't hide it. "Lady, I've just been through the same storm you went through. My wife is 150 miles away from here wondering if I'm alive and if our house is still standing. Something I'd like to know, too. Instead of taking the time to call her, or check out my own house, I came here. I just spent half an hour with the late Mr. Catlett, in an apartment where the temperature is somewhere north of ninety-five degrees. On top of that, I'm a volunteer—that's what the 'Reserve Deputy' on my shoulder means. So let's try and keep the conversation as friendly as possible and we'll all be better off." Frankly, I was proud of myself. Because what I really wanted to tell the *faccia brutta* was to go fuck herself. Let her call the sheriff and complain—if she can find a phone that works. What's he going to do, fire me?

"I'm going to let the office know what's happened here. I advise you to salvage what you can that's important, valuables, papers, insurance policies. If you have an ice chest, take whatever is going to spoil with you. And leave. Listen to the local radio stations. They'll tell you when the power is back on. Till then, it don't makes any sense for you to try and return."

I didn't wait for anyone to say thank you. I just walked back to the car, climbed in, started the engine, popped a DDP, and just sat there with the AC running full blast for a minute before I put it in gear and drove home, dreading what I was going to find.

Turns out, I'd done a lot of worrying for nothing. Except for some missing tiles, the roof looked okay. No water damage inside the house—gotta pat myself on the back for spending the big bucks on shutters. And *Inamorata* had a few bruises and a busted windshield, but otherwise, she done fine.

chapter 9
fly

L ess than a day after Charley whacked us, there'd been an influx of a couple hundred cops from jurisdictions all over the state. There were squad cars from Tallahassee and other departments in the panhandle, from Fort Lauderdale on the east coast, and pretty much every place in between, large or small. The Charlotte County Airport looked like a military base, with tents for the visiting cops, electrical workers and other emergency personnel who'd come in force.

The biggest surprise was the arrival of a couple of tractor-trailers from Outback Steakhouse complete with cooking crews. They set up a mobile kitchen at the airport that operated around the clock. Any time of day you could get a great burger or a steak—all for free. For people who'd been maxing out on canned tuna and peanut butter, Outback was a godsend. They were so well prepared that they even brought housing tents for their crews. I put Outback on my short list of long-term thank yous, just below the Salvation Army.

But not everyone who showed up to help was so well-intentioned. Seems as though the county had been invaded by a strange species of toothless entrepreneur, coming in from as far away as Texas with chain saws in their pickups and larceny in their hearts. We'd already been told of a little old lady who got charged ten thousand dollars—why the hell she had that much cash around the house is beyond me—to have a tree taken off her roof.

On the second night AC—After Charley—I was sent with Dave Hofer, a veteran reserve deputy, to guard a Port Charlotte liquor store. Looting was becoming a problem, and we'd been trying to keep coverage on this place because aside from the local gun shop—whose owner had sprayed the front of his building with a warning that looters would be shot first, questioned later—the liquor store was a prime target.

Around dusk, we parked our squad in back of the place, and the two of us climbed into the cab of a Ryder truck parked right in front of the store. I popped a DDP from the stash I was keeping cold on FEMA ice, and was about to hit Hofer up with some questions about the Rolex Man situation, when he reached into his shirt pocket and pulled out a few sheets of paper. "I meant to give you this earlier. The captain said you'd been waiting for it."

I unfolded the papers and saw that it was the autopsy report on Catlett. "What? You been keepin' this from me?" He just smiled. I read the first sheet quickly: John Catlett, 83 years of age, white male in apparent good health. Physical description, the usual stuff.

I flipped to the next page and there it was: Cause of Death. Exsanguination, from glass embedded in his thigh, severing the medial circumflex femoral artery. Jumping to the last page, I read that the medical examiner had ruled the death accidental.

"Bullshit," I blurted out. When I looked up out of the corner of my eye to see Hofer's reaction, he started laughing.

"What's so funny?" I asked, defensively.

"You are. Captain told me your theory that the guy was offed. You know he's not buyin' it, don't you?"

"Yeah, but he's not looking at the evidence."

"Evidence? The guy was standing in front of a sliding glass door on the fourth floor of an apartment building watching a hurricane go by. The slider gets clobbered by whatever and the glass shatters."

"I thought that glass wasn't supposed to shatter," I said, unable to come up with anything better.

"When was that place built? I'm guessing before Andrew. The codes were weaker—and apparently, so was the glass."

It really pissed me off that he could be so smug, and deliver a witty line at the same time, but that's Hofer. He's an anomaly. One of the first things I noticed when I moved here was that most people didn't have a sense of humor. He's the exception that proves the rule.

"Okay, but hear me on this." My voice was rising now. "I know someone was in that apartment after the guy was cut. We got no way of knowin' whether he got clobbered on the head when the glass broke, and someone took advantage of the moment and slit his leg open with a piece of glass to make it look like an accident."

Hofer was looking outside the truck cab, then turned back to me and said, "You gotta tone it down. In case you forgot, we're trying to catch real bad guys, not imaginary ones."

I started in again, but this time I tried to whisper. It wasn't working. "Look, if *you* had *seen* the *footprints* from the door to the *body*, *you'd* be upset too with this *bullshit* autopsy report." That's almost impossible to do, whisper and scream at the same time. Try it. You'll fry your larynx.

"Fly, relax. Is it possible that someone was in the apartment after the guy croaked, but left because he didn't want anyone to know he'd been there?"

"I suppose so, but it *doesn't make any*...it doesn't make any sense. A guy is bleeding out, neighbors are hiding in their apartments, someone goes in, sees the guy—*who might have still been alive at the time*—takes a close look, and leaves? Somebody is hiding something."

"I'll agree with you on that, but that doesn't make it murder. Just for the hell of it, why don't you go over to the medical examiner's office and see if they saved the piece of glass they pulled out of his thigh. Maybe get it checked for prints."

"Now you're telling me something--" I stopped in mid-sentence, because at that moment we both heard a dragging sound outside the truck. I pointed toward the rear, and Hofer nodded yes. He motioned me to be quiet, and we both slid down in our seats. I pointed at my gun, and he shook his head no. Then mouthed, "Not yet." He's probably thinking of the paperwork we'll both have to fill out if we draw our weapons.

A moment passed, then two of the stupidest losers in Southwest Florida walked past the truck, and climbed into the store through the broken glass door. Dave motioned me to sit still. "Let's just watch these assholes and see what they do."

"They're going to steal booze, that's what they're going to do," I said, a little louder because both of the geniuses were inside and couldn't hear us. Hofer pointed behind our truck. I got it. We needed to know whether they had a third guy in their vehicle. He nodded his head and we each opened our door, slipped out, and walked slowly toward the rear of the truck. Nothing. Across the frontage road, however, was a parking lot, and in it were a couple of vehicles, a van with a busted windshield that had obviously been here before the storm, and an old Ford pickup. Empty.

Hofer came over to me, "What do you want to do? Grab them as they come out the door, or wait until they load the stuff in the truck?"

I thought back to my training at the academy. "Let's watch 'em load the truck. It'll make for a better case. If we bust 'em too soon, they could say they were just sightseeing."

He looked at me and smiled. "Good answer. Let 'em do the crime so they get the time." he whispered. We both crossed the road and hid behind the van. In a few minutes, the geniuses came out of the store, each carrying two cases of booze. Hofer looked at me as if to say, "enough?" I shook my head and smiled.

"Let'em work harder."

We watched them bring out three loads of stolen booze. As they were putting a couple cases of Keystone beer into the pickup, we came out with our guns drawn. "You are two of the dumbest mooks I've ever seen," said Hofer. You would've thought we'd hit 'em with a ten zillion watt spotlight.

"Stealing *Keystone*?" I said, mocking them. "You're ripping off a liquor store and you take the cheapest, most watery brew in the place? There oughta be an additional charge for having no taste."

"Shit, you ain't gonna bust us for takin' a little taste. Our house got torn up by the storm, and we got nothin' left," said one of the thieves.

"Even if you were stealing food for your wife and kids, I'd have a hard time letting you skate. But beer and booze? You make me sick." Too judgmental? Nah.

"Look officer, our dad is a disabled vet, and he needs his whiskey for the pain. That's the onliest thing that keeps him go-in'. I'm tellin' ya, honest," said the second thief.

Now I was seriously pissed. It's bad enough that these scum-bag lowlifes were looting a store that got blasted by the storm, but now they're telling me that we should give them a pass be-cause their dad is an alky vet who needs the booze. Not a chance.

"You're looking for sympathy, aren't you?"

"Well, yeah, if you could give us some, it'd be cool."

"Well, I can't give you any, but I can tell you where to find it." I didn't wait for one of these dumbasses to ask where. "Sympa-thy—it's between shit and syphilis in the dictionary," I said, with satisfaction, even though the line wasn't original. The look I got from both of them ranged from *huh?* to *whut?* That's when Ho-fer spoke up.

"You want to book these guys, or cut 'em a break. It's up to you."

"I wanna book 'em. I wanna charge them with enough felony counts to make their life miserable." I stopped in mid-rant and looked at Hofer closely. "You're not buying their story about the alky dad, are you? You don't really want to let 'em go. Tell me you don't."

"Like I said, it's up to you. You can't see clear to cutting them slack, we'll take them in. Not a problem," my partner responded.

"You know what bothers me?" I asked, and then offered the answer without waiting for a response. "My first felony collar, and there's not even a struggle. Not even any resisting arrest without violence. They just folded." Hofer just looked at me, shaking his head sadly.

We made them carry all the liquor back into the store, and in a moment of pity, gave them each a bottle of warm water.

Wouldn't want our felons dehydrating on us. And that was it. Anti-climactic.

Two hours later, having tossed the booze burglars into the county lockup, where showers were being given from a fire hose spraying down on the recreation area, I made it home to find Jinx on my couch, wearing headphones connected to his iPod. "Let me guess: it's Benny Goodman doing *Sing, Sing, Sing* from the 1938 Carnegie Hall concert."

"How'd you know?" he responded in mock amazement.

"Because you listen to that same fuckin' song at least once a day, maybe more, right? I think you're queer for Goodman—even if he is dead. You probably dream about doing things to yourself with his clarinet."

"That's the only recording I've found that makes me feel better every time I hear it. If I really need help, I back it up and listen to Ziggy Elman's solo on *And the Angels Sing*, which reminds me of every Jewish wedding I went to while my grandparents were alive."

"When did you get back to Punta Gorda? And where's my wife?"

"I only got back an hour ago, and both our wives are still living it up on the east coast. Sophia gave me the key and told me to make myself at home. She said to tell you she's fine, she misses you, but not enough to come back until there's air conditioning, drinkable water and phone service. My wife, on the other hand, doesn't want to come back until she knows there are at least three restaurants and a day spa back in business. They're both doing fine. The dogs, too."

"Jinx, you're looking at a man who made his first felony bust tonight."

"You're serious?"

"Serious as a mob bookie on Monday. Locked them up and threw the key away. Can you believe that they heist a liquor store and steal Keystone? But we got 'em in jail. You know my motto, 'if you can do the crime, you can do the time.'

"And I always thought your first arrest would be cardiac."

"Mock me, liberal. But who you gonna call when the bad guys take over the town?"

"I'm not mocking you. I want to hear all about it. Every stinking detail. And speaking of stinking, I need a shower. I reek."

It was the most honest self-evaluation Jinx had made since I've known him.

"We still got no running water here. Grab some towels from the linen closet. We'll go to the Mack's place."

We were walking to the car when Jinx says, "If I wanted living conditions like this, I could have gone to Afghanistan."

"No, you're wrong" I told him. "In Afghanistan, our guys have AC, hot chow, and electricity."

We jumped in the car and began the twenty minute drive down to Burnt Store Marina, which didn't have power, but unlike Punta Gorda, did have running water. Our friends Bob and Linda had a house there, and even though they were up north, they'd left a key and told us to make ourselves comfortable. That meant we could take cold showers to our hearts' content. Actually, cold water in August down here is in the eighties, so it was no hardship, and we had it better than a lot of people who were making do with moist towelettes.

"Wait a second. Jinx, what're you doing to us?"

"I'm not doing anything. The wind is blowing onshore, the tide is going out, and we're in the pass. You wanna drive?"

"Damn right, I wanna drive. Going through Boca Grande Pass can get squirrelly. Switch seats. Besides, now that we've reached the point where you've come back to Punta Gorda to be with the manly men, I know you're dyin' to tell the story. Just don't screw it up. I'm gonna be listening close."

jinx

"Drive the boat, Fly. And try to stay out of their way," I said, pointing to a couple dozen fishing boats drifting through the pass in pursuit of tarpon. I've got this handled." And I turned to the newbies, who had taken advantage of the handoff to refill their drinks, and began.

You're probably surprised that Fly hasn't bothered to fill you in on the post-Charley status of his first love, *Inamorata*. That's because the damage he discovered was minimal when he got home after toe-tagging Catlett—the dead guy in that condo. There was some minor dinging to the gel coat, a few missing cushions, and a cracked windshield, nothing to get upset about, all things considered. And he was in no rush to get the repairs made because with all the debris that wound up in the canals— roofs and pool cages primarily—he would have been a fool to try and take her for a spin before the authorities cleaned up the waterways.

Anyway, where was he? Oh, yeah. I'd just come back, we had driven down to take a cold shower in Burnt Store Marina, and we needed to get something to eat. "What do you feel like for dinner?" I asked Fly, more to see what kind of smartass answer he was going to give me than because we actually had choices. The Salvation Army canteen truck had been going street to street, sort of like the Good Humor man, but instead of ice cream bars they were passing out baloney sandwiches, hot coffee and bottled water. None of the local restaurants had survived Charley unscathed. Even if they weren't trashed, they had to dump all the food that spoiled when the power went out. Best guess was that it would be six months before most of them got the damage cleaned up, rebuilt and reopened.

"Let's go down to the dead lakes," he said. "I hear the developer has put up a tent and is feeding anyone who shows up. And it's supposed to be pretty good, too."

The dead lakes are a series of landlocked lakes around which this developer had planned to build a small city of six hundred or so condos in four story buildings. Everyone knew that if he could get the Army Corps of Engineers—and everyone else with permitting power—to allow him to dredge a canal through the mangroves a short distance from the lakes to navigable depth in

Charlotte Harbor, the value of those condos, which would then have docks with harbor access, would triple. Spending twenty-five or fifty grand to set up a tent and give the residents of Punta Gorda Isles along with all the first responders free meals during the hurricane emergency was relatively cheap PR. He was being smart about it, too. People asked him what he wanted—did he want letters written to city hall or elsewhere—and he just smiled and said no.

chapter 10
jinx

Ten days after Charley whacked us, and with one nervous eye on the Atlantic Ocean where hurricanes spawn, Sophia and Laura returned home from their combination evacuation/shopping trip. I had driven to Weston to pick up the girls, who'd been living it up driving a rented convertible, and when I pulled up in front of Fly's house, our wives feared the worst. We'd told them what to expect, but they'd fallen under the spell of the Weather Channel's hurricane cowboy, Jim Cantorre, who managed to do every live shot from Punta Gorda in front of a mobile home or manufactured housing park that had been turned into an aluminum scrap yard by Charley.

Sophia immediately set about counting trees down, lamp posts missing along the dock, and taking inventory of holes through the garage door where tiles or 2x4s had penetrated as though they'd been fired from a cannon.

Apparently expecting to see a roof stripped bare of concrete barrel tiles, she began arguing with Fly about the roof. "Why do you say we need a new roof? It looks fine, except for a couple of missing tiles."

"It looks fine. But if you climb up there, you'll discover that all the tiles are loose. You can lift up an entire row just by lifting one tile. The wind got under the tiles, lifted them, pulling the screws out of the underlayment. So while the roof looks okay, another storm could blow those tiles right off. *Capisce*?"

Having Sophia back home meant that Fly was going to be continually nagged with unanswerable questions: When will the adjustor be out? How long will it take to get a check from the insurance company? When will a roofer come out to begin work? Nevertheless, he admitted to me later that it was good to have her home. During our two weeks batching it together, we both actually missed the nagging.

Finally, Fly said that the adjustor from their insurance company would be out in a few days, and that would give them their first indication of how much of a fight they were in for.

"Why would we be in for a fight?" Sophia asked innocently. "We have insurance. I know we do. I write the checks."

By the way, the reason I'm just talking about the Moscone's house and not ours, is that, believe it or not, we didn't have any damage.

"But you're Mr. Jinx—how can that be?" interrupted Aronson.

Good to see you're paying attention to details, counselor, but you missed a critical point. I am not jinxed myself. My jinxedness only affects others in proximity to me. Go fishing with me, you'll get a hook in your hand. Or the boat will run aground. Or all around us boats will be catching fish, and we'll get nothing. So it's not surprising nothing happened to our house—the place was built like a bunker. With the shutters down, it *is* a bunker.

Now where was I? Oh, yeah. Sophia is expecting an adjustor to show up and for Fly to charm him. With a weariness that I knew would only get worse, Fly finally said, "You're right, dear. Jinx and I are gonna take the mutt for a walk. Why don't you throw those burgers on the grill." See what several dozen decades of marriage does for a guy?

Fly had just put the last hamburger patty on the grill when the phone rang.

chapter 11
jinx

I thought you said the regular phones weren't working," Sophia shouted from the kitchen.

"That's what I said," Fly yelled as the phone continued to ring.

"Well it's ringing," she responded, stating the painfully obvious.

Shaking his head in the world-weary way known to husbands around the globe and across centuries, Fly said, "Yes, it is. It would be nice if you answered it."

"Oh," Sophia replied, as though the notion was something that would never have occurred to her without his suggestion. The phone rang once more, and Fly could hear her pick it up in the kitchen. A brief pause, then she shouted, "Honey, it's for you. Steve Duke at Westchester Gold."

Turning back to the phone, she said, "He's coming, Steve. The cameo Paul got from you? It's absolutely be-you-tee-ful." Like Fly, she pronounced it the way she heard it near any exit along the Garden State Parkway growing up, with four syllables. "I love it. If you ever get earrings to match, let Paul know—but don't tell him I told you. Oops. Here he is."

She handed Fly the phone and he looked at her quizzically. "What shouldn't he tell me?"

Sophia ignored the question, and walked back to the kitchen.

"Steve, what's up? You back in business?" asked Fly.

I'd met Steve at the temple and became a customer, and then I introduced Fly to him. Over the past couple of years, they became friendly when Fly shopped for the various doodads he bought for Sophia. The first time Steve saw Fly in his deputy sheriff's uniform, he asked what the deal was. After Fly filled him in, Steve promised to call if he got wind of anything suspicious. Given that his place was combination antique shop, art gallery, jewelry store and pawn shop, all sorts of people came in, many of whom are more likely to have their pictures on the walls at the post office rather than at the local yacht clubs.

Westchester Gold had been thoroughly trashed by Charley, and until the sheriff had posted a couple of cops outside the place on a 24/7 basis, the wreckage was being pawed over by the underbelly of Charlotte County society. Seems that the redneck grapevine had put out the word that the storm had popped open Steve's safe and scattered gold, diamonds and pearls. The rumor, of course was unfounded. Casting pearls—or anything else of value—before two-legged swine is not condoned by his insurance company, which requires that anything of value be shipped out of state, under bond, whenever a storm threatened. So while the safe was there, it was bare.

Less than a month after Charley, Steve moved the store into a newer strip mall that had survived the storm, and he was back in business. The place wasn't elegant, but that didn't matter. What we really missed was AJ, the blue and gold macaw who greeted customers with a screechy "buy a diamond" or "buy a Rolex." I have a feeling that the purpose of bringing AJ to the shop everyday was to occupy husbands so they wouldn't rush their wives who were busy trying on earrings and bracelets and other expensive baubles.

After Fly had made the de rigueur post-Charley small talk, Steve told him that a kid, maybe seventeen or eighteen years old, had brought in a small drawing to sell.

Not being an art scholar and unfamiliar with the terminology, Fly said, "Drawing? Not a painting? A drawing, like kids do in school?"

"Yeah, just like kids do in school. But this one was signed by a guy named 'Picasso,' and on the New York auction market, it's worth upwards of seventy-five K."

"Where'd the kid say he got it?" Fly asked.

"He said it had been in the family, and that his mom asked him to sell it."

"Did you buy it from him?"

"I did," said Steve. "I knew what it was worth, and I offered him fifty K. I felt it was a fair price, even though I knew I could turn it around and make close to fifty percent on my money in a couple of weeks. Hey, I'm entitled to make a profit," he said, simultaneously sounding defensive and guilty.

"Hey, hey, Steve, you don't owe me any apologies. You probably could have screwed the kid really bad. It's just strange that a kid is selling something that valuable."

"Fly, that's why I'm calling you. When it came in, I checked locally, and then online to see if it had been reported stolen. You know the FBI has a pretty good handle on the stolen art market. But it was clean. So I told him if he'd leave it with me for a couple of days so I could have it authenticated, I'd buy it. He didn't have a problem with that. I took it up to Sarasota, and it checked out."

"You know who he is?" Fly asked, intrigued by the whole thing.

"I thought I did. Took a copy of his Florida driver's license like I always do. He asked to be paid in cash. Didn't want a check. Didn't want me to wire transfer the money. I mean fifty large is a lot of cash for a teenager to be walking around with. Bad things happen here for a whole lot less. I told him I don't keep that kind of cash in the store, and he said that it was no problem. I should tell him when I'll have it and he'll come back. It didn't fit the M.O. of a gonif trying to fence stolen goods. So I didn't check out the license right then. Just before I called you, I got a friend to run it. It comes back phony. But you gotta understand, I wanted to make the deal. We had a lot of damage and lost a lot of uninsured merchandise in the storm. I could use the money."

"Steve, I keep tellin' you. You don't owe me any apologies for doing business and making a profit. What did he look like?"

"Pretty much like the picture on the phony license. Seventeen or eighteen. Hispanic looking. Dark hair. The photo doesn't show it but he's trying to grow a mustache. Medium height. Solid build. I remember that he was very polite. This was not some barrio gang banger up here from Fort Myers. He spoke good English, not accented. I'm just sure he had Mexican blood in him—well, Hispanic for sure, don't know if it's Mexican."

"Steve, I'll be over first thing in the morning."

Fly spent the night feeling like he had an itch that he couldn't scratch.

chapter 12
jinx

Fly and I were waiting outside the door when Steve Duke unlocked Westchester Gold promptly at 10 a.m. He'd been feeling introspective; perhaps he should have gone to the detective captain, Paul Sandler, and asked to be assigned to the task force that was working hurricane-related crimes, but pride was keeping him from giving up on the Catlett case. Besides, he knew there was no way Sandler would let a volunteer with no prior law enforcement experience get involved in that stuff. In the meantime, maybe this tip from Steve would turn into something that might interest the sheriff. A fifty grand art theft would be big news in Charlotte County. Of course it might turn out not to be a crime, but it was definitely a mystery.

We walked into the new store, took one look around and Fly said to Steve, "I'm assuming this is temporary. 'Cause it's a shithole."

"Nice to see you, too, Fly," Steve shot back.

Despite Fly's rotten bedside manner, he was right—Steve's place *was* a shithole.

But after Charley, a lot of merchants were glad to be doing business out of any kind of hole.

The bicycle store down the street had set up shop in a couple of surplus shipping containers. The old Romanian shoemaker was working on a folding table in front of his storefront, which the building inspectors had red-tagged as unsafe for occupancy. He used a portable generator for power and snuck inside to work when the rains came. The little barbeque restaurant that had been in business forever was gone, but the owner had set up his portable smoker at a gas station that had been blown down, and was doing a pretty good business at lunchtime. I figure it was only a matter of time before the health inspectors found him and shut him down, which would be a shame. Hey, what's a little dirt on your barbeque when your house was gone with the wind?

"Steve," Fly said after looking around, "you out of the jewelry business?"

"Just temporarily. Our stock is still in a vault in New York. But nearly all of our business now is pawn. I had a feeling that after the storm, people were going to need cash, so we rented this place, and we're staying busy."

I didn't see the parrot, so I asked. "Where's AJ? I miss him."

"He's at home. There's too much dust and *schmutz* in the air here. I don't need a parrot with black lung disease."

"But the air is good enough for your wife and kids to work in?" Fly said, with lots of mock. The three of us played this ball busting game whenever we saw each other.

"I should let them stay home and loaf because of a little dirt? Who's gonna work the counter? Besides, nobody does a better job with pawn than Barb. She's a *pawn star*." Steve cracked up at his own joke, and then, without so much as a transitional phrase, he got down to business. "So, you want to see my Picasso? It's a little gem."

"I'm not here for my health, that's for sure." Fly faked coughing up a double loogy as Steve went into the back room. In a minute he was back with the piece.

"You weren't kidding when you said it was a *little* gem, were you?" The drawing was no larger than a sheet of 8½ x 11 typing paper. With the ornate gold leaf frame, the whole thing was maybe 20 x 24. The blue paper turned out to be the cover of an exhibition program titled "The Private World of Pablo Picasso." The artist had used green, white, blue and yellow crayons to draw a face—not even one of his profile/frontal faces. Near the top, he'd written "pour Bill," and at the bottom, it was dated in the late fifties and signed "Picasso" in blue crayon. Fly was unimpressed.

"You paid fifty grand for this? My granddaughter could have done it."

"It was a bargain. Others like it—not exactly the same—have sold for eighty."

"You paid him in cash?"

"That's how he wanted it. Cash."

He picked up a folded piece of paper and handed it to Fly It was the copy of the kid's phony driver's license.

"Steve, this is none of my business, so forgive me for asking, but don't you—like, need a signed receipt or something for the feds? Don't you have to send out a 1099 at the end of the year?"

"You're right, Fly. It's none of your business. But basically, all Uncle Sam is concerned about is that I pay taxes on my profit. And I always do. The paperwork…" His voice trailed off and he gave a shrug. It reminded Fly of being at his friend Joel Weisberger's house when they were kids. His mother did that same kind of shrug. The shoulders come up and the head and neck tilt to one side, while the hands do a sort of it-doesn't-matter thing.

"Can I hold it?" Fly asked, wanting to look closely at the drawing.

"Try not to drop it," Steve said, handing it to him.

After staring at it for ten or fifteen seconds, his eyebrows furrowed, he muttered something—nothing more than a prolonged hmmmmm, because Steve said, "Hmmmmmm what?"

"You have no idea who the kid is that sold it?"

"None. The kid went out of his way to make sure of it. He was driving a beat-up pickup truck. If Florida required front license plates, I would have written it down. But he pulled into a space right in front of the store, and when he left, he backed all the way out onto the street and pulled away. There was no way to catch the plate numbers. Sorry."

"You should be sorry, you goddam moneylending *gavone*. You coulda made my life easier, but noooooooo." A pause, then,

"Steve, thanks for tipping me off. I'll let you know what happens."

As we turned to leave, Steve's wife, Barb, called after Fly, "I think we're going to have earrings coming in to match the cameo you bought Sophia. I'll put them aside for you." He waved at her and didn't stop moving. He'd been down that road before, and it always cost him money.

As soon as we got in the car, Fly said, "I seen that drawing before. Not the actual drawing. A photo. BC."

BC—that's before Charley.

But Fly couldn't figure out where. I suggested getting an iced coffee while he let the problem percolate. We drove over to the only convenience store open for miles and I went for the coffee while he sucked down a Diet Dr. Pepper from the ice chest in the back seat. By the time I got back to the car, he'd figured it out.

"Jinx, when the *Sun* did an article about Catlett, just before I had the run in with him at Dean's, they showed pictures of some of the art in his condo. I think the Picasso was in one of the photos. But I gotta make sure. We gotta go over to the newspaper."

As Fly drove over to the offices of the *Charlotte Sun*, he became even more convinced. It was going to be a simple thing to get a copy of the article, see if he was right, establish that the drawing had been stolen from Catlett's condo, and go from there. But nothing was simple AC. Much of the *Sun*'s paper library had been destroyed by the hurricane, and even though it had all been transferred to digital storage, they were months away from being able to have a way to find it and a place to view it. It was a dead end.

Sitting in his car outside the *Sun,* Fly began to piss and moan. "Hey, dipshit," I said, "you're not thinking straight. What's the first thing I showed you first time you came over to the house?"

"Jinx, I'm in no mood for your games."

"C'mon, think!"

"I don't know—wait a sec—you pulled out those books of your old newspaper clippings and made me suffer through the highlights of your worthless life."

"Right. And..."

"Wait! I need to find the reporter who wrote the story. He probably keeps clippings," he said, already halfway out the door. Fly went back into the newspaper office, and explained to the receptionist what kind of story it was, she told him it was likely written by one of two feature writers. They both happened to be in, and when he mentioned Catlett's name, one of them owned up to having written it.

She fished through her desk drawer, and in less than a minute, Fly was holding a copy of the article, looking at a photo showing the dead asshole smiling as he pointed to the Picasso hanging on a wall in his bedroom. It was all Fly could do to keep from smiling back at him. The reporter made him a photo copy, and he thanked her while fending off her persistent inquiries into what it was all about with a vague promise to get in touch with her if it turned into anything important.

Back in the car, Fly confessed that even though he was now certain a crime had been committed, he didn't know what to do because he might have blown his credibility with the detectives. Before I could counsel him—and a good thing, too, because I had nothing useful to say—his cell phone rang. He listened for a minute, said yes, and hung up.

"What?"

"Gotta get home and put on my uniform. The sheriff was actually paying attention when I told him I wanted to help the insurance fraud guys. I gotta meet one in an hour at Dean's. And by the way, someone just shot an insurance guy."

chapter 13
sophia

I need to interrupt here, because you need to hear the story Paul told me when he came home to change into his uniform," said Sophia.

"Oh boy, this is going to get ugly," Fly retorted from the helm. "Jinx, I need you to drive the boat."

As the switch took place, Sophia began.

"Paul walked in the door and was in an all-fired hurry to get out of his clothes. By the way, you should know that everyone but me calls him Fly. Even the grandkids call him Papa Fly. But to me, he's always been Paul. Fly just isn't dignified, but it's been a losing battle. Anyway, I followed him into the bedroom as he began putting on his uniform. He hadn't said a word to me. So I looked at him. 'What's going on?'"

"The sheriff called me. They need me to work."

"I thought you were going to work on the boat this afternoon."

"I was, and now I'm not."

"Paul, you're keeping something from me."

When he answered, his voice had risen. "I'm not lyin' to you."

"Paul, I didn't say you were lying to me. I said you were keeping something from me. Lying will come next. What's going on?"

"Something happened—a shooting."

"Shootings happen in Port Charlotte. Usually over drugs," she said, then bored in. "What's different about this one?"

"It was in the Isles. An insurance adjustor. He's in the hospital."

"And the work they want you to do, does it have anything to do with the shooting?"

"No," he said. Paul figured that if he answers me quickly, emphatically, that gives him the best chance of getting me to stop asking questions. He was wrong.

"What do they want you to do?"

"Okay, Sophia, I'll tell you if it'll make you happy. They want me to baby-sit an insurance investigator, drive him around to a bunch of different houses where they suspect fraud."

That did it. I knew my husband was nuts, but until that moment, I didn't know he was crazy.

"Paul, have you completely lost it? Someone just shot an insurance man and you're going to go driving around with one?"

"Look, Sophia, I'm not going to be in a car that has Allstate or State Farm painted on the sides. I'll be in a squad car. And I'm going to be in uniform. Whoever shot that guy is certainly not looking to kill a cop. Not in Florida. I'll be fine. Now let's drop the subject."

"Why do you have to drive him around?" I asked him.

"Because Charley blew away nearly all of the street signs, and until someone goes out and spray paints street names on the pavement, a stranger has no chance of finding his way around. Hell, I got lost coming home the other day."

I didn't believe a word of it, but there wasn't anything I could say to change his mind. So I just told him to be careful, and to call me. All right, Paul, now you can tell them what happened. They'll see I was right to be worried.

fly

"Yes, dear. You're right. I was wrong. I apologize. And I'll pick up the story right where you left off, if we live that long. Jinx, you're bouncing the crap out of us, what's going on?"

"You told me to expect one to three footers. We're getting hit by three to five, sometimes bigger," Jinx shouted back from the helm.

"Then bring her around and we'll go back to the Intracoastal. It'll be a smoother ride to the restaurant. And don't swamp us when you make the turn. Now, where was I?"

I made what turned out to be a very quick stop at the Sheriff's office, got my marching orders, and drove over to the new Dean's where I parked on the rubble of his old place alongside half a dozen cars and pickups with insurance company logos on the doors. I remember sayin', "Why don't they just paint a target on the side?" as I picked my way to the entrance. Let me explain for a second about *the new Dean's*. Remember we said that the old Dean's South of the Border needed to be cleaned and burned? Charley took care of it. The owner said it would be back, but I don't think anyone really believed him. The new Dean's was purely an accident. Before the hurricane, Dean— there really is a Dean—had opened up a bakery/coffee house in a newer building fronting right on 41 just half a block from his old place. The new concept was a loser, but the building withstood the storm. Taking the hint from God, he immediately killed off the bakery, and gave birth to Dean's at Hurricane Charley's.

Replacing the stylish torn green Naugahyde booths were wooden chairs that were uncomfortable as hell. Because of a bureaucratic technicality that had to do with the number of seats in the place, they couldn't serve booze under their old liquor license, just wine and beer. And as if we didn't suffer enough with a goddam hurricane, without the income from hard liquor, Dean stopped offering free chips and salsa, for which I'll never forgive the *stunad*.

Looking around the place, I saw a couple of booths filled with the guys who went with the logos out in the parking lot. I guess even Dean's limited post-hurricane menu was an improvement over the Salvation Army Canteen truck. Most of the other tables and booths were filled with locals I recognized, including a few who belonged to our newcomers club. And there were a handful of low-lifes probably in town to see if they could hustle more old ladies out of their savings. Off in a corner booth where he could watch the door was a man sitting alone. As soon as I caught his eye, the guy gave me one of those casual, one-fingered salutes that immediately rubbed me the wrong way. He was tall and thin, with salt and pepper hair in a modified military cut, wearing gray slacks, and a white, open-collared short sleeve dress shirt. I walked over to him.

"You're wearing a uniform," he said.

That's how he says hello? I didn't get it, but managed to resist my first inclination, which was to bust his balls for his powers of observation.

He followed up with, "I just didn't expect a uniformed cop. Actually, I didn't want a uniformed cop."

"You got something against cops?" This was getting off on the wrong foot, and one of us had to back off. Fortunately, the insurance guy blinked first.

"Sorry, no. That's not what I meant. Let me start over. I'm Elvin Melton with the Underwriters Group." He stuck out his hand—the one he'd semi-saluted with.

I shook it and said, "Paul Moscone. Most people call me Fly."

"Moscone. Fly. I get it. Probably better than Guido."

I nodded at his linguistic sophistication. "With a name like Elvin, you should talk. What am I supposed to call you?"

"Vin works just fine. Not Vinny. Never Vinny. Let me explain about the uniform thing. Doing what I do—insurance fraud investigation—I get a lot more done without looking like I'm a cop. Truth is, I rarely work with the locals on a job. So when I said that thing about the uniform, it wasn't personal. Just surprise. Guess I forgot to tell the chief when I asked him for someone to help me navigate around here."

I was about to answer when the lovely Maria came by with a coffee pot. Without asking, she refilled Vin's cup. Then she looked at me. "I'm a sucker for a man in uniform. Wait a second." I didn't know what she was thinking. But she turned and dashed back to the refrigerator. Then came back to our table and put down a glass with ice and a can of Diet Dr. Pepper. She looked at Vin, and said, "He's special."

The DDP was a surprise. I guess Maria's way of saying thanks for coming to her defense. All I could do was shrug my shoulders and grin. Vin looked at me. "Do I want to know why you're blushing?"

"It's a long story. Maybe I'll tell you in the car." I turned back to Maria. "You know that guy who was bothering you…" I didn't get to finish the sentence.

"I heard what happened to him," she said. "It's terrible…" Her voice choked, she mumbled a "sorry" and ran back to the kitchen.

"Sounds like a helluva story," Vin said.

"You can't even imagine. Look, I only live ten minutes from here. We can stop there, I'll change, and we'll be on the move in support of truth, justice and the American way—or whatever it is we're going to do. One thing though. My wife isn't happy that I'm driving you around since the shooting. So if she's there, be cool, *capisce*?"

We both ordered burgers, made small talk while waiting for them, and when they arrived, wolfed them down. Vin paid the check, and then he followed me back to the house. Thankfully, Sophia was out running errands. I slipped into my closet and changed back from Superman to Clark Kent. "This better?" I asked, modeling an untucked Hawaiian shirt, khaki pants, and sneakers.

Vin nodded in the affirmative, adding sardonically, "The gold mirrored aviators make the outfit. That your undercover look?"

"You want a Diet Dr. Pepper or the real thing?" I asked, ignoring the rap on my eyewear, and grabbed my fourth or fifth DDP of the morning.

"No thanks. I've got cold water in the car. The office asked me to take a look at a house in Tropical Gulf Acres first. You know how to get there?"

"I can find it. Why don't you leave your car here and I'll drive?" Vin agreed and we threw his folding extension ladder and ice chest in the back of the 4Runner. I turned on the portable sheriff's radio, did a quick radio check, and then backed out of my driveway.

The address Vin gave me was for an area just south of the city limits, to the east of US 41. While it has a name, technically it's unincorporated Charlotte County, and it had been hit bad by Charley.

After several minutes of driving in silence, Vin spoke. "There are no people. Where is everyone?"

I didn't have an answer, so I changed the subject. "You heard anything about the shooting?"

"I heard it was an adjustor—Florida Gulf Casualty—but that's all I picked up when I called the office. You know any more?"

"They say he'll be okay. Anyone ever take a shot at you on the job?"

"A shot at me? No. Someone came after me with a machete. And I have had a shotgun pointed at me. But no one ever actually pulled the trigger."

"So—" I paused so we could both stare at a mobile home wrapped around an oak tree—"so, you'd say this sort of thing that happened here is unusual."

"The shooting?"

"Yeah, the shooting."

"Yeah, I'd say it's unusual. Not necessarily unexpected, but unusual."

"You mean you go out expecting stuff like that to happen?"

"I'd be foolish not to. But do I think we're in any danger, which is what you're trying hard not to ask out loud? Not especially."

I opted to let it go and just drove on in silence, pissed that Vin could read me so well. Eventually, he said, "Look, unless you want to sit in the car and wait for me—which I suspect you don't—we've got to have an understanding. Don't speak unless I ask you to. Don't answer any questions. Don't react to anything I say or do—unless you're sure what I want you to say. If the homeowner asks who you are, just say you're my partner, and let it go at that. The people we're going to see are named—" he paused to flip through his paperwork—"Ludwig. You know anyone named Ludwig?"

"Only Beethoven, but I'm sure he'd live in the Isles."

chapter 14
fly

In less than two minutes we were in a block of nice but not expensive ranch-style homes, stucco over concrete block walls, asphalt shingle roofs. "There's the house on the left," Vin said, "but keep driving." I continued slowly down the block as Vin looked at the damage to homes on both sides of the street and made notes.

"Okay. Turn around, go back and pull into their driveway. How are you with heights?" he asked me.

"No problem. Why?"

"You'll see."

We parked, got out, and while I got the ladder out of the back, Vin rang the doorbell. It was quickly answered by a man wearing jeans and a Miami Hurricanes T-shirt who came outside, closing the door behind him. Vin handed Mr. Ludwig his card. I walked close enough to hear the conversation getting off on the wrong foot.

"About time you guys got here. Your adjustor was out here a week ago. I don't know why he couldn't write it all up and give me a check like he's s'posed to do. He said he needed to have you come out and look at the place. You're here. Knock yourself out."

On the ten-point hostility scale, the guy was already around a six, but there was no reason for any attitude—yet. Vin just listened. When Ludwig stopped talking, Vin played with his paperwork for a bit, then said, "You're claiming damage to your roof, and water damage inside your home. How'd the water damage happen?"

"How the hell you think it happened? We had a friggin' hurricane. It tossed something through the sliders out back, broke 'em, and everything got soaked."

Vin was writing things down, playing it slow and methodical. He was all business, not unfriendly, just business.

"Why don't you show me the damage inside the house? We'll look at the roof when we're finished. That way I won't go tracking any dirt inside."

"Hardly matters. The place is ruined anyway. It's all going to have to be replaced, painted. New carpeting. Just c'mon inside."

Vin turned to follow Ludwig, and motioned for me to come along, so I grabbed a clipboard out of the car, just to be carrying a prop. It's a lesson I learned in the army.

Ludwig was right. It looked as though the storm had blasted clear through his house. Wind damage everywhere. Stuff blown around. A TV in the bedroom was upended onto the floor. I followed Vin as he checked out the living room and the two bedrooms first, photographing everything on a throwaway film camera, then making his way to the rear of the house. Just like Ludwig said, one of the sliding glass doors was shattered. Vin walked around slowly, opening kitchen cabinets, making notes.

"It was a fuckin' mess when we came home after the storm. Dishes and glasses broken. Took me and Cheryl a day to clean it up so we could walk without getting cut. I put a big piece of cardboard up to cover the hole in the door. Took it down so you could see better."

"I appreciate that. You make a list of everything damaged by the storm?"

He reached into his pants pocket and handed Vin several folded sheets of school notebook paper. "We listed it all.

Vin flipped through the list, then looked up at Ludwig. "You certainly did."

"You wanna go up on the roof now?" Ludwig asked, missing the sarcasm.

"That sounds like a good idea," said Vin, motioning for me to head toward the front door. Once outside, we unfolded the ladder and carried it around to the side of the house and set it up. Ludwig followed, watching. "You first," Vin said to me. I gave Vin a look and he just nodded.

I climbed up, trying hard not to slip as I made the transition from the ladder to the sloping roof. Vin followed. We both took a look around, and then Vin set off toward the peak of the roof, motioning me to follow him.

"What do you see?" he asked me

"A roof missing a lot of shingles."

"What else do you see?"

"I'm not sure what you mean."

"Look around the neighborhood. Take your time."

I did a slow 360-degree pan of the nearby homes, and suddenly a light bulb went off above my head. "Looks like Hurricane Charley had a personal grudge against this *jadrool*. This is the only house within sight that lost its roof."

"Now look around this roof, look carefully, and tell me what you see."

I looked, slowly. "Scrape marks all across the plywood."

"If you wanted to remove shingles from a roof, what would you use?"

"Probably a shovel or a spade."

"Bingo. It's time we introduce Mr. Ludwig to the facts of life."

We climbed down the ladder and walked around to the front of the house, where Ludwig was waiting.

"Got hit pretty bad, didn't we?" Ludwig said to Vin.

"Mr. Ludwig, have you been up on your roof since the hurricane?" There was nothing gentle in his tone.

"Yeah, sure. I wanted to see how bad the damage was."

"When you were up there, did you happen to look at your neighbor's houses?"

"No. Why should I?"

"Well just look at them from down here. How many homes besides yours need a new roof?"

"I'm not a fuckin' roofer. How the hell should I know?" The hostility was not warranted by the question. I waited to see if Vin was going to lop his head off.

"Can you tell me how it's possible that the only house on your street that needs a new roof because of Hurricane Charley is yours?" The question hung in the air like a swarm of insects on a muggy evening.

Vin didn't move. He just drilled Ludwig with his eyes.

Finally, Ludwig spoke. "I don't know."

And Vin stuck it to him. "I think you do know. The hurricane didn't make those shovel marks in the plywood. Those marks were made when you scraped the shingles off your roof." And he let it sit, again.

Ludwig tried. "Well the storm blew some of the shingles off."

Vin countered, "Please Mr. Ludwig, I've been doing this job for twenty years. Don't insult my intelligence."

"So what do we do now?" Ludwig asked, still not quite throwing in the towel.

"We talk about what you say happened to the inside of your house. What actually broke the glass on the slider?"

"I don't know, honest. We evacuated to my wife's sister's house in Kissimmee, and that's how we found it when we came home."

"That's how you found what?"

"The broken glass into the kitchen. Everything thrown around, wet."

"Mr. Ludwig, I'm trying to work with you here, but you're just not telling me the truth. How did the television end up on the floor in the bedroom?"

"The wind?" The way he said it, it was more a weak question than a statement.

"I don't think so. That television weighs what—at least fifty pounds? How did the wind throw the TV onto the floor, but didn't move the pictures hanging on the walls?"

And that's the moment that Ludwig caved. I had to turn away so Ludwig wouldn't catch me smiling.

"Okay, suppose you're right. How do we settle this? Or are you going to turn me in?

"You want to know what the law says I do?" Vin asked.

"No. But you're going to tell me anyway."

"First, let's agree that you tried to defraud your insurance company by claiming that the hurricane damaged your roof, when you actually got up there and damaged it yourself. Do you agree?"

"Okay, I agree."

"Then you're admitting that you committed a felony. Just want to be clear what's going on here."

Ludwig wasn't looking happy. Vin continued to ruin his day— maybe his year. "Since that's the case, the law says I can disallow your entire claim—even if it was the hurricane that tossed a rock through your sliding glass door and then soaked everything in the back of your house."

"But that part is legit. Charley did that."

"Doesn't matter. If you attempt to defraud your carrier, we're within our rights to void your entire claim. That's the law in the state of Florida. It's up to you to give me a reason not to do that. Otherwise, my partner and I are going to drive away and file the paperwork closing your claim."

"I don't know what to say. We need to live in the house. We got nowhere else to go, my wife and me and the kids."

"How old are the kids?" Vin asked

"Six and eight, a boy and a girl."

"You have a job?"

"I did, but not since Charley."

"What did you do?"

"Sold cars. At Gator Motors near downtown."

That's when I nearly burst a blood vessel from trying not to laugh. I had tears in my eyes holding it back. The guy was a freakin' used car salesman at a place with a reputation slimier than a slug's skid mark on a dew-covered driveway. But I knew if I even twitched, Vin would kill me, so I faked a cough and walked out to the backyard. But I didn't wanna miss what came next, so I got myself under control quickly and came back in, standing with my hands at a fairly stiff parade rest position, stern-faced, listening.

"How did your place of employment do in the storm?"

"Not so good. All the cars on the lot got dinged by flying crap. And the showroom was wiped out."

"Then I'm sure it won't be too hard for you to get some of your colleagues from work to help you blue tarp your roof. I wouldn't wait for the Corps of Engineers to do it. You wouldn't want the roof leaking on your family, would you?"

"No, sir."

"Now let's talk about the rest of the damage. I'm going to do something I don't have to do, and frankly, you don't deserve it. But I'm guessing that your wife wasn't part of your plan to defraud us, was she?"

"No, sir, she didn't know nothing about it. When I went up on the roof, I told her I was scraping damaged stuff down."

"I'll tell your adjustor that he can pay you a fair price to replace the shattered sliding glass door, and we'll also cover the cost for you to get some plywood and board it up today. We'll also pay to replace the carpet that got soaking wet—but you and your friends are going to have to remove it before it begins to stink up the house. That means today." Vin looked down at his paperwork, then scanned the kitchen, dining area and living room. "Okay, then…"

I couldn't tell whether Ludwig was grateful that Vin appeared ready to leave, grateful for getting what he got, or was just beginning to understand that the rest of the damage—including the TV in the bedroom—was coming out of his pocket. He looked back over his shoulder at the living room. "That's it?"

"If you're not happy, I can tear this up and give you nothing. Either way I'm required by law to file a report with the proper authorities. It can be accompanied by a letter saying you've withdrawn your claim and are cooperating, or not. Your choice."

"What good does a letter do if you're turning me in anyway?"

"No prosecutor is going to take the case when he sees that letter. It'll keep you out of jail. So? What's it gonna be?"

"It's fine," he mumbled, "I'll sign."

"I'm going to go out to the car and complete the paperwork that you and your wife are going to sign. While I'm doing that you can explain to her what you did." And with that, Vin nodded at me to follow him, and we walked out of the house, around the side, collected the ladder and put it in the back of my SUV.

I got in the car, started it up, and turned on the AC full blast. The temperature and humidity had already climbed into the mid-nineties. When Vin had settled into the passenger seat, I almost shouted at him. "Why'd you let that *stugots* used car salesman off the hook? He's a goddam felon; he admitted it. We should have slapped the cuffs on him and hauled his ass to the county jail."

"Look, we're not in the same business. You gotta get that through your head. Your job is to serve and protect or whatever crap they've got painted on the side of your squad car. My job is to make money for my company."

"But he's a felon. Why not make an example of him? Why give him a goddam nickel?" My voice was not only getting louder, it was getting higher. Nearby dogs were beginning to howl.

He rolled his eyes and heaved a tired sigh. "Who do I work for?"

"What? You work for Underwriters Insurance."

"And who does Underwriters Insurance work for?"

I was sure it was a trick question, but I was too wound up to think like the puzzle guy on NPR. "For its customers or clients or whatever the fuck you call us *stunads* who pay premiums."

"Wrong. Underwriters Insurance works for its stockholders. And they expect us to make a profit. Not every year, of course. Hurricane Andrew was a bad year. But then we upped our premiums and did very nicely for the next decade or so. Now they tell us to expect more cats."

He saw the blank look on my face. "Cats?"

"Catastrophes. Catastrophic occurrences. Hurricanes. Torna-does. Floods. Fires." He had a rhythm going, and was picking up speed. "Frogs, locusts, lice, hail, darkness, blood, boils and…"

I jumped in and completed the list, "Slaying of the first born. Hey, I had to pick up something after being the token gentile at my friend's Passover seder for the last coupla years. But you were telling me about catastrophe insurance. I'm all ears."

"Insurance business 101. We don't want to pay fraudulent claims. But we also don't want to end up in front of a jury against one of our policyholders, because when that happens, we mostly lose. Juries hate insurance companies. Even when we're right, we're wrong. You ever hear the expression 'bad faith' in connection with insurance?"

I shook my head slightly in the negative. I was ignorant, but didn't want to advertise the fact.

"Let's say we deny Ludwig's entire claim—which we have every right to do. But suppose he finds some scumbag ambu-lance chaser—how hard is that to do down here?"

"I once counted. In the Charlotte County yellow pages there were sixty pages of ads for lawyers—PI, medical malpractice, slip and fall, nursing home abuse. Sixty damn pages."

"So he has no trouble finding a lawyer who takes the case on a contingency. The lawyer sees Mrs. Ludwig, two cute little kids, and asks for a jury trial. 'Ladies and gentlemen of the jury, we're going to prove to you that this cold, heartless insurance company took the Ludwig family's premiums for years, and then when it came time to pay a claim to keep them in a home that would pro-tect them from the elements—keep the rain and wind out, keep mold from filling the house and making them sick—it refused to pay.' You get the picture?"

"But…but…" I was stuttering. "That's just wrong. The law says once he's nailed for fraud, you don't have to pay."

"But now we're in civil court, not criminal. A year or two from now, after everyone in Punta Gorda has been through the mill with their own casualty carriers, you think you could find a jury of your peers who'll side with an insurance company against a homeowner—even a jerk like Ludwig?"

"Point taken."

"That's not all. In addition to paying whatever judgment the jury comes back with, the company has to pay a law firm to handle the suit, it's got to pay me to spend my time in court when I could be out in the field protecting its interests. You getting it yet, Fly? It's all about the bottom line. Don't look for justice anywhere but under 'J' in your Funk & Wagnalls."

"It's just not right. You do the crime, you're supposed to do the time. It's black and white."

"Shades of gray, my friend. Shades of gray. That's what makes the world so interesting."

chapter 15
fly

We drove back to Dean's for lunch after taking a quick detour toward Tuckers Grade because I needed to see if the storm had blown away Bada Bing, the only porn and adult toy store in south Charlotte County. They were already back in business, and judging from the cars in the parking lot, business was good. I guess not even a hurricane can keep a good man down.

Vin could tell that I was still upset by what he'd done with Ludwig. "You're not saying much," he observed, after we'd both ordered the quesadilla-light lunch plate.

"I've pretty much said everything."

"Did I tell you that before I went into the fraud business, I was a homicide cop?"

Now he was talkin'. Like Jinx said, homicide was the dream I never got to follow. I still couldn't think of anything better than being a homicide detective. Go after the worst of the worst, find 'em, get the goods on 'em, and watch 'em get sent away for life without parole. Some people think the death penalty is better, but you want my opinion—spending thirty or forty years in a cell is worse than a lethal injection.

But something wasn't right. "Wait a sec," I said. "You were a homicide dick, and you're okay with letting scumbags beat the system? What happened to you? Something must've happened. C'mon?"

"I was on the job for ten years. Put a lot of scumbags away."

"And?" I asked, knowing that the devil was always in the details.

"And, I got a little too aggressive. So I was invited to leave."

"How—too aggressive?"

"Aggressive enough that I could have ended up as a guest of the state. With a wife and two young kids, that didn't seem like a viable option. So I offered to leave quietly. After some time off, I got recruited to become an insurance fraud investigator. I didn't get to pound on bad guys, but the profit sharing made up for it. And eventually, I discovered that this kind of private law enforcement was just as satisfying."

"You're kidding, right? You know you can't bullshit a bull-shitter."

"No, I'm not kidding. I can even watch *Law and Order* reruns without getting misty-eyed."

"At least you had the opportunity to do it for a while. I'm trying to get it off my regrets list."

I could tell Vin was now confused, so I explained. "You know what they say about dying with regrets? You wanted to go to China, but you didn't. You wanted to become a great golfer, but you didn't. You wanted to get back on good terms with your family, but you didn't. I want to feel like I did something useful for society—not just be a great computer salesman. And what I really wanted to be was a homicide dick. But here I am in Punta Gorda, with my life winding down. I still want to get that off the regret list. And maybe I can. Maybe we can cut a deal."

"How so?" he responded, his eyebrows coming together in a near unibrow.

"I need your advice on this case. Well, officially, it's not even a case, but I know it should be." Rather than continue to confuse him with evasive talk, I laid the whole story out for him. Tracks in the ceiling insulation. The downstairs neighbor I knew was lying. The coroner's report that said it was an accidental death.

"Let me see if I have all this straight," Vin said between bites of the recently arrived quesadilla, and then pretty much repeated back to me everything I just told him

"You've got it. All of it. Except when I hear you say it, it makes me wonder whether or not I'm crazy. I just know something wasn't right when I walked into that condo."

"Let me ask you something. You think you've got good instincts? Has there ever been a time where you knew something was rotten, everyone else said it was okay, and you were right?"

I waited till I finished chewing to answer. "When I was a salesman, my instincts about people were dead on. I could tell when we were being played about half a second after it happened."

"And you feel like that on this one?"

"Absofuckinglutely. When that neighbor said he hadn't been upstairs—when his wife said she and her husband hadn't been upstairs—they were lying. I know it. When I saw the trail of insulation leading to their apartment door, I was certain. I don't need Goldilocks dropping breadcrumbs in the forest in order to follow the trail. But this was pretty close."

Vin glanced at his watch, and must've realized that we'd been having a leisurely lunch while crime was waiting to go unpunished, he looked at the check, dropped a twenty on the table, and motioned for me to follow him out. He grabbed the check so fast it surprised me. Hey, don't be so quick to judge—I'm used to eating with Jinx. The last time he grabbed a check Truman was president.

As we walked back to my car, Vin said, "Help me out this afternoon, and if we have some free time at the end of the day, take me over to the scene of the crime. Maybe I'll get a hot flash."

I was about to respond when a pickup truck with an Everglades Southern Insurance Catastrophe Team sign on the side whipped into the driveway off of 41 on two wheels and slid to a stop in the gravel. The guy inside wasted no time getting out of the truck. "Motherfucker!" he shouted to no one in particular. "Some bastard took a shot at me."

Vin was on the run to him before I could even think of reacting.

"What happened?" asked Vin.

"I was coming down Marion from PGI, and just as I got to the bridge closest to Fisherman's Village, I heard a shot and a bullet went through the windshield on the passenger's side. Scared the crap outta me. I nearly lost control, but managed to straighten out and stomped on the gas. Got the hell out of there."

The guy was wearing a blue, button-down denim shirt with a logo on the pocket. He musta forgot his Right Guard that morning, or it wasn't up to the rigors of attempted murder. As he talked, he kept mopping his brow, but I could tell it was more out of nervousness than need. Vin led the guy over to one of the chairs on the patio. "Did you see where the shot came from?"

"Naw, it could've come from anywhere. All I know is it was close enough for me to hear the shot; the windshield cracked right after it."

"You piss anyone off lately?" asked Vin.

"You're kidding, right?" he said. "I'm an insurance adjustor. My life is about pissing people off—at least that's what they think."

During this exchange, someone had run inside to get a couple of the sheriff's deputies who'd been having lunch, and they came flying out the door and over to the small crowd that had gathered. I knew both of them, and introduced them to Vin, who related what he'd been told, then backed away. "Let's go," he said. "Life just got a whole lot more exciting around here."

chapter 16
fly

I got a favor to ask you," I said to Vin. We were headed to an address in the older section of the Isles, premium sailboat property—no bridges to go under on a relatively short trip out to the harbor.

"Since you got me wearin' civvies, and we're using my personal car, would you mind very much if we stopped and picked up my buddy Jinx so he can ride along? He's a retired newspaper guy and he's always looking for a story to write freelance. It gives him somethin' to do, and with the bills our wives ran up while livin' large on the east coast, and me working pretty much fulltime right now, he's getting lonely."

Vin bought the pitch and I headed toward Jinx's house, going down Marion Avenue which took us through what looked like downtown Baghdad post shock and awe. The old mall seemed as though it had been hit by artillery fire. The small restaurants and shops on the quaint street were boarded up. The town clock had stopped at 4:35—a minute or two after Charley slammed into the city. People had been talking about redeveloping the downtown area for years. It looked as though nature had done what the government couldn't do: accelerate the schedule. I couldn't help but wonder how long it would take to rebuild. And whether my great grandchildren would live to see it.

Just west of downtown on Marion, a lot of the older homes in the historic district had taken a real beating. Roofs were ripped off, letting you see inside. It was the sort of thing that you're used to seeing on television, but not where you live.

And the place was deserted. No one was here trying to clean up, trying to fix things up so more damage wouldn't occur with the next rainstorm. It was eerie.

I finally broke the silence by asking a silly question. "Vin, how come you use those throwaway cameras to document stuff. Shouldn't you have gone digital—that way you can email pictures to your office?"

"Digital would make sense to me, but the higher ups think that digital photos can be tampered with—and they can be. So they want us to use film cameras. It's stupid—because what matters is my judgment about what I'm seeing, the pictures are just support. If they think they can't trust me, that I'm faking claims and doctoring photos to make a buck, they ought to get a new investigator. It's the bean counters. What can I say?"

A dead silence passed between us. It wasn't broken until Vin said, "Go ahead. Ask."

"What?"

"Whatever you're thinking about. You haven't said a word for at least two minutes."

"I'm wondering about the shooting. Do you think that Everglades South guy was the target, or was it random?"

"What if someone just doesn't like insurance adjustors?"

"You're kidding, right?" Vin didn't respond, causing me to say, "Okay, you're not kidding. But Vin, aren't you jumping to a conclusion without any facts?"

"That's exactly what I'm doing. But when you've done this crap for a while, you develop instincts. And my gut tells me that guy wasn't personally singled out by the shooter. He was a target because his truck said he worked for an insurance company. There's a lot of people here who resent paying money year after year to their insurance carriers and getting nothing back. And in a few months there's going to be a lot more. I hope your PD is up to the job of catching the perp."

I didn't respond. I had my doubts whether the locals could find their ass in of circumstances, and these clearly ain't the best of circumstances. Not that they don't try hard. They just don't have the technology or the manpower that big departments have.

A few blocks farther west on Marion, Fishermen's Village came into view. In the early 1900s it had been where the fishing boats brought their catches. And nearby, there'd been a wharf that ran into the harbor so boats could load cattle bound for Cuba. The place had been converted into a tourist destination. Lots of water view restaurants and cute shops. And the upstairs had a bunch of timeshare condos. As I checked out the place I had another holy shit moment.

"*Madonna mia!*"

"What?" Vin asked in response to the shouted epithet.

"Holy shit!" I translated. "The top floor is gone. Not just banged up. Gone. Ripped off. MIA. And all that wreckage is somewhere at the bottom of the harbor." I was stunned.

When we arrived at Casa de Jinx, we found him wearing a bathing suit, sitting next to the pool on his now-screenless lanai, listening to NPR on a small transistor radio. "Your house did okay in the storm," Vin observed.

"Just some minor roof damage. And this—" he gestured to the lanai supports which had been bent or ripped apart by the wind. "For us, Charley was pretty much a major inconvenience. When the power comes back up, life will go on. We got lucky. This time."

It took Jinx two minutes to throw on some clothes, stick a freshly charged battery in his camera, and we were off.

"Let me tell you what we're about to do," said Vin. "You know my favorite type of loss?" He paused. "Anyone?" Another pause while Jinx and I pondered the question. "Well, I'll tell you. Total loss. You walk in, you look around, and you write a check for the policy limits. Nice and clean. You know my least favorite loss?"

"I can't imagine." After seeing Fishermen's Village, I really didn't feel like guessing games.

"Everything else. It's always a fight for someone. Either I fight with the homeowner. Or the homeowner fights with a contractor who says we didn't really pay replacement value. And then we fight with the contractor because we assume they're taking advantage of the situation and jacking up prices."

"Come back to the homeowner for a minute," Jinx said. "When my adjuster came out, I asked him what percentage of people in PGI he thought were trying to scam their insurance companies. You know what he said?"

"Sixty percent." Vin didn't hesitate. He just said it like it was a figure in a government budget report. "It's what we expect. Insurance fraud is the second biggest crime committed by nice, middle and upper class folks. You know what's in first place?" He didn't wait for one of us to venture a guess. "Tax evasion."

I digested that for a moment, and then said, "Yeah, but what gets me is that these *jadrools* brag about insurance fraud."

"I've seen it lots of places," Vin continued. "There must be something about major catastrophes that brings out the best and worst in people—sometimes even in the same people. The guy who's helping his elderly neighbor cope, out of the goodness of his heart, is the same guy trying to bullshit us with a bogus claim. Don't ask me to explain it. The industry has studies that prove it."

"What's with the claim we're headed to now?" Jinx asked.

"The adjuster told me it's pure fraud, and the guy has a major attitude."

"So let me ask you a question," I said. "You're going to interview some rich *stugots* who's living in a house that probably cost 800K to build, and it's on a million dollar lot right on the harbor. I guarantee you that the prick is going to have a Mercedes or Jag or Beemer—maybe one of each—sitting in the driveway. And whether he's into sail boating or power boating, there'll be something moored behind his house that cost him more than his trophy wife's new tits, ass, lips and the diamond solitaire on the hand she jerks him off with. His attitude is going to be that he can buy and sell you five times over. You're just an investigator. If you were up north, you'd be wearing a buy-one-get-one-free suit from the Men's Wearhouse. And the schmuck you've got to interview is not gonna like the way you look. So how the fuck do you get the upper hand?"

"*Stugots*. Schmuck. Prick," Vin repeated. "Jinx, I had no idea your buddy Fly is tri-lingual. And I'm not a therapist, but it sounds like he's got a few unresolved anger issues."

I was *not* getting the answers I wanted, and he was beginning to annoy me. "Let's leave my issues out of it. I just wanna know how you handle this guy."

"I'm used to it. When's the last time you ran into a humble, mannerly person with a ton of money? When you're dealing with jerks, you just have to work your way around them. Sometimes, you've got to be blunt."

"How blunt? 'Cause I like blunt."

"Sir, I think you saw Hurricane Charley as an opportunity to have your insurance carrier pay to remodel your home. That's blunt."

"How do they respond to blunt?"

"I'd say that things tend to get real shitty real quick."

I thought about it for a second. "This could be fun. What do you want us to do?" During the remainder of the drive Vin explained in detail how he might have me help. It wasn't the good cop-bad cop routine that I expected. Thanks to television, everyone is on to that game. Initially, Jinx was going to have to wait outside. Vin invoked the two's-company-three's-a-crowd rule.

Checking the address Vin had provided, I pulled into the driveway of a high end house directly on the harbor. As we got out of the car, a pickup with the Allstate logo on the side drove past and pulled into a driveway across the street and two doors down. Vin gave his good ol' boy one fingered salute to the driver, who returned it. "You know that guy?" Jinx inquired.

"Nope. Just professional courtesy."

"You boys have fun. I want to hear all about it when you get back," Jinx said. Then he cracked open the book he'd brought with—the paperback edition of *How We Die* by Dr. Sherwin Nuland. His choice of reading matter gives you guys a little insight into his glass-half-empty personality. You might wanna keep that in mind if you're thinkin' he'd be fun to hang with.

As we walked up to the front door, I realized that my pulse was racing. This wasn't homicide, but it *was* the real thing.

Seconds after Vin rang the doorbell, it was opened by a well-tanned man in his late fifties wearing Bermuda shorts, a Tommy Bahama collared shirt, and a pair of three hundred dollar Bruno Magli sandals. I know the price 'cause I looked 'em up. The guy took Vin's card, looked at it, and tossed it carelessly on the table in the foyer. "You're late," was his opening gambit.

Vin was cool. He made a point of looking at his watch, even though he'd checked it before he rang the doorbell and knew it was a couple of minutes before one. "I thought our appointment was for one o'clock. Yes?"

The man ignored the response and went directly into a rant. "We've gotta get this place fixed. The adjuster your company sent out was a bonehead. He should have handled it. There's no reason my wife and I should have to endure this disaster for a second more than we already have."

Vin tried small talk. "Are you and your wife living here now?"

"No. We've booked a suite at the Ritz in Sarasota for a couple of months. It was a pain in the ass to drive down here just to meet you. Let's get this over with."

So much for small talk. "Sir, could you walk us through the house and point out the damage you're claiming was caused by the storm?"

That's when the guy lost it. "I already took your adjustor on a fucking tour of the house. Here's the way it should be: I paid the premiums, now you write a check. Let's cut the bullshit."

I could see the wheels turning in Vin's eyes. Okay, Elvin, my boy, I thought, let's see what you got.

"Sir, if it was that simple, you'd have your check and I wouldn't have been sent here. I've been an insurance investigator for twenty years. I'm here because I *am* an investigator, because we have a problem with your file, your claim, which I've discussed at length with our adjustor. Now, looking at the house you live in, the car you drive, the big boat out back, and the houses your neighbors live in, I'll guess that you've got more money than God. But, Mr. Whitstone, most of the claims involving fraud activity that I've handled over the years have involved people with a lot of money *just like you*. I don't think that this situation we're in is because you need the money; it's because you see an opportunity to put one over on the insurance company. Maybe you even think you're entitled to a big settlement because you've paid your premiums faithfully for years. Now if you want me to process this claim, I need to inspect the damage. Even though our adjuster already has been out here."

Vin stopped talking. Just stopped dead. Didn't ask a question, didn't give the guy any slack. Just stopped and stood there staring at him, waiting. You could hear the sounds of mullet jumping in the canal behind the house. Then, from down the block, the sound of a chainsaw ripping into downed trees. There was no problem hearing it. All the sliding glass doors that had comprised the rear wall of the house were missing.

Finally, the guy spoke. "Go ahead. Look at whatever you want."

chapter 17
fly

And we did. Vin noted that the sliding glass doors were missing, that the kitchen cabinets were delaminating, that water had gotten inside them. The extra large projection TV in the media-slash-game room was upended; the pool table felt was soaking wet and showing the early signs of growing a moldy beard. The king size mattress in the master bedroom—which had a gasp-inducing view of the harbor through windows which were still glazed—held enough water that it squished when he sat on it. And clothes in both walk-in closets had clearly been soaked and were also sprouting mold. I'm sure if the place had been carpeted rather than floored with Italian marble and porcelain tile, the carpeting would also be squishy wet.

As we walked back to the living room where Whitstone had been pacing, Vin surreptitiously shook his head at me, then turned and said, "Mr. Whitstone, can we sit down at the kitchen table to discuss this?"

Whitstone didn't answer, but led the way into the kitchen where he used a dishtowel to wipe off a chair for himself, and then tossed the towel at me. The guy had all the charm of Vladimir Putin. After cleaning off the chairs, the two of us sat down facing a *strunz* I was beginning to think of as the perp. Hey—a guy can dream, can't he? Vin had told me that if it came to a sitdown, my role was just to stare daggers at the guy. I wasn't to say anything unless I got the signal.

Vin played with his notebook, shuffled some papers, took a pen out and carefully laid it on the table, parallel to the edge of the notebook. Then he took a small cassette recorder out of his pocket, turned it on, and told Whitstone that the meeting was being recorded. When he finished setting the stage, he folded his arms across his chest and looked directly at Whitstone. I expected Vin to say something, but he just stared. Five seconds, ten, twenty. It felt like an hour and a half. The sound of the chain saw just seemed to get louder. Hell, it was so tense I was ready to jump out of my skin. Who would snap first? It was the perp.

"Well," Whitstone said, all attitude, "what's it going to be?"

"I think you should tell us."

Whitstone snapped. "I'm not telling you shit. Either whip out your checkbook or I'm getting my attorney on the line right now."

"Sir, I hope you do, because I think your lawyer would probably explain the laws of the State of Florida to you."

"What the fuck are you talking about?" Vin didn't have him on the ropes—yet.

"Tell your attorney that there's an insurance investigator here saying you have intentionally misrepresented your claim in violation of Florida Statute 626. If you'd like me to speak directly with your attorney, I'll be happy to do so. What I'll tell him is that he needs to investigate the fraud charge, because if he supports you, under the law he can be served with the same arrest warrant. The crime is a felony, punishable by up to five years in state prison for each count. And there are multiple counts here."

I didn't know whether Vin was bluffing, or whether he really had him by the short and curlies. But he deserved an Oscar for the performance.

Vin wasn't finished. "You might also remind your lawyer that I'm not an adjustor. I'm an investigator, and under that statute I am required to report suspicious claims to the state insurance fraud department, and when I report this one, there's a good chance you're going to be arrested.

The perp began to sweat, first on his upper lip, then on his forehead.

"You know, hurricanes are beautiful," Vin continued, enjoying Whitstone's discomfort. "The law changed back in 1997. Insurance fraud in Florida used to be a third-degree felony, which is punishable by up to five years in prison and a $5,000 fine. Used to be, first offense, they wouldn't do anything. But it's now part of the larceny statute. You know what that means?"

Vin paused to see if Whitstone, who was beginning to slowly twist in the wind, was going to say something. He didn't, so Vin continued. "It means that $0 to $20,000 in fraud is third-degree; twenty K to a hundred K is second-degree; and above $100,000 and you've hit the big time. Now you're talking about hefty fines, which I'm sure wouldn't bother a rich man like you. But along,with the fines, you'll do fifteen years. And it'll be in Raiford or Charlotte Correctional. You're not going to do the time on your lanai at home with a bracelet on your ankle. You won't like your new neighbors, trust me on that one."

"Why do you think it's fraud?" Whitstone asked belligerently, right after he wiped the sweat from his eyes with the back of one hand.

"Where do you want me to start?"

"Start wherever the fuck you want to start."

"Okay," said Vin, "let's start with the sliding glass doors."

The perp smirked. "I told you, the storm tossed some shit through them. There was broken glass all over the place."

"After you saw all the broken glass, what did you do next?"

"What do you think I did? I cleaned it up."

"Where is it?"

"Where's what?"

"The broken glass. The trash collectors haven't been here since before Charley hit. All through Punta Gorda, there's debris piled in the swale near the street. I looked. I didn't see any broken glass in front of your house."

"I don't know what happened to it. I spent hours cleaning the shit up. Maybe it was in the stuff I dumped in the canal."

"Don't play me, Mr. Whitstone. Let's move on. How did you get so much water damage to your cabinets? The roof seems to have held up quite well, so it didn't rain in your house."

"You see the sliders missing? The wind blew water in here. It soaked all the cabinets. You can see the damage."

"Mr. Whitstone, do you have any enemies in the neighborhood, people who would have had access to your home after the storm?"

"Why the fuck would you ask that?"

Vin remained calm. "I just want to determine whether you think any of your neighbors might have come in here with a water hose and soaked the place down."

"That's crazy. We had a friggin' hurricane in case you didn't notice."

"I noticed. But I have doubts as to whether we've got a legitimate claim here. But I tell you what I'm gonna do. I'm going to cut a piece out of that cabinet—the one right behind you that's delaminating. And I'm going to send it to our forensic laboratory for analysis. If the water that soaked that cabinet came out of a hose, there's going to be chemicals in there from the water. God doesn't put chemicals like chlorine and fluoride in rain."

Vin looked at me. "Paul, would you please go out to the car and bring in the power saw. You might want to put the fresh battery on it." For a second, I was confused. We didn't have any saw in the car. Then I realized Vin had just given me lines in this drama.

"No problem, Vin," and I began to push my chair back from the table.

And that's when Whitstone cracked. "Wait a sec," he croaked. "Let's talk about this." I pulled my chair back in.

"What is it you want to talk about?"

"We need to work things out here. Why don't you go ahead and make a decision. Pay me what you think you owe me."

"Let's talk about the sliders. How many were there?"

"Eight. Floor to ceiling. They were special order. Twelve feet tall. I don't remember what we paid for them. But they were custom…"

"Of course they were."

"What? You think you can walk into a builder's warehouse and buy those? They were custom made. We had to wait four months to get them."

"Really? Mr. Whitstone, where are the frames for those eight floor to ceiling twelve foot tall sliders? Did you dump them in the canal too?"

Whitstone turned pale under his tan. He said nothing. Vin just stared at him. Didn't say a word. Just stared.

Still nothing from the perp, who now looked like he was about to lose his lunch. Vin flipped through some papers in his notebook and withdrew one, sliding it across the table until it was in front of Whitstone.

"Do you recognize this?" Whitstone said nothing. Vin went on, "That's your signature at the bottom, isn't it?"

The perp looked shell shocked. He gave half a nod. I was straining to read the document across the table. All I could tell is that it was a receipt from one of the local self storage places.

"Mr. Whitstone, would you like to tell me what you put in the storage unit you rented on August 16, three days after Charley? Or should I tell you?" He hung one of those long pauses in there. Then picked up where he left off. "As I said when we first arrived, people like you don't defraud insurance companies because you need the money. You do it because you think you can. You have a warped sense of entitlement. And you could care less that major fraud is part of the reason that premiums for yourself and all of your neighbors keep going up. What were you going to try and get from us for each of those glass doors?"

"They cost six grand apiece. Look, isn't there any way we can make this all go away. Any way?" By the time he said "any way" the second time, he was pleading. There's no way I can describe how good it made me feel to see the bastard grovel. Vin had a sharp stick up the guy's ass. The only question was how high he was going to shove it.

"Yes, we can make it all go away," Vin said. Whitstone looked shocked. Vin reached into his notebook and pulled out a one page document. "This is an acknowledgment that you attempted to defraud your insurance carrier. It also says that you waive your rights to any claim at all for damage to this property that may actually have been caused by the storm." He paused to let it sink in.

"You mean I get nothing?"

"Why does that surprise you? We're not going to waste our time trying to sort out the damage the storm caused from the damage you caused. And the mere fact that you've acknowledged an attempt to defraud gives us the right to deny your entire claim. If I thought that your family was going to suffer because of that denial, I might offer something. But you've got them living at the Ritz-Carlton in Sarasota, so you're not moving the needle on my sympathy meter."

"Do I have a choice?" he asked. I was surprised that he hadn't figured it all out by now. You'd think that a business guy who's made a fortune—probably screwing his customers—would understand leverage.

"Sure, you have a choice. You're not being coerced. I'm from your friendly, neighborhood insurance carrier. I wouldn't do that to you. You can refuse to sign this paper. You can call your attorney. Regardless of whether you sign or not, I'm still required to file a report with the state. They're not too happy with small cases, but you've hit the big time. I'm guessing that if I work out the cost of the custom cabinets you destroyed; add in the TV, the bedroom furniture, the pool table, all of it, we'll hit a hundred thousand dollars easy. The Division of Insurance Fraud pays attention to six figure cases. You know why? Because they make excellent examples and get lots of media attention. If the Charlotte County attorney won't bring it, the state will. You're looking at five years hard time. It's your choice, and you've got thirty seconds to make it before my associate and I walk out of here."

I had turned away from Vin to look at Whitstone's reaction to the come-to-Jesus speech when a loud crack tore through the air that had me diving for the floor. Damned startle response never goes away. I shouted, "That's a shot."

chapter 18
fly

It came from out front," Vin instantly responded. We both raced for the front door, but before I could get it open we heard a car barreling down the street, taking the turn at the corner on two wheels. Vin yanked on the door, forgetting that new hurricane building codes require that they open out. "Other way," I shouted.

The first thing I saw as we spilled out of the house was Jinx on the ground next to my car. For a nanosecond I thought he'd been shot, but then I realized that he was looking through the viewfinder of his camera which was pointed down the street.

"Jinx, you okay?"

"I'm fine. But I shoulda stuck with film. This friggin' digital camera takes six hours to boot up. I didn't get anything."

Vin was scanning the nearby houses when he noticed the Allstate pickup. "Over here," he yelled at the two of us as he took off on a dead run down the driveway. We raced across the street and over the lawn toward the vehicle. It was instantly obvious what had happened. The driver's side window was blown out and the Allstate man was slumped over the wheel. He'd taken one to the head. I shouted to Vin, "Check him, but I don't think we need EMS. I'll call it in."

I raced for the car and grabbed the portable radio from the center console, hitting the push-to-talk. "This is Reserve Officer

Moscone. Shots fired." I gave the address. Told them the victim was DOA and that the shooter got away in an unknown vehicle leaving the scene at a high rate of speed.

Under normal circumstances, there'd only be four patrol cars on duty at any given time. But post-Charley wasn't normal and there was no telling how many cars were available to flood the area. When the investigators arrived, Vin and I told them what we'd seen and heard—which wasn't much—and we returned to Whitstone's house to complete the insurance paperwork leaving Jinx to answer their questions. All the joy I had felt over making that prick's life miserable had dissipated.

Back in the car, the three of us rode in silence for a few minutes, making the lefts and rights to get us out of the cul-de-sac neighborhood. Finally, Vin broke the silence.

"Fly, what're you thinking?"

"I don't know. Why?"

"Of course you know. Seeing a guy with a bullet through his head got to you."

"I seen it in Nam."

"Punta Gorda isn't Nam."

I didn't answer. Vin was right; I just didn't want to admit it.

"It's my second dead body in weeks." I wanted to tell Vin to back off. The ex-cop was getting inside my head, and I didn't like the way it felt.

"In a big city, you could have a couple in a day," Vin said.

"You trying to needle me?"

"Needle? No. Just doing an assessment that we used to run on rookies. You'd prefer to change the subject?"

I reached in the cooler and took out a DDP. "Either of you want one?"

Vin scrunched up his face. "Not even if my cardiologist prescribed it and said it would make me live forever. So—you want to talk about the shooting? Either of you?"

"I'm all talked out," Jinx replied. "I answered the same questions for three different people. Seemed like a lot of wasted effort." His annoyance registered.

Right then I didn't want to talk about anything, and said so. I came to a stop sign and just sat there for a second. Then I cut loose at Vin. "You son-of-a-bitch. Why didn't you tell me you had him by the nuts? When did you get the storage receipt? How did you know?"

Jinx didn't have a clue what I was talking about, but I figured he was a journalist—he could pick up the story from the conversation. Except there was no conversation because Vin didn't answer me. I repeated my questions.

"Why don't you drive to the condo where the guy died during Charley, maybe we can learn something." Vin said.

I made a right and pulled away, torn between being pissed that Vin didn't trust me enough going in to tell me that he had the guy dead to rights, and admiring the way he handled the whole thing.

"Remember that I told you our adjustor knew the guy was a thief?" Vin asked. "What I didn't mention is that after he left Whitstone's house, he knocked on a few doors in the neighborhood. We train them to do that. There's an old Yiddish proverb that goes, 'Don't judge a man by the words of his mother, listen to the comments of his neighbors."

From the back seat, Jinx said, "I'm listening to old Jewish proverbs from a cop with a Scottish name. Who woulda' thought?"

Vin turned his head and looked at Jinx. "Oy vey!"

Then he turned back to me. "We know that a guy who is rotten enough to commit deliberate, major fraud, is probably not a great neighbor. Probably has a lot of attitude. And people are more than willing to help screw a neighbor who's gone out of his way to be an asshole. Sometimes the neighbors have seen something. Other times, the asshole has bragged about how he's screwing his insurance company. In this case, one of the neighbors said that a couple days after the storm hit, there was a U-Haul truck in Whitstone's driveway, and four or five Mexicans were helping him load it."

It still wasn't clear to me. "So how'd you track where he took the stuff?"

"Fly, it's not rocket science. If he took those doors out in order to file a claim that they were destroyed, sooner or later, he's going to bring them back. Why would he want to truck them halfway across the state? He wouldn't. He'd put them in a local storage place. So I pull out the yellow pages and begin calling all the self-storage outfits within five miles. They'd answer, and I'd say, 'I'm Vin Melton with Underwriters Insurance, and I'd like to know if the unit that Greg Whitstone rented has some things in it?' They look through their registry and if they say, 'Oh, you must be mistaken. He's not here,' you thank them and call the next one on the list. Sooner or later, you're going to get the right one. Then it's just a matter of going over, flashing ID—it doesn't even seem to matter what the ID says—and usually, they'll give you a copy of the contract. In this case, it was an inside unit and they offered to let me climb a ladder and look through the mesh on the top, although that's not even necessary."

I was blown away. "You make it seem so simple."

"It is—after you've been doing it for as long as I have."

"So why didn't you tell me before we got to his place."

"Fly, we only met six hours ago. I didn't know how you'd react in a situation like this one, and I didn't want to take any chances that you'd blow it."

From the back seat, Jinx piped up. "You could've asked me for a reference. I wouldn't have given him a good one—but just the same, you could've asked."

I wasn't in the mood for Jinx's attempt at humor. So I ignored it and said to Vin, "Now you know."

"You're right. Now I know." But Vin could see that I was still upset. "What?"

"You could throw these guys in the county lockup. They're goddam felons. But you let 'em off. It ain't right."

"Sorry, but life is like that sometimes," he responded. "That's not to say that I don't have little ways of sticking it to him."

"Like what?" I asked, intrigued that maybe Vin might not be such a wuss after all.

"When I nail a guy who seems remorseful, I tip him off that as soon as my report goes in to the company, his insurance is going to be cancelled. And I tell him that as soon as I drive away, he ought to be on the phone trying to get a new policy, so that when he fills out the application, he doesn't have to check 'yes' when it asks if he's ever been cancelled or non-renewed. That at least gives him a shot at getting coverage."

"You didn't tip off Whitstone?" I asked in a voice bordering on the soprano side of disbelief.

"You're not serious?" Vin asked, with a smile on his face.

As we pulled into the parking lot for the condos where Rolex Man died, I said "I'm not sure what we're going to find here. I'm guessing that they've moved his stuff out of the unit—at least the valuable stuff. Getting in shouldn't be a problem. Vin didn't respond. He was just taking it all in.

As the three of us walked up the stairs to the penthouse apartment, I told Vin about the Picasso and how it had turned up at Steve's store. When we got to Catlett's apartment, the door was still hanging open. Ceiling insulation was all over the place. No one was around. Vin stepped through the open doorway and stopped. "Tell me exactly what it looked like when you walked in here after the hurricane."

We did a very slow walk-through during which Jinx shot a bunch of pictures. I took about ten minutes to describe everything I remembered. Vin listened carefully, then asked, "What's different now?"

"The body's gone, of course. The crap on the floor has been kicked all around. When I walked in that day it was clear that there were footprints from the door to the bed."

"Did they go directly to the bed? Or did someone take the grand tour?"

"That's a tough one, to be honest. There were footprints near the broken slider in the living room, and they went to the bedroom. But the dead guy could have made those. The only ones that didn't make any sense what with everyone denying they'd come into the place were the ones from the bed to the front door."

"Could you tell that they came in and went out? Were there tracks in both directions?"

"Vin, it wasn't like that. It wasn't like someone making a path through new snow. You might see a footprint here and there, but mostly I just seen sort of a trail."

"Any chance it was the stiff who walked to the front door, and then back to the bed?"

"I doubt it. First of all, there was no blood trail in that direction. Second, he was bleeding like a stuck pig. I have to believe all he could think about was getting a tourniquet on his leg and lying down. The phones were working when he got hit, but there's no indication he tried to call 911. And no one heard him yelling for help."

"Why would he stay here? There were warnings. Why didn't he get the hell out?"

"What I read in the newspaper is speculation by friends who guessed that he didn't want to leave his *stuff*. He'd been written up in the papers for having a lot of antiques and valuable art-work—stuff that was too big to throw in his Caddy."

"The newspaper article about him before he died—it said where he lived? And that he had a valuable collection?"

"Yeah. I see where you're going, but I don't think anyone came in here to rip him off. He was wearing the Rolex Mariner that I seen on him at Dean's. I lifted up his left arm to look at it when he was lying on the bed. If someone's coming in to rip off the place, they're not going to leave a Rolex."

"When you were up here, could you tell if any of the antiques or paintings you'd seen in the paper were gone? The Picasso?"

"Nah, the place was pretty much blown around. And honest-ly—with a dead guy lying there, and people out front that I needed to question, I didn't think of taking an inventory of what was here."

"Fly, why are you so convinced that the guy was murdered?"

"You ever get a feeling in your gut that something is wrong but you can't put your finger on it?" I didn't wait for an answer. "That's the feeling I got when I came in here that first time. Mostly, though, it's from knowin' that someone came in here right after the storm."

"Okay. Let's go." Vin didn't say another word as we sweated our way down the stairs to the car. Fly started it up and cranked the AC on high, then grabbed a towel from the backseat to wipe off his face.

Vin busied himself getting a bottle of cold water out of the cooler, twisting off the cap and taking a swig. Jinx did the same.

"Fly…" Vin said, and then took another swig. "Fly, I've always told my partners that they need to go with their gut. I've only known you for a day, but I like what I see. Let's assume your instincts are correct. Where do you go from here?"

I put down the towel, cracked open another DDP and almost drained the can. Then I belched. "That's what I was hoping you could tell me. I mean, just because you might have beat confessions out of a few scumbags doesn't mean you don't know anything about homicide investigations, right?"

Vin just shook his head. "Fly, how'd you pass the psych test to become a volunteer deputy or whatever the hell they call the program?"

"I've been asking him that for months," Jinx said. "Apparently, they do have standards. But they're low."

"Did you ever consider that I was perfectly sane till I began hanging with you?"

"Not even for a second," Jinx replied.

"Hey, Vin, considering what happened today, I gotta ask you something serious. You said that you'd been threatened with a machete and a shotgun. I thought Whitstone might try to pull something like that. He didn't seem to have his laces knotted."

"It happens. But I'm ready. Even in a nice place like PGI." He leaned over and pulled up his right pants leg. Strapped to his ankle was a small revolver. "S&W .38 caliber Chief's Special with a two inch barrel. If I can't stop him with five hydro-shocks, I deserve whatever is coming my way. I showed you mine, now you show me yours."

I was taken aback. "You know?"

"You're kidding me, right? First of all, you're new on the job. What's a new cop's favorite toy? Second, I give you credit for having brains enough to know that there's no telling how someone is going to respond when we drop by with the message that he's a fucking thief and he's not getting a penny of my company's money. Third, why else would you wear a butt-ugly Hawaiian shirt like that if you weren't hiding something besides a pot belly. So let's see it."

"Fly actually thinks that shirt is smart and stylish. It's actually a couple steps up from the wife beater undershirt of his youth," smirked Jinx.

"We called 'em Italian smoking jackets, you *stunad*." I lifted the shirt and pulled the gun out. "It's a Glock 27—.40 caliber. Only weighs twenty ounces plus the rounds. Ten shots." Checking the safety, I stuck it back in the holster. "You ever have to use a gun? Since you left the force?"

"Never. But I've drawn it a few times. Once on the guy who came after me with a machete when I told him that the holes in his roof weren't made by hailstones, but by a ball peen hammer. Another time it was in a rural area and I managed to stumble into a meth lab. That could've ended unhappily, but the guy was high and fortunately, he was the only one home." He changed the subject. "So, you know how to use that thing?"

"I'm pretty good on the range, when the target's close," I said. "But I'll be honest with you, I don't know how I'd do pointing it at a person. This isn't Nam—and anyway, I was a kid then and didn't know any better. But I figure that if I need to use it, I'll find the strength. And as long as I'm hanging out with you while someone is running around killing insurance guys, I feel better having it with me." I put the car in gear and began driving toward the center of town.

"Wouldn't be a bad idea for me to get some range practice while I'm down here? You up for that? Or you afraid I might embarrass you?" Vin said, a smile crinkling his face for the first time that day.

I rose to the challenge. "Any time you want. Nine mils at ten paces."

chapter 19
fly

Vin was silent for a few minutes, then said, "I'd like to go back to the sheriff's office and find out what's going on with these shootings."

"Then we need to drop Jinx off at home. Besides, he's had enough fun today for someone his age," I responded.

"Just when I was beginning to get a feel for the story, you're shutting me out?"

"I'd take you with us," I said sincerely, "but I don't want them asking me all sorts of questions about you. 'Specially not with what went on today."

With Jinx safely at home, I headed to the cop shop, fielding suggestions from Vin along the way.

"You said Rolex Man's apartment was filled with valuable stuff—antiques, artwork. Where'd it go? You've got to find out. My thought would be to call the medical examiner and find out who they released the body to. Then track it from there. Sooner or later, you'll end up talking to a lawyer who's handling the guy's estate."

"Anything else?"

"Yeah. The question the cops on TV always asks the dead man's wife. 'Did he have any enemies?' Try and track that down. You know he was an asshole, but did anyone hate him enough to kill him? Did he have any friends you could ask?"

There was a very long pause before the light bulb went off over my head.

Vin noticed the raised eyebrows and wide eyes. "What?" he asked.

"Lacey Drawers," I said, as though Vin would understand what I meant.

He didn't. "What are lacy drawers?"

"Not what. Who." I provided a full explanation which included a thorough description of Lacey's recently acquired anatomical enhancements, the better to play her role as Punta Gorda's Black Widow.

Back at the sheriff's office, I checked in with the captain, and then we headed down a hall filled with metal file cabinets recently relocated from a section of the building blown apart by Charley, ending in a room where the detectives hung out. Lt. Lew Albert, who'd taken our statements at the murder scene, looked up from his notes. In lighter moments, we called him Loo Lew just to annoy him. This wasn't a lighter moment for him.

"Fly, you guys think of anything else?"

"No, Loo, but Vin wanted to ask you a couple of questions." I nodded in the insurance investigator's direction. "He spent some time in homicide up in New York."

"I'm guessing they have a bit more help in New York than we've got here," Albert said. "You got any ideas?"

"Don't know enough to have any ideas. One dead. One hit. One miss. And the only thing that ties the three targets together is that they all worked for insurance companies as adjustors," said Vin.

Vin scratched his chin for a second, then said, "I'm guessing you've already begun trying to figure out who the vics pissed off. No way you can adjust cat claims by the bucketful and not have that happen." Vin asked a half dozen more question while I just listened quietly. Yeah, I know. It's against my nature. But Jersey guys know that sometimes it pays to keep your mouth shut and your ears open. Sophia's been trying to get me to do that for years.

chapter 20
fly

I don't mean to interrupt," Jinx said, interrupting, "but we're here." None of us had noticed that he'd slowed the boat almost to a stop and was waiting for another vessel to back away from the dock. Hickory Dickory was legendary for its incredibly dumb but unforgettable name, and its gumbo, which was good enough to warrant a forty-five minute drive from Punta Gorda if you didn't feel like coming by boat. Laura and I hadn't been here since before Charley, and were looking forward to it. The gumbo is all I could talk about since we began planning the trip.

"You don't really think I'm going to let you bring her in, do you?" I said, quickly moving to take the helm that Jinx was more than willing to vacate.

"Fly, you want me on the bow to help tie us up?" Jinx offered, realizing it was a mistake about a millisecond after it left his lips.

"Jinx, I don't want you going anywhere near the bow," I shouted. "That side deck is only six inches wide. Twenty years ago, you might have been able to make it. And even if you managed to make it to the bow without falling in, you'd never be able to toss the line to the kid on the dock. I've seen you play baseball with your grandkids. Pathetic."

By the time I finished abusing him, Sophia was already making her way to the foredeck. We had the routine down pat, so I really didn't need Jinx's help.

"Don't feel bad for my husband," said Laura, "they do this to each other all the time. They thrive on the abuse." She looked at the two couples who had been taking it all in, but directed her comment only to the wives. "Men." The women nodded as though it was a code that meant something only they could understand.

Jinx did know enough to head for the stern, toss a bumper over the side, and secure the stern line, but he knows better than to expect a thank you. "Okay," I said from the bridge. "Be careful getting off. Jinx, instead of daydreaming about gumbo, you might want to be useful and help the ladies."

jinx

"Wait a second, Captain. Rushing them off the boat is no way to treat our guests. This is a special moment."

I flipped up the rail, stepped off the boat, and made a formal announcement. "If you'll all come right this way…" I helped the women disembark, and watched the men follow. "Ladies and gentlemen, I want to be the first to welcome you to—wait for it—Hickory Dickory's Dock." I tried to hide a look of smug satisfaction. Sophia and Laura just shook their heads. Fly rolled his eyes, but I could tell he knew I'd taken the moment from him and he was annoyed. And the newbies? I didn't know whether they were just stunned by the magnificence of it, or just didn't get it. Unfortunately, I quickly learned it was the latter.

"Hickory Dickory's dock?" asked Rich, oblivious to the humor.

"Oh, you know," Laurie said, poking her husband in the arm, "we said it all the time with the babies. Hickory Dickory Dock, the mouse ran up the clock…"

Then all four of the women finished it off, "The clock struck one, the mouse ran down, Hickory Dickory Dock."

"That's pathetic. It don't even rhyme," Fly complained, as he stepped onto the dock and took the lead toward the restaurant.

Laurie was undeterred. "Hickory Dickory Dock, the bird looked at the clock. The clock struck two, away she flew. Hickory Dickory Dock."

"All right, Laurie, that's enough," Rich mumbled, clearly embarrassed.

Our group was seated almost immediately, and a basket of incredible jalapeno corn muffins, garlic rolls dripping with olive oil, and warm mini-baguettes with a crunchy crust arrived simultaneously with the menus. Fly didn't wait for the newcomers to ask for recommendations. "You've got to have the gumbo. It's better than anything we ever had in New Orleans." The menu described the gumbo as "a sublime combination of crab, shrimp, okra and tomato with just the right touch of heat."

"I'll go along with Fly on that one," I said. "Their gumbo is fantastic. Huge shrimp, and lots of crab legs filled with meat. Get the full bowl, a side salad, and unless you're starving, it's a meal."

The waitress took our order. Only Kim skipped the gumbo, something about being allergic to okra. Sounded to me like she got turned off by the gooey slime that shows up if it's not cooked right. In Hickory Dickory's gumbo, that's never a problem, but I wasn't in the mood to try to change her mind. I knew she'd be happy with the blackened fresh grouper sandwich.

We hadn't gotten very far into small talk when the gumbo arrived, along with Kim's dinner salad. Fly took one look and went apoplectic. "Wait a minute," he said as the server was about to leave. "This isn't right. Where's the crab legs? I didn't get any crab legs in my gumbo." Then he looked over the rest of the table. "No one has any crab legs. What happened? You reached the bottom of the pot and just gave us what was left? This isn't right."

Sophia had put her hand on his arm in an effort to quiet him down, but it wasn't working. He was so busy complaining, he didn't hear the server, a cute blonde in her early twenties whose nametag said she was Emily from Tennessee, saying, "Sir...sir...I can explain, sir."

Finally, Fly sputtered out, and Emily was able to make herself heard. "Sir, we had to stop putting crab legs in our gumbo because a woman choked on a piece of shell and sued us. I'm sorry."

"Did she die?" Fly asked, with no apparent sympathy.

"No, nothing like that, although the manager did do the Heimlich Maneuver on her and she spit it out."

"Then why did she sue?" Fly asked, working himself into a state of red-faced indignation.

"I don't know why she sued, sir. I do know her husband was a lawyer, but that's all I know. Would you excuse me, please? I need to take care of another table." And with that, she pretty much ran away.

But Fly wasn't finished. He turned to Rich Aronson, the trial lawyer from Chicago. "This isn't right. I don't get crab legs in my gumbo 'cause some bimbo married to some Rambo of a lawyer—" he almost spit when he said the word—"wasn't smart enough to know not to eat the shell."

Aronson, who'd undoubtedly heard better anti-lawyer rants in his career than Fly's bimbo Rambo gumbo outburst, looked at him calmly and said, "What's your point?"

"My point is that because of some sleazeball lawyer, I don't get a crab leg in my gumbo."

"And next you're going to tell me that you pay more for medical care because your doctor does tests you don't need so he doesn't get sued. And that your car insurance costs too much because lawyers take phony cases and get settlements. And we already heard that homeowners insurance premiums are sky high because of...oh wait...that had nothing to do with lawyers. Just sleazy homeowners. You probably didn't notice it's the lawyers who go after those sleazeballs on behalf of the insurance companies who keep your premiums from going even higher than they are."

Everyone at the table had stopped their side conversations to listen to the guy. In fact, everyone at nearby tables had stopped talking and was listening, too.

But Aronson wasn't finished. "You know, it takes a lot of nerve for an Italian from New Jersey to be stereotyping anyone. Bada Bing! I'm waiting for your best lawyer joke. I know it's coming. C'mon. Whatta youse got?"

"Geez, you bustin' my agates now? I didn't expect you to take it personally," said Fly. I could tell he was secretly glad that Aronson had some *cojones*. "But since you asked: Two lawyers are shipwrecked on a desert island for months when a beautiful mermaid appears. One lawyer says to the other, 'Hey, let's screw her.' The other immediately replies, 'Out of what?'" The look on Fly's face, which was now back to its normal shade of light tan from bright red, was one of satisfaction. It wouldn't last long.

"Not bad. But I can top it," Aronson said.

"You're going to tell a lawyer joke?" Fly asked quizzically.

"No, a client joke. Ready? A client, who cruelly fired his faithful lawyer, is defending himself at trial for having been caught by a game warden just as he blew a Spotted Owl into a flurry of feathers. After convicting him of the charges, the judge—well known for his environmental sympathies—gravely announced that since the species concerned is in danger of imminent extinction, he would have to make an example out of the defendant. But before he pronounced sentence, he asked if the defendant had anything he wished to say.

"The client said he was very sorry for what he'd done, but that he was totally destitute and needed the bird to feed his hungry children. All he had to his name, he said, his voice cracking with emotion, was the little bit of bird shot he had left for his shotgun.

"The judge wiped a tear from the corner of his eye, and after regaining his composure, told the defendant he would let him go with a warning this time. The client beamed with pride as he started out of the courtroom. Just then, the judge called out, 'Oh, by the way, what does a Spotted Owl taste like?'

"The man's face came alive as he turned around and said, 'Your honor, it's hard to describe. Sort of a cross between a Bald Eagle, a Whooping Crane and a California Condor.'"

Fly looked at Aronson in disbelief. Then turned to me. "This guy has agates after all. He might be okay."

It fell to me to explain what Fly meant. "We were worried that you couldn't take it. But you passed the test." I turned to the other guy at the table, Robbie Beiler, and said, "Be ready. You never know when he's going to come after you."

"Come after me? I didn't realize I had to pass a test to retire down here," Beiler responded.

"You don't," Fly said, gruffly. "But you should. You'll see for yourself. It won't take more than a few food-and-friends dinners for you to figure it out. Unless you're like them." The *them* was not specified, and Fly's little nod away from our table wasn't enough to explain it. So I jumped in, again.

"We'll have breakfast next week—just us guys. Meantime I'll send you a copy of Man Rules so you'll understand."

chapter 21
fly

Back aboard *Inamorata* with Jinx at the helm, I picked up the story the morning after the Allstate adjustor was murdered.

The mutt began yapping shortly after ten in the morning, followed momentarily by the sound of the doorbell. From the master bedroom, I yelled, "Sophia, that's Vin. Will you get it?" I was running late because I was still going through the shirts in my closet, trying to find one that might hide the gun yet get me through the day without suffering more ridicule.

By the time I got to the living room, Vin and Sophia were on first name terms and deep in discussion, which caused me no end of concern.

"You're not tellin' her anything about me, are you? Cuz that would be unacceptable."

"As a matter of fact, I'm not," Vin replied. "I was just asking if you'd looked at your computer this morning, and she said you hadn't. That for the first time in a long time, you'd slept through the alarm clock. I guess that's what a real day's work will do for you."

"Don't be so smug. It wasn't the work. It was the new pill I'm taking for my prostate. I can't believe it. I peed before I went to bed, and didn't have to pee until I got up this morning. This is going to be a great day."

That's when I noticed the look on Sophia's face.

"What? What is it?"

"There's another hurricane coming this way," Vin said. "Frances."

"You're shitting me." I looked at Vin's face closely. Then at Sophia. Back to Vin. "Okay, you're not shitting me. I thought when Danielle and Earl went elsewhere, we were done for the season. Now we're getting Frances? Which way is that bitch going?"

"According to the tracking maps, if it follows the computer models, it'll hit the east coast near West Palm Beach then come across the state. It's projected to go west northwest, which would take it toward Tampa, but…"

I didn't let Vin finish the sentence. "Yeah, I know. Charley was supposed to go to Tampa, too, until he decided to visit Charlotte Harbor. How much time do we have?"

"It's still six or seven days out. A lot can happen. Meantime, I've got one more fraud case I'd like you to go with me on."

That's when Sophia came to life again. I had been watching her out of the corner of my eye. I thought she was mesmerized by the talk of us getting whacked by another hurricane, but that wasn't it. She looked right at Vin and asked, "You're not getting him involved in anything where he could get hurt, are you? I read in the newspaper about the killing." Since I was behind Sophia, she couldn't see me point to where Vin knew my gun was hidden, and then shake my head in warning. Translation: "She has no idea I'm carrying a gun, and you better not be the one to tell her. She thinks I'm just chauffeuring you around PGI. Don't say anything that will make her think otherwise."

Later I told Jinx, "I've gotta hand it to Vin. He was good. See, if he'd been too quick to deny that we could get into any trouble, Sophia would pick up on it, know she was being patronized, discuss it with Laura, and there'd be hell to pay when I got home.

And oh yeah, she'd worry all day long, for which I'd also pay a steep price sooner or later. But if Vin did the old hommina-hommina routine, she'd know he was full of crap."

What Vin did was perfect. He said, "Mrs. Moscone, I'm sure you're nervous about your husband being a cop—especially at his age. I have to tell you, Fly's instincts are right on the money. If you'd seen him yesterday when we nailed a guy for attempted fraud approaching a hundred thousand dollars, you would have been proud. He can think on his feet, and despite the fact that I know he just started doing this stuff, he acts like he's been doing it for years."

Sophia had tears in her eyes. "Now you've done it," I said to Vin, and punched him in the shoulder. "You made her cry." Then I walked over and gave Soph a big hug—being careful to make sure she couldn't feel the Glock tucked into my waistband under a more subdued tropical shirt than the apparent atrocity I'd worn yesterday. "It's all good, honey. Really, it is." She kissed me, and then impulsively stood on her tiptoes to kiss Vin on the cheek.

"You're not getting involved in the murders, are you?" she said to me, more as an instruction than a question.

"No, dear, I'm just assigned to drive Vin around. You can re-lax." And before the conversation could develop, I moved to-ward the kitchen, "C'mon, Vin, our appointment's in ten minutes." And without waiting for a response or even checking to see whether Vin was following, I cut through to the laundry room, then into the garage, hit the clicker to open the door, got in the SUV, backed out and waited for Vin to climb in.

As he did, Vin said, "She's really emotional. I'm surprised she signed off on you doing this cop work."

"You know they came out and interviewed the two of us to-gether. I'm sure she would have liked to tell them that she doesn't agree with me doing this, and that would have been the end of it. But this thing with me having been sick cuts two ways. On the one hand she doesn't want me taking risks and getting hurt. On the other hand, she knows how much I always wanted to be a cop—a detective actually—and she knows I gave it up in order to take a job that paid a whole lot better and would provide better for my family. So she sees letting me do this as a way of making up for that. But if she would've felt the gun under my shirt, I guarantee you'd be on your own this morning. And by the way, I wanna thank you for telling her about the new hurricane."

"Sorry, I figured since you guys were now hurricane veterans, the next one wouldn't get you all bent out of shape."

"Vin, how long you married?"

"Twenty-five years. That's a running total. Why?"

"You didn't learn anything about women in twenty-five years? All you did by telling her about a new hurricane is trigger the worry gene. Right now she's checking the Weather Channel and calling her girlfriends. By the time she finishes, they'll have whipped it into a Category 10 storm heading straight for our front door."

"Sorry."

"Was your wife all that relaxed and happy when you were working homicide?"

"She wasn't. Maybe that's why she became my ex-wife after five years. I married my second wife when I began doing insurance work."

"All right, it is what it is. I'll have to try and smooth things over when I get home. What criminals are we not going to lock up today?"

"How 'bout if I make it up to you? You take the lead on this morning's visit."

Suddenly, my palms got sweaty, like a teenage boy whose girlfriend tells him he's gonna get lucky tonight.

chapter 22
fly

I wanted to tell Jinx about my personal triumph over the fraud artists Vin had sicced me on, but he and Laura had to drive over to the east coast to have dinner with the Zimmermans and thank them for the use of the condo. They came home two days later, and Sophia invited Vin to join the four of us for a barbeque.

Over drinks on the screenless lanai, I began telling Jinx the story, which I knew he wouldn't buy. "Hey, Vin is my witness, right?"

Vin nodded in the affirmative.

"Wait a second," Jinx said in total disbelief, "you're telling me they stuck a dining room chair through the ceiling and tried to say Charley did it?"

"That's what the *jadrool* said."

"But it's so f-ing stupid," Jinx responded. "Vin, she really thought you'd buy it?"

"I have yet to decide whether they do it because they think I'm stupid, or they're just a few pancakes short of a stack. I think one of the reasons they do such dumb things is that they don't spend a lot of time thinking it through. A hurricane comes through, and they think *damage*. So they trash the place. They don't consider that hurricane winds are not random. They have a pattern. They move in certain ways. We have a pretty good idea what wind will do once it gets inside a house."

"I would have never thought about bringing in a garden hose and wetting down my own house," I said.

"Fly, let's not pretend you're an altar boy." Vin raised his eyebrows and looked over at Jinx. "He told me some stories about his misspent youth under the boardwalk."

I tried to defend myself. "Yeah, but I was a kid. Kids do dumb things. That's what being a kid is for."

Vin changed the subject. "You know what I'm surprised we haven't had a lot of calls about? Boat fraud."

"Hurricanes do destroy boats," I interjected.

"And sometimes they have help doing it," said Vin. "Because at some level, most people really and truly want to get rid of their boats. It's the old joke…"

Jinx popped in, "Second happiest day in a guy's life is when he buys a boat. Happiest day is when he sells it. You'll notice I'm an exceptionally happy man."

I ignored his self-professed happiness, and turned to my own issues. "Do you know what a pain in the ass it's going to be to get the gelcoat fixed on my boat? And replacing the windshield that cracked? I haven't had time to check, but I guarantee you, I'll still be working on getting it fixed when the next hurricane season starts."

"And you'll still be whining about it," said Jinx. He looked over his shoulder toward the kitchen to make sure that the women were well out of earshot, then turned to Vin, "You think they'll solve the murder *before* next hurricane season? Or at all?"

"I can't say. How impressed should I be with the investigators here in Charlotte County? Even if they're top notch, you don't have the resources we had in New York."

"And I'm not so sure they're top notch," I added. "Long time ago I was talkin' to a Punta Gorda cop; had twenty on the job with a gold shield in New York, then retired down here. I asked him something about solving murders and he said if you wanna get away with murder, do it here. That could've just been talk, but who knows?"

"You got any ideas?" Jinx asked.

With a covert glance toward the kitchen, I responded. "I've been thinking about the shootings. We've got one dead and two that coulda been. All insurance adjustors. All in their vehicles, which all had company logos on them. And it looks like they were all shot from a distance, probably with a rifle. Maybe a sniper rifle with a scope. Lots of retired military down here."

I turned to Vin, "You disagree?"

"Nope," Vin answered. "I'm just puzzled by someone taking out a mixed bag of adjustors. Someone has a general grudge against the species. It would be easier to solve if the vics were all from the same company. At least that would narrow the suspect list down to a couple thousand or so. I just can't figure this one out—not with the information at hand."

"I'm trying to remember what the TV DA's wanted detectives to bring them," Jinx said. "What was it? Means, motive, opportunity? Something like that."

"You're right," Vin replied. "In this case our perp has got plenty of opportunity."

"Yeah, that narrows it down a lot," I added, sarcastically. Then I just stood there, open-mouthed, like a thought had just struck me between the eyes.

"What?" Jinx asked.

"This may be obvious, but I think our shooter is local, someone who lives here, someone who knows his way around the Isles."

"There are a lot of people who might know their way around but don't live here," Vin tossed back. "Mailmen, UPS and FedEx drivers, garbage truck drivers, all sorts of service people, plumbers, electricians, even landscape workers. I wouldn't limit the suspects just to residents."

"But listen to me," I said. "None of those types you mentioned could disappear quickly. There's only a couple of streets that actually get directly out of the Isles and back to US 41. But someone who lives here could take a shot, drive three minutes back to his house, click a button and disappear into his garage."

I glanced toward the kitchen and saw Sophia and Laura headed toward us. "So—how 'bout those Cubs?"

"What about the Cubs?" asked Laura, a diehard Cubs fan going back to her childhood on Chicago's North Side, as she walked out onto the lanai with Sophia right behind her. "You're not putting down my team, are you Paul?"

I took a shot at saving myself. "Nah, I'm not putting down the Cubs. I don't believe in picking on the handicapped."

Sophia stepped in to save me, putting a tray of ribeyes in my hands and pointing toward the grill. "Cook!" she ordered.

"Yes, dear," I muttered like a well-trained husband, and went off to do as I was told. Over my shoulder, I could hear Sophia starting up a conversation with Vin, and it made me nervous.

"Paul says you used to be a homicide detective up north. He's told you about his suspicions?"

"You mean with the dead guy in the condo? Yeah, he took me over to look at the place."

"You think there's any merit in what he believes—that it might be murder? Or is he letting his imagination run away with him?"

It's always nice for a guy to hear his wife expressing doubts about his sanity, emotional stability and intellect to his guy friends. She has no idea how they'll use it all against me the first chance they get.

"I don't know, Sophia," Vin said. "Let's just say the circumstances aren't especially clear, and since the medical examiner has already ruled it an accidental death, if it is murder, Fly is the only one around who's going to dig it out."

"I see," said Sophia, in one of those judgmental tones that husbands the world over know all too well.

Vin caught the tone. "Look, Fly has great instincts. I gave him a lot of rope today just so I could see what he'd do with it. You'll notice…" he pointed at me sweating over the steaks, "no rope burns around his neck. He did a great job nailing a crook. I just wish I could make him happy and toss the bum in jail."

"He told me about that. It just doesn't seem right. All the people who live by the rules, and someone tries to steal from their insurance company and basically gets away with it. And what happens? Our premiums go up."

"Wait a second," said Vin, "they aren't getting away with it. They're going to pay for everything they damaged. I'm not doing them any favors on stuff that the storm destroyed. And their insurance is going to be cancelled. The notation in their file will be such that *if* they find a company willing to write them a policy, the premium will be only slightly lower than the national debt."

From the other end of the lanai, where I have to say I was doing a more than respectable job of making certain the steaks were a perfect medium rare by the professional touch method, I turned and shouted at Vin, "I want to see them do hard time."

Vin listened, turned to Sophia and said, "He's like a broken record."

"You're telling me? Try living with him," she responded.

"Okay," said Vin, "then *why* do you put up with him?"

"It must be his charm. It took me about thirty years to get used to it. Now it's sort of like not hearing the trucks going by when your house is only thirty feet from the highway."

chapter 23
fly

The next morning I put on my uniform, signed out a squad car, and then stopped by Jinx's house to pick him up before driving over to the medical examiner's office. Jinx waited in the car while I went in and asked to see the file on the dead guy. The clerk asked no questions, which is just how I hoped it would be. I smiled a lot, photocopied the information I needed, and left.

What I'd been looking for is what Vin had suggested I get—the name of the person who authorized release of John Catlett's body to a funeral home. I got back in the car, turned to Jinx and said, "You're not gonna believe it," as I handed him the paperwork.

Jinx took one look and said, "You're right. I don't." The executor of Catlett's estate was a local attorney whose name is Strom Thurmond. No, I'm not kidding. That's the guy's name.

"How in hell are you going to meet with him and not break into hysterical laughter?" Jinx asked. I didn't have a good answer.

Fifteen minutes later we were back at my house where I got out the Yellow Pages. The fifty or sixty pages of ads for attorneys were slightly absurd for a county of fewer than 150,000 people. There in the midst of full page ads suggesting that lawsuits are the answer to whatever ailments or affronts you may have suffered, real or imagined, was a modest little bold-faced listing that read:

THURMOND, STROM ATTORNEY AT LAW

The address was in downtown Punta Gorda, smack in the middle of an area hit hardest by one of the vortices in Charley's eye wall.

The highest measured wind during the storm was a whopping 173 MPH, just down the street from Thurmond's office. From a helicopter it's easy to see the swath cut by one of those vortices. One side of a street, everything's blown apart. The other side of the street is open for business. It's like nothing happened. You could liken it to the way a tornado sweeps through a town, and lots of folks here have been saying that Charley spawned tornadoes. But the experts say there were no tornadoes near the eyewall. There were vortices. It don't make any difference to the stores who got hit whether it was one or the other, but if I'm not precise in choosing my words, Jinx busts my balls. The question of the day is on which side of the street is Strom Thurmond's office?

I picked up the phone and dialed the listed number. On the second ring, a pleasant-sounding woman answered, "Attorney Thurmond's office."

"Hello, this is Deputy Paul Moscone with the Charlotte County Sheriff's Office. I have a matter I'd like to discuss with Mr. Thurmond."

"I'm his assistant, Lisa. He'll be back in the office in half an hour. Would you like to come over, or talk with him on the telephone?"

I said I'd rather meet Thurmond in person, made certain that his office was still on Sullivan Street in the downtown area, and said I'd be there at 10:30. She asked if she could tell her boss what I wanted to talk about, and I said that it had to do with a former client of his, John Catlett.

Fifteen minutes before the appointment, I parked the cruiser half a block from the office. The building needed some repair work, but it hadn't been beat up too badly. Across the street was blue tarp city, and it was clear that roof tarps weren't going to be enough to save some of the structures.

"If you're gonna come in with me, we gotta have a reason," I said.

"Not a problem. I'm retired. I'm working free-lance on a magazine article about the aftermath of Hurricane Charley and I'm shadowing you on this aspect of it."

"That actually sounds believable. He'll never go for it."

"Sure he will. And if he doesn't want to talk with me in the room, I'll leave. Don't worry about it." We agreed, and at precisely 10:30, I pulled into the small parking lot behind Thurmond's building, and we walked inside. Lisa looked up, smiled, and said, "Go right in. He's expecting you." She didn't even ask who the guy in civvies was. I thanked her and we walked into a modest office with a window that gave the occupant a nice view of the devastation. Behind the desk was a slender man, jet black long hair pulled into a ponytail, frameless eyeglasses, probably in his mid-fifties, wearing a short-sleeve white shirt and knit tie with a squared-off bottom. I used to wear those—forty years ago. A wrinkled navy blue suit coat was draped over one of the chairs at a small conference table. I sniffed the air a couple times. Damned if he wasn't burning patchouli incense. *This* Strom Thurmond had some hippie in him.

As we entered, he stood up, and we could see he was wearing jeans. He came around the desk and stuck out his hand, "Deputy Moscone, I'm Strom Thurmond."

What am I supposed to say after a line like that—not that in his lifetime he probably hasn't heard every response possible? He must have caught the look that flashed across both our faces when he said his name. "Everyone reacts that way. At least everyone over forty."

I introduced Jinx, who said he was writing an article, and when that didn't elicit a negative response, said, "I gotta ask. How'd you get that name? You related?"

"You want the long version or the short one?"

"As long as you're not billing by the hour, we'll take the long one." It was a lesson I had learned from my days as a salesman. If you want to get information, get the client talking about himself.

"Can I offer you some tea? I just brewed a pot of Red Zinger." Jinx and I looked at each other, accepted, and made ourselves comfortable while he ducked out to get the tea. I'm guessing that asking the receptionist to pour would have been exploiting the working class.

After settling back in behind his desk, Strom began. "My family is from South Carolina, the Charleston area. They lived there since forever. I have ancestors who fought with Robert E. Lee. I found a diary one time that seemed to indicate we were slave owners and had a fairly large cotton plantation, but no one I ever asked would own up to it. The family name wasn't Thurmond back then. It was Thurston.

"Just before World War II, Strom Thurmond became a circuit court judge, but after Pearl Harbor, he signed up and got himself a commission in the army, and was assigned as a JAG officer. Well, my father had some college and somehow, he was assigned to be Thurmond's law clerk. Maybe someone in personnel thought it would be funny to have Thurston clerking for Thurmond. Dumber things have happened in the army, right?"

It was a question that didn't require an answer, so we just nodded our heads and encouraged him to continue. I was having a bit of buyer's remorse on the long version of the story, because it was beginning to look like I'd be in Diet Dr. Pepper withdrawal by the time Thurmond finished.

"Anyway, the two of them spent the rest of the war together. After dad came home, he went back to work in my grandfather's restaurant, and as far as I know, never saw Thurmond until he began his campaign for South Carolina governor in '46. Dad did some campaigning for him, and I guess tried to impress the women with the fact that he was tight with the new governor." He paused, looked at us, and asked, "This taking too long?"

"No, but I'm curious where it's going," Jinx replied.

"Okay, I'll get there soon. Right around this time, the civil rights movement was starting up. You know, the Klan was still active, lynchings weren't uncommon, and Truman was on the way to desegregating the army. That's what probably did it for dad. That and seeing his old commanding officer lead a walkout of Southern Democrats at the 1948 Democratic Convention. Dad was involved with a girl around the same time, and it looked like they were going to get married. I'm not sure if this happened before or after he proposed, but he told the girl—my mom—that he was really proud to have served with the governor in the war. And my mom said that since she was going to have to change her name when they got married, why doesn't dad also change his name—from Thurston to Thurmond as a way of honoring the governor and what he stands for."

I could actually hear Jinx rolling his eyes when Thurmond said that, but he covered it by coughing a couple of times. To my credit, I managed to maintain a poker face.

"So that's what happened. A few years later, when I was born, they named me Strom. Growing up in South Carolina, it wasn't a hindrance or anything. But when I applied to colleges in the north, in the 1960s, and they saw where I was from, it caused some problems. People make all sorts of assumptions, as I'm sure you can imagine. Then they see the pony tail and get really confused. At heart, I'm the pony tail. But I'm too stubborn to change the name.

"Even here, I get clients because of it. And I'm sure I've probably lost clients because of the name. So that's my story."

"That's a story all right," I said.

"So what can I do for you? Lisa said you had some questions about John Catlett?"

"What can you do for me? You can tell me about Catlett."

He pursed his lips and shook his head. "Now there's a guy who hired me because of the name."

Jinx piped up before I could respond. "Not exactly a freedom rider?"

"No," Thurmond answered. "A night rider, maybe. John was a bigot, not to mention that he was definitely not a nice man. On more than one occasion I had to tell him that if he didn't stop talking about spics and niggers, he could take his legal business elsewhere."

"But he stuck with you?"

"Yeah, I guess he got his rocks off knowing that Strom Thurmond was his lawyer and the executor of his estate. And frankly, his checks always cleared. So I didn't toss him out. Maybe I should've, but you know how it is—everyone is entitled to counsel, although I confess to not being overwhelmed by sadness when I learned he was one of the few people to die in Charley. So back to why you're here? What's up?"

"You've obviously seen the medical examiner's report saying the cause of death was an accident." The lawyer nodded in assent. Then I hit him with, "I'm not so sure it was an accident."

That knocked Strom right back into his chair. It gave me an opportunity to explain that my investigation was absolutely unofficial, that I'd seen things that led me to believe that at least one person had been in the condo after Catlett was cut by flying glass, but since the body was found wearing a fifteen-thousand dollar Rolex, theft didn't make sense as a motive.

At the mention of the Rolex, Strom jumped in. "There was a lot more than a Rolex in that place when he died. I had to inventory it all, get it appraised, and then jump through a few legal hoops to transfer ownership to the beneficiary."

When he said "beneficiary," my ears twitched. Someone stood to gain from Catlett's death, and I was about to find out who. I tried not to appear too eager, but it was hard. Visions of sugarplums were dancing through my head. Well, not quite sugarplums. It was more like a wedding cake on a turntable, and instead of one cheap plastic bride and groom at the top, all around the cake were little plastic figurines. But I could only see their backsides—with their hands cuffed behind them. And it was going round and round and round like the rotating dessert display at the Tick Tock Diner on Route 3 in Jersey.

Here it came. The big moment. I let Jinx pop the question: "Who was his beneficiary?"

Strom answered as though it was no big secret. "Catlett left everything to the church. The parish here in Punta Gorda. Sacred Heart. The one that got destroyed by Charley."

Talk about the air going out of a balloon. We were both stunned. "The church was his only beneficiary? No heirs? No friends? Lacey Drawers didn't get a cent?" The question was a semi-test: how much did the lawyer know about his client's private life. He passed.

"Nope. You know Lacey?"

"Let's just say I know of her. Saw the two of them together once at Dean's."

"She called me not long after John died asking about his will. She wasn't happy when I told her what I just told you."

"I'm shocked," I responded, unable to convey an ounce of sincerity with that declaration.

Strom then continued with his story. "When John came in here to make out his will and said he wanted to leave it all to the church, I asked him about heirs, and he said he had none. I didn't question him further because—well, he wasn't the kind of guy who was going to answer a lot of questions he thought were unnecessary. He asked me if I'd serve as executor of his estate because he said he didn't have anyone else. I said yes, frankly, because it generates a pretty hefty fee. Getting all the stuff appraised was a real pain in the backside."

I was still processing the shocker. "Everything goes to the church?" I mumbled, half statement, half question. What sunned me was having my theory of the crime blown to smithereens.

"Yeah. Everything. I got lucky with the appraisals, though. Steve down at Westchester Gold was able to do the fine arts, antiques and jewelry. I think the pastor is actually using him to sell the stuff, or take it to auction in New York."

"Steve's a good guy. I've been doing business with him since we moved here—not that I buy a lot of jewelry."

"Once all that stuff was taken care of, it was just a matter of dealing with the boat, the Cadillac and the condos."

"Did you say 'condos'? Plural?"

"Yeah. Catlett owned the unit he lived in and three more in the same building."

"Do *you* have to sell it all and give the church the money, or is that the parish's problem?"

"The will says it can be distributed 'in cash or in kind,' so I left it up to Father Tim. He said they'd deal with it. I guess they've got a couple of attorneys and some brokers who are parishioners, and they'll get them to handle it all pro bono. So that's what we've done."

I thought about everything he said. The vision I was now getting was of a large boat named *My Theory*. And when I looked closely at the hull, it was riddled with holes and sinking fast.

"Maron!" It escaped my lips before I could stop it.

Then Strom asked the million dollar question. "So why do you think his death wasn't accidental?"

"I gotta be honest with you," I said, "It's just a hunch that something wasn't right. I was hoping you'd be able to tell me something that pointed to a motive for killing him, but no such luck. You're telling me no one other than the church profited from his death. Sure, you got a pretty hefty fee for handling the estate, but you don't look like the murdering type. Besides, Catlett was eighty-four and you were going to get the fee sooner or later. You wouldn't commit a capital crime just to speed things up." I paused, thinking through the entire scenario, and then added, "You wouldn't, would you?" It wasn't intended to be a serious question.

"No, I wouldn't. But in case you're wondering, I'm not desperate for John's money. And that's easy for you to check."

"No, I'm sorry. I didn't suspect you. I was just thinking out loud. I just know something isn't right. I'm stymied."

I stood up, ready to go, and then delivered the Peter Falk/Columbo line. "Oh, one more thing." I reached into my pocket and pulled out the newspaper clipping with the photo of Catlett and the Picasso drawing.

"You ever see this?"

He took it from me, looked at it closely. "Nope."

"You never saw it? Never knew Catlett had it?"

"Nope. Should I have?" Strom's face wasn't showing any signs of stress. If he skimmed the Picasso from Catlett's collection and hired some kid to fence it for him, he wasn't letting on.

"Strom, I forgot to ask if you had a list of the artwork in Catlett's collection."

"I've got a list of the artwork we gave to the church, if that's what you mean."

"Not exactly. When you did his estate planning, he never gave you a list of everything in his collection?"

"Nope. I asked for it, along with the provenance of each piece, but he said it was too much trouble to find the paperwork. I remember him saying that he wasn't getting anything out of giving the stuff away after he's dead, so why should he bother?"

It seemed that with each new fact I picked up about Catlett, he became more and more of a prince. That's spelled with a C-K, not an N-C-E. I thought for a second. "Do you know who handled the insurance on Catlett's condos?"

"I do, and I see where you're going with it, but it's going to be a dead end. You're thinking that he must have had scheduled coverage on all his fine arts and antiques—the valuable stuff. You're out of luck."

"What do you mean?"

"He never had them insured. You have no idea what it was like dealing with him. He was a prick, through and through."

Surprise, surprise. Strom spells prince the same way I do.

Then he volunteered, "I asked him for a copy of his insurance on the artwork, and I'll never forget what he said. He was sitting right in that chair you're in when he said it. 'Fuck insurance. I've got no one I'm leaving this stuff to. I just like to look at it and brag that I own it, and I'm not going to be around forever. If something happens to it, who gives a shit? Why should I write those leeches five figure premium checks every year?'

chapter 24
fly

When I got home I gave Vin a call. An hour later, we met at the Cecil Webb Public Shooting Range which was just fifteen minutes from my house near the entrance to a state wildlife management area. The place was home to several thousand wild pigs that were fair game several times a year, and the range was frequented by all sorts of shooters. On any given day out here you could find serious pistol competition types, cops practicing for their annual qualification, ex-military who get off playing soldier with their own AR-15 or AK-47, and various other gun enthusiasts who have concealed weapon carry permits and get Viagra-type results when they fantasize about blowing away bad guys who were dumb enough to try and rob a local store while they were in the place.

"You ever shoot anyone in Nam?" Vin asked me, as he pulled a couple of silhouette targets from the trunk of his car.

"Yeah. Women, children, old men, the occasional water buffalo. What kind of question is that?" I asked, clearly annoyed. It was a question a lot of returning vets got from anti-war assholes looking to pick a fight, especially assholes who had found a way to dodge the draft without consequences.

"Settle down, big guy. I'm just asking if you could pull the trigger on another human being. It's one thing to walk around with that Glock under your shirt; it's another to know you could use it effectively if you had to."

"If I had to, I could."

"When cops do it, it's up close and personal. It's not spray and pray like in the jungle."

"I said, if I had to, I could."

"All right, then," said Vin, recognizing a tone he hadn't heard in my voice till that moment. "Let's see if you can hit anything. What kind of ammo they give you to shoot?"

I took my Glock out of its case, put it in the holster on my belt, and locked the case in the car. "Standard issue is the .40-cal Speer Gold Dot, 165 grain hollow-point."

As I said it, Vin reached down, lifted his pant leg and pulled his .38 S&W Chief's Special from its ankle holster.

"You're going up against me with *that*?" I asked. "Dick Tracy leave it to you in his will?"

"Yeah. You got a problem with it? Maybe I should use a pea-shooter instead?"

"I thought that *was* a pea-shooter. You can actually hit a target with it?"

"Unlike your fancy automatic, this one always goes bang. You wanna bet dinner on it. Winner picks the restaurant?"

"You're on," I said, exuding confidence. "How close?"

"Hell, most officer-involved shootings start at around twenty feet. How's that sound?" Vin said it with way too much confidence.

Now I was beginning to sweat that he might actually be able to hit center of mass, despite the two-inch barrel. "Twenty's good."

We waited until the range officer gave the all clear, walked out and pinned up the silhouette targets at the twenty-foot mark, then walked back to the firing line. That center of mass area, a four-inch by two-inch vertical oval looked pretty small.

"Five shots, tightest group wins," Vin called out. "Who's going first?"

"Age before beauty," I said, stepping back.

Vin nodded, took his position, legs spread shoulder-width, facing the target. In his big hands, the little .38 almost disappeared.

He gripped the gun, arms level, rolled his shoulders forward, and cracked off five shots, barely stopping in between to reacquire his sight picture. "Let's go look," he said, popping open the cylinder and clearing the brass.

We waited for the all-clear, and then walked down range. Not only were there five holes in the COM, the group could be covered by a silver dollar.

I was lost in thought on the long, slow walk back to the line. With the Glock still in its holster, I turned to face my target. That's when I heard Jerry Renfroe's braying voice. The asshole from Dean's. No, the *other* asshole. "You can actually hit that target?" I wheeled around and saw him standing there with Dave Hofer, the volunteer deputy I was with when we busted the guys hitting the liquor store. Renfroe was holding a huge revolver at his side. I glanced at it, then up at his face, and shook my head in disgust. That's when he spoke again. It was the Dirty Harry speech.

"Being this is a .44 Magnum, the most powerful handgun in the world, and would blow your head clean off, you've got to ask yourself one question. 'Do I feel lucky? Well, do ya, punk?'"

I turned back to the range just as it was cleared for fire. Checking the mag in the Glock, I assumed the isosceles shooting stance, and fired five shots in rapid succession. Then a single.

"That's six," said Vin, curiosity in his voice.

"I know. The last one was for him," I said, pointing at Renfroe. I cleared the Glock and set it on the counter. "Let's see what I hit."

Vin and I walked to the target. Five in the COM, in a grouping that could be covered by a half dollar. A small half dollar. And one more right between the eyes. I took down the target, wheeled and walked back to where the grin had been wiped off Renfroe's face. Handing him the target, I said, "Here ya go. Guess I was feeling lucky after all." Then I looked at the .44. "Nice gun. You know what they say about guys with guns like that, Jerry. Big gun, little dick." I looked at Hofer. "Lemme know if he hits anything." And to Vin, "I'm thinking dinner at the Verandah in Fort Myers. I'll pay for Sophia. Let's go."

As I started walking toward the parking lot, Renfroe called after me. "Nice shooting, Moscone. But handguns aren't really my thing. This is just for fun."

chapter 25
jinx

My turn now.

Fly and I both knew that we caught a break with Hurricane Frances. But I have to confess, the stress was getting to us. Just three weeks after Charley whacked us, Frances pretty much followed the skinny black line in the middle of the cone of stupidity and went where she was supposed to go. That doesn't mean, of course, that we didn't have the car packed and the house buttoned up. Maybe I shouldn't say "we." Laura and Sophia had the van packed, and they were close to spending the night in it as a way of encouraging us to self-evacuate, which is what the emergency management types call voluntarily getting the hell out of Dodge. It is not to be confused with the term the gastroenterologists use for the night before a colonoscopy.

If we had to run, the plan had been to repeat what Sophia, Laura and I had done with Charley—head south and then east to the Miami area. Only this time, Fly would be going with us. Sophia finally laid down the law, and in the interest of preserving peace in the family, he agreed.

Hurricane Frances came ashore late on September 4, between Fort Pierce and West Palm Beach as a Category 2, with winds of 105 MPH, downgraded from the Category 3 status it had when it passed over Freeport, Grand Bahama Island and put the airport there under six to eight feet of water.

Everyone who thinks one land falling hurricane is just like another needs to pay attention. Frances was huge. The eye was roughly eighty miles across, nine times larger than Charley's, and it was slow moving, maybe only five miles an hour forward speed—which was about a third of Charley's 14 MPH when it hit us. Frances diddled her way across the state well north of us, causing nearly nine billion dollars in damage. By the time it crossed the west coast into the Gulf of Mexico, she had been downgraded to a tropical storm.

Frances brought us some heavy winds, maybe some gusts that hit sixty or seventy miles an hour. The big concern here was that the debris and loose roof tiles laying around from Charley would get picked up and tossed around, causing more damage. Bottom line—we got lucky.

Salladé was all over radio and TV reminding everyone that they need to restock their hurricane supplies and maintain their vigil, because the hurricane season doesn't end until December. It's funny how people react to a guy they thanked for saving their lives less than a month ago. I actually heard folks saying he was grandstanding, that he loved being the center of attention and that's why he was trying to scare us. "After all," one bone-headed woman said, "Punta Gorda has only been hit once since Donna in 1960. It'll be another forty-five years before we get hit again." Her husband nodded his agreement, but I couldn't tell if he was being a *schlemiel* or just doing a silent "yes, dear."

When I pointed out that Frances could have jogged south and easily whacked us only three weeks after Charley, they accused me of being a Democrat who wants the government to run his life and tax us all to death. Now I could tell. He *was* a *schlemiel*. These are some of the same folks who were at the front of the FEMA truck line to get free ice and bottled water after Charley hit. Hey—don't ask me to explain it. Putting up with seasonal stupidity is the price we pay for living year 'round in such a beautiful place.

The night that Frances was raising hell less than a hundred miles north of us, Laura and I went to the Moscone's for dinner. While the women had coffee in the kitchen, Fly and I went down to the dock, got on board the boat, and enjoyed the breeze. On a

normal summer night, we would have been eaten alive by mos-
quitoes or no-see-ums, but the annoying little bugs are grounded
when there's a 30 MPH wind. While I lit a cigar, Fly broke into
his secret stash of Remy VSOP, poured us each a healthy shot,
and kept the bottle handy as he bared his tormented soul.

"Jinx, I was sure Strom would tell me that some *jadrool* stood
to inherit a couple million bucks when the son-of-a-bitch
croaked, and I'd be able to lock him up for murder. But when he
told me that the church got it all, I was crushed."

"I'm here for you," I responded, buried my nose in the snifter,
then took a healthy pull on the cognac.

"Hey, Be-Bop, stop mocking me," said Fly, in disgust.

"I'm not mocking you, although I feel compelled to tell you
that you're getting real annoying. Or more annoying than usual."

"Are you going to listen to me, or do I have to resort to talking
to my wife?"

"Let's not get carried away. I'm listening. What's the problem?"

"Okay. The problem is that I was certain that something wasn't
right with the dead guy. So when Thurmond told me that the
church was Catlett's sole beneficiary, there went the theory."

"No," I said, "there went *a* theory. "You're certain that someone—at least one person—had gotten to the body before you did,
right?"

"No question. There were tracks in the insulation on the floor.
If I'd only had a camera with me."

"Never mind about the camera. You know that the Picasso that
had been in the apartment went missing. What you need to figure
out is who got to the body ahead of you, and why? Is there a
connection between those two facts? "

Fly shook his head. "Jinx, I don't know how to do that. I need
a break."

Just then, Laura called us from the lanai. As we stood up, I pat-
ted Fly on the back. "Buddy, maybe you'll get a break in the
case. Maybe you won't. Cut yourself some slack. You've never
done this before. Most guys don't do on the job training by
themselves on a murder case. All I can tell you is what a mentor

of mine told me years ago, when I had my first real job in the news business. He said to trust my instincts. And if I believe that I have good instincts, to never kill my own story."

I could see that Fly was getting frustrated, since none of the advice I could give was going to solve his problem—or the crime. "So I'm supposed to keep butting my head up against a brick wall, just because I think I'm right?" he asked.

"Yeah, if you want to be playin' this game, that's what you're supposed to do. And one of two things will happen: your head will turn to mush, or you'll punch a hole in the wall."

"You don't expect me to pay you for advice like that."

"Hey, it's the best I can do. And since I'm the only one in PGI who'll put up with you, it's also all you're going to get. Deal with it."

For a few seconds, Fly said nothing in response to my admonition. I looked at him and knew something was eating at him, and asked, "What?"

"There's something wrong with me, with the way I am," he responded.

I could tell he was serious, not screwin' with me. "Why do you say that?"

"Look, I spent a couple of days with Vin and I watched him carefully. I know where he comes from, he told me. But he seems to be able to rein in the need to kill the bad guys, or at least crush them. He's satisfied with a lot less. Just seeing that they don't get away with it is good enough for him. He doesn't need to punish them. But the whole reason I wanted to be a cop, the whole reason I went through the academy at my age, did the exercises, studied the law, passed the tests, is so I can put away bad guys. I need it all. Jinx, why can't I be as comfortable as Vin with *some* justice? Why does it have to be the death penalty before I'm satisfied?"

"Fly, now you're scaring me. In the few years I've known you, you've never been that introspective. I can't answer your question. Maybe it has to do with something that happened when you were a kid. Maybe you should see a shrink. Come to think of it, didn't you have to see a shrink to get into the volunteer deputy program?"

"Yeah, I did. And I was honest with the guy, too. You know what he told me?"

"What?"

"He told me that a lot of guys become cops because they want to put away bad guys. That's their motivation. Deep down, they hate bad guys. Firemen—the guys who become firemen—you know what they want?" He didn't wait for me to answer. "They want to be heroes. They're consumed with being good guys. You know something, Jinx? I never wanted to be a fireman."

chapter 26
fly

The next morning began the way a lot of mornings begin for guys all over the world. I was getting blamed for something over which I had absolutely no control. Sophia—who I dearly love—decided that it must be my fault that Merkin Casualty hadn't yet sent a check to pay for replacing our tile roof. "Honey," I said plaintively, "I can't make those *mamalukes* move any faster. I've made all the phone calls to all the people I can find. You know what they all say. 'You're on the list.' If I had a dollar for every list I was on, we'd—" I just stopped. I couldn't think of anything we could do with maybe ten or fifteen bucks that would impress her. The only good thing about that moment for me is that Jinx wasn't around to see me at my pathetic worst. I told him about it later, in excruciating detail. "Never mind," I said to Soph. "Just don't blame me. You're always blaming me."

Sophia took it all in, and then said what wives all over the world think—but probably don't say. "I have to blame somebody." That's what marriage is about. To all you kids out there: don't say you weren't warned.

As luck would have it, the phone rang a little after eight. It was the latest in a series of Merkin Casualty adjustors. He'd been assigned to investigate our roof claim and wondered if he could come over right away. "Right away?" I asked? "How do you take your coffee? How would you like your eggs? Potatoes or grits? Biscuit or toast?" He told me that wouldn't be necessary—and sounded very businesslike doing so. No sense of humor. Not even when I poked him about the company name.

When we first moved here, we knew nothing of what we've since learned is called "Florida Time." All tradesmen—electricians, plumbers, painters and the like—operate on it. And while I had no specific information about insurance adjustors, I had to assume that if the guy was working in Florida, he was on it, too. Even if he came from out-of-state, he likely caught the Florida Time virus. It works like this. If a tradesman says he'll be at your place tomorrow, figure on seeing him in two or three days. And don't expect a phone call rescheduling. *Tomorrow* means "in the next couple of days." It's our equivalent of the Mexicans' *mañana*.

Now, if a guy says he'll be there first thing in the morning, that means he thinks he'll make it by late afternoon. If you get out of bed and see that it's a nice, sunny day with light winds, and you want to know if or when the guy is going to show up, you need to check the tide table for Charlotte Harbor at Punta Gorda. If it's winter time and the tide is incoming or high, that means there'll be water in the canals and harbor, and the guy is going fishing. He'll probably have to be back at his dock before low tide, because if he isn't, there might not be enough water to get his boat on the lift. So if you know when low tide is, you can figure the guy will show up at your house shortly thereafter. There is one other complication: if the guy doesn't keep his boat on a lift or in the water, but trailers it to various launching ramps, none of the above applies.

Okay, that leaves the kind of call I just got, the one where the guy says, "I'll be right over." This is a tough one, because no specific time was given. Instead, the *stunad* said, in essence, "I'm in the car and on my way." That's about as good as it gets. He's not likely to change his mind and go fishing. He didn't say he had to drop the kids off at school, or do a couple of errands for his wife first. The vehicle was drivable, and he said he'd be right over. Down here, that's cause for a friggin' celebration. We learned to lower our expectations. Post-catastrophe etiquette does not require common courtesy on the part of those *giamokes* whose income depends on coming to your home. But—this is important, pay attention—you, on the other hand, would do well to be courteous, or at least civil, no matter what club you want to hit the guy with. Me, I like a lob wedge. It'll take a cleaner divot out of his skull. I'm just sayin'.

Two DDPs and a chocolate chip biscotti later, the doorbell rang. The mutt barked and raced from the kitchen to the front door, then back to the living room for a couple of laps around the couch. I knew there was no point in trying to shut him up until he'd stuck his nose in the guy's crotch, so I opened the front door and said, "Don't worry about the mutt, he only bites insurance people." No reaction from the guy. "Just kidding," I said, thinking that if he'd write us a check now, I'd greet him the same way the mutt did. I'm desperate. Soph was making me nuts with the roof thing.

For what seemed like a full minute, the guy—he said his name was Larry Johnson—stood on the little front porch flipping through papers. I restrained myself and waited quietly, which I'm sure you realize by now is totally against my nature. Finally, Larry spoke. "It says here that we've agreed to pay $8,200 for replacement of broken tiles on your roof, but that you believe that's not adequate. What's the problem?"

I should have excused myself at that exact moment, taken a couple laps around the house with the mutt, and then done some deep breathing exercises. Anything to keep from ripping off Larry's head and shitting down his neck. Figuratively of course. I'm not a violent person. I don't need to be; I got a gun. But what's going through my head is that it's been more than a month since Charley roared through here, and as far as I could tell, while my neighbors were seeing good hands, me and Soph had been getting an extended middle finger. You gotta gimme credit though. I just stood there and remained calm. Really against my nature. So here's what I told the *stugots*.

"The problem is that three different roofers have been out here—do you know what a miracle that is? To have gotten three roofers to actually come out here—and climb up on my roof. And they all came to the same conclusion. Which is, we need a complete new roof." I stopped and waited to see what Johnson would say.

"Well, Mr. Moscone, our roofing consultant counted the broken tiles, and since they equal no more than ten percent of your entire roof, we're only allowed to authorize replacing those specific tiles."

"*Those* specific tiles?" I sputtered, pointing to several spots on my roof. "*Those* tiles? That's what the last guy said. What's the name of your roofing consultant?"

"I'm not required to give you that information." More of the middle finger than the good hands. Again.

"Okay, then I'll tell you. He gave me his business card. His name is Lamont. Bud Lamont. And he's not a roofing consultant. He's just another *gavone* sitting on his ass drinkin' coffee and eatin' donuts in your Port Charlotte office. He's not a licensed roofer. He's not a licensed home inspector. As far as I know the only license he holds is drivers. And you want to know something else? When Bud came out here to evaluate my roof, he didn't bring a ladder with him. And he declined my offer to use mine. So your roofing consultant *who isn't* gave you a written report that says I don't need a new roof without even going up there to examine the damaged one. Now what do you have to say?"

Johnson didn't say anything. He walked off the porch out onto the lawn and looked up at the roof. Then he walked about ten feet to the left, and looked up again. I followed him at a respectful distance—probably close enough to reach him with a driver but not a wedge—and waited. Did I tell you I hate friggin' golf and golfers? Never mind. Finally, I couldn't take it any more. "You can't see what I'm talking about from the ground. You want to use my ladder?"

Johnson turned, and miracle of miracles, said, "Yes, if you don't mind."

In anticipation of this moment, I had the garage clicker in my pocket. Faster than Jinx can say, "Yes dear, you're right" to Laura, I had the garage door opened and brought the extension ladder over to the side of the house. "It's easier to get up on the side. Let me tell you what all three of the roofers said." Johnson nodded, and I barreled on. "First, can I ask where are you from?"

"Is that important?" he responded, rather abruptly.

"It might be. Are you familiar with tile roofs?"

"I'm from Oklahoma, and no, not really. We don't have 'em where I come from, and this is actually the first cat I've worked where they're prevalent. Usually I work tornado alley, do a lot with floods in the Midwest, hailstorms in winter. Don't know how I've managed to avoid it, but this is my first catastrophe in Florida."

Inwardly, I breathed a sigh of relief. Maybe there was a chance to actually deal with this guy, if I could control the anger I was· feeling at his company for sending out *stunads* who have no friggin' idea what they're looking at. I decided to try the nice approach and see what happens.

"Mr. Johnson, the gold standard for hurricane codes in Florida is Miami-Dade. After 2002, they said that the only way to install concrete tile so it can resist winds up to 140 miles is with special foam. Use that foam properly, and Mr. Universe couldn't pull a tile off the roof. But the roofs here in Punta Gorda were installed to the state code that went into effect after Hurricane Andrew in the early 1990s. The tiles are screwed into the wood decking, which has been covered with a waterproof membrane— something like tarpaper—and then tarred over.

"When Charley came through, the winds got under a row of tiles and lifted them up, just ripped the screws right out of the decking. But think about this. When a row of tiles lifts, the row above it lifts, and the row above that. Then the wind stops for a couple of seconds, or changes direction, and the tiles drop back down a little cockeyed. But they're no longer screwed into the roof. They're just sitting there. Some of them are cracked, and those are the ones your company says you'll replace. But nearly all of them are loose, waiting to turn into ten pound missiles the next time we get a storm. And the holes where the screws had been are now just holes. Some of them might be plugged with tar, but some of them are going to let water in. The only fix for this according to all three roofers who came out here, is to take off the roof down to the bare wood and start over. And eight grand won't cover that job."

I couldn't read his face, which surprised me because I'm usually very good at reading people. But the adjustor must have been paying attention, because he asked a good question. "Did they tell you what the job would cost?"

"I got three different estimates. The low is thirty-two K, the high is thirty-nine K, and the other one is in the middle, thirty-five K."

"That's a lot of money. Is that what these roofs really cost?"

"No, that's what these roofs really cost after a hurricane tears 16,000 roofs off buildings in a single county. Before the hurricane, this roof might have cost twenty, twenty-two K. But now they've got us all by the balls. Even when they give you an estimate, there's no guarantee that they can come right out and do the work. So you might have to write this so I can get the first company that's available. Otherwise, I'm likely to be calling you back here to look at water damage inside the house."

As soon as I said it, I knew I screwed up and gave the *jadrool* an opening. Johnson's tone changed. "Mr. Moscone, you realize that under the terms of your policy, it's your responsibility to take action to prevent additional damage, and if you don't, it's not covered."

I moved to within lob wedge range. "And under the terms of the policy, it's your obligation to put the house in the condition it was in before the storm."

"But that doesn't mean we're required to give you a new roof. We've offered to repair it. You've declined."

I wanted to stick that lob wedge where the sun don't shine. But Soph woulda been proud a me if she'd seen it. I tried to get him back on track. "Do me a favor. Climb up there and lift up a couple of tiles and see what happens."

To my surprise, the guy put his notebook on the ground, checked to see that the ladder was sturdy, and went up. He swung off it and onto the roof as though he'd actually done it a few times, and climbed up until he was about ten feet from the edge. I watched as he reached down with both hands, grabbed the edge of one tile and lifted. Voila! Not only did the tile he was lifting come up, but four or five tiles out to each side, and a couple of courses above the tile he was lifting rose up.

"Unscrewed, right?" Only after I said it did it dawn on me that the phrase could have applied not only to the tiles in their present condition, but the condition Soph and me hoped to find ourselves in as Mr. Johnson drove away. I visualized standing there with a check for about thirty-five thousand bucks in my hands. What a putz I was.

The adjustor come down from the roof, took the ladder down and without asking, carried it back to the garage. I pointed to the back wall, and he leaned it there, came back out and took his notebook, which I had picked up from the lawn. "Mr. Moscone, everything you say about the tiles being loose appears to be correct. But I'm not authorized to say that we'll replace your roof. It's a tough case. Some of the roofs I've seen have lots of tiles missing, and it's easy to show my supervisors a photo and get them to okay replacement. But a photo of your roof wouldn't show very much damage."

I was beginning to get the idea that when his visit was over, we would not be unscrewed. "What's all that mean?" I asked, trying to keep a defeatist tone out of my voice.

"It means, I'm afraid, that I'm going to have to ask for the zone office to send out a roofing consultant to examine your roof."

That's when I just about lost it. "But this time tell me you're going to send out a real, honest-to-God licensed, experienced roofing consultant, not some *giamoke* whose business cards are still wet. Please tell me that!"

He clearly didn't like that. "Mr. Moscone, there's no need to lose your temper."

I had a quick flash where I thought that the guy shooting insurance adjustors may be a folk hero, but I brushed it aside. Time to attack. I was tired of playin' Mr. Nice Guy. "No need? No need? Maybe you'd like to meet Mrs. Moscone and explain that to her." I stopped and thought for a moment. "No, that wouldn't be a good idea. She doesn't have the self control that I have." Then it dawned on me that maybe Vin had given me the tool to fix this problem. I switched to my Deputy Moscone voice. It was bee-you-tee-full.

"Mr. Johnson, you know what's going on here? I think your company is acting in bad faith." I watched his face carefully for any sign of understanding. "Yes, you've been stalling us for several weeks. You sent someone out and said he was a qualified roofing person when he clearly wasn't. Now they send you out and you tell me they'll have to send someone else out. Meantime, we're living with a damaged roof. We've already had a second hurricane go by, and probably more to come—there are still almost three months left to the season. Who knows what could happen? Yes, I think we have all the elements needed to file suit against Merkin Casualty for acting in bad faith. Remember when I said that 16,000 buildings in Charlotte County need new roofs after Charley. You know who lives in those buildings? The people who'll be on the jury in our lawsuit. And there won't be more than a handful that had good experiences with their insurance companies. So is that what it's gotta be? Moscone vs. Merkin for bad faith?"

I stopped talking and looked at him closely. The guy was flipping through papers, then stopped when he seemed to find what he was looking for. I was sure it was all bullshit—a play for time while he tried to figure out whether I represented a serious threat or not.

Then I pulled a primo move to help the guy along. Even Jinx was proud'a me when I told him. I reach into my pocket, come up with Strom Thurmond's business card and offer it to him. "Maybe you'd like to talk to my lawyer before you make a decision?"

Johnson waved off the card. "That won't be necessary. If you'll give me copies of those three estimates, I think we can resolve this matter to your satisfaction."

I almost forgot the first rule of sales: when the customer says yes, stop selling. Forgetting that the Merkin Man had no sense of humor, I actually said, "In my lifetime? Or my children's?"

"By the end of the week you should have a check."

But noooooo, I wasn't ready to celebrate yet. I heard the horror stories; I knew that even though a quote for a roofing job said it was good for thirty days, there was weasel language in there that allowed them to raise the price due to market conditions. And the demand for concrete roof tile was exceeding the supply; something about all the concrete America makes being shipped to China for some dam they're building. "What happens if the quote doesn't hold because the price of materials keeps going up?"

"When you send us the appropriate documentation, we'll discuss it with your roofer and if we have to, we'll pay it."

"Just like that? You'll cave and pay it? C'mon, don't kid a kidder."

"Mr. Moscone, we need to resolve your claim in good faith. And we're willing to go to whatever lengths we have to in order to get your house repaired and make you happy."

Once again I began visualizing. This time all I could see was Sophia's face. She was saying, "Paul Moscone, just shut up." She was waving her finger at me—and the visualization morphed into the Wicked Witch of the West. You know the scene, where she tells Dorothy, "I'll get you my pretty!"

Suddenly, I snapped back to reality. "That's great, Mr. Johnson. Wait right here and I'll get you copies of those estimates." As I ran to the front door, I was actually smiling. Yeah, ladies and gentlemen, a big, crooked, toothy smile.

chapter 27
jinx

That night, Fly called to tell me about his apparent victory over the forces of evil. He knew something was wrong when I didn't high five him through the phone as soon as he told me how he had sprung the bad faith argument on the adjustor.

"What's wrong?" Fly asked. "I can tell, there's something bothering you. Give."

"You haven't been on your computer lately, have you?"

"No, why? Somebody go postal on another insurance adjuster?"

"At the risk of being insensitive, that would be relatively good news," I responded.

"Oh, no," Fly said, "not another one." It was a hopeful statement, not a question.

"Another one."

"What's the story?"

"The usual for this time of year. A tropical wave southwest of the Cape Verde Islands, moves west and gets stronger. I didn't bother you when it became a tropical storm. This one's Ivan. When it was still over a thousand miles east of Tobago, early this morning, they upgraded it to hurricane. This afternoon, it became a Cat 3 storm. The hurricane center said something about such quick strengthening being unprecedented at such a low latitude."

"Jinx, there's something you're not telling me. Give."

Fly knows when I'm holding back. I guess there's just something in my voice that gives it away. It's what makes me a crappy poker player. I've got more tells than my wife, and she hasn't won a poker hand since she taught our kids to play when they were ten years old. "They just put out the five day forecast. We're in the cone."

I said it quietly, just let it lay there and marinate. There was silence on the line for a mini-eternity. "Where's the skinny black line?" he asked.

"You're not going to believe it. It's following Charley's track. It's coming right for us."

"But I still have loose tiles on my roof. It can't come here." Fly sounded whinier than he had with the insurance guy, and I told him so. "A third hurricane in a month? I think I'm entitled to whine. A lot." Then there was nothing but silence. I thought I could hear him breathing heavily.

"Fly, you okay?"

"I'm fine. I'm just thinking what a *stunad* you are."

"Excuse me?"

"*Stunad*. Moron. You gave up earthquakes for this. And you brag about it. How many times have I heard you say, 'At least with hurricanes, we get a warning'?"

"Well, it's true, isn't it? Would you rather not know?"

"Sometimes, I think I wouldn't mind knowing a lot less. I suppose you've looked at the spaghetti tracks online." Fly knew I wouldn't have called him without checking at least three different web sites, to see how half a dozen different computer models were projecting the path of this storm.

"Well, they're not totally all over the place," I told him. "They all have the storm coming into the Gulf, but one has it going west southwest to the Yucatan. Two more show it making a right turn to the northeast. They're the ones that put it on the same path as Charley. The others are in the middle—they can't decide between Texas, Louisiana or the Panhandle."

"*Ba-fungool*," Fly shouted in disgust.

"Hey, don't tell me where to stick it. I'm just the messenger."

"You'd think that if this was really science, they could all agree on where the friggin' hurricane is going to go. But nooooooooo."

I expected Fly to continue on a rant, but instead he just told me to hang on. Thirty seconds later, he was back.

"Jinx, all she did was look at my face, and Sophia knew. We been married way too long. If you haven't told Laura, better do it before they talk to each other. Let me go look at the computer. Then we can figure out what we're going to do. If this thing could follow Charley's track, I might be leaving with you. One time was enough." He hung up before I could bust his balls about not sticking around to experience another hurricane. That's okay; next time we talk I'll tell him he owes me for being kind. There are no free passes in our relationship.

I wasn't looking forward to explaining what was going on to Laura, but then the phone rang. Without even looking at the Caller ID, I yelled, "Honey, it's Sophia for you." Problem solved: I won't have to break the news to my wife.

This would be as good a time as any to give you my theory about the roles of men and women in a marriage, because I'm certain there are women who will take offense at my assumption that it's the guy's job to decide to evacuate, when, and where to. But that's the way it is, like it or not.

When Fly called the night before Charley hit to warn me that the track had changed and it was coming here, I got off the phone and told Laura what was happening. You know what she said? "I'm not leaving." The facts didn't matter. Her house was her nest, it was the safest place she knew, and she wasn't leaving it for the unknown. And that was before I explained that we were going to have to drive through the early bands of thunderstorms, right into the area where tornadoes were being spawned.

It comes down to this: men and women are different. Fly and I talk about this all the time. I could make a strong case that we're not even part of the same species, and anyone who says we are is making a political statement, not being honest.

By the time Laura got off the phone, I'd flipped on the TV.

The breaking news headline was that our buddy Salladé had gone before the Charlotte County commissioners and asked for a phased evacuation order for the entire county. He'd already issued a mandatory evacuation order for mobile home parks. While the anchors were still explaining how the staggered evacuation would work—it started with areas closest to the water and moved inland, more or less—I reached for the phone. Before I could hit speed-dial, it rang.

I just pushed the button and said, "You heard?"

Fly had heard. "We need to go," I said. "The question is where?"

Turns out he was a couple of steps ahead of me. "We can't head to the Miami area. The storm could come in south of Punta Gorda and head straight across the state. We'd be right there. And we can't go to Tampa or Orlando. They're both just a jog off the path that brings it here."

I was getting annoyed. Sometimes, all I want are the answers without having to show my work like my high school trig teacher, Mr. Silverman, used to demand. I interrupted, "So where are we going?"

"We're going to Jacksonville. It's in a perfect place. From there we can run north, south or west, depending. A dozen couples from our boating group are going there. Supposedly, the Holiday Inn near the airport has space—and they allow dogs."

The pet issue was a real problem, since there were more families with pets evacuating than there seemed to be hotel rooms available for them. "I'll call as soon as we hang up. When do you think we should leave?"

"Before noon tomorrow. The roads are going to be jammed. There are a lot of folks who rode out Charley who aren't sticking around for Ivan," Fly concluded without mentioning that he was one of them.

For Fly, the only thing good about this new storm is that it was coming during a lull in his investigation into the Catlett case. I'd given him the advice about not killing his own story, but the ending he was seeing isn't the one that he wanted. He'd called Vin at his home near Tampa and discussed it with him. Without being a smartass, Vin said, "Welcome to homicide. That's why we have cold case files." Vin told Fly about half a dozen cases he'd worked where his instincts went one way, and the facts either went in the opposite direction, or just froze things in place. "Looks like your case is frozen," he told Fly, adding, "My best advice is to find something else to work on. If this case is meant to be solved, a clue will pop up. If not, you can't let it eat your guts out."

Then Vin asked about the sniper case, and Fly bottom-lined it for him, promising to call back to discuss it when we finished dealing with the next inbound hurricane.

Before the newscast ended, Laura was taking a half-hearted stab at gathering the stuff to take with us when we evacuated. We already had all our important papers in the plastic box, which she moved to a spot near the front door. Then she started packing a suitcase. I knew that if I continued to watch the news or got on my computer to check things out, I'd be in trouble, so I cheerily said, "I'll get all the photo albums ready," and began the job of gathering them up and packing them into a soft-sided piece of luggage.

I knew I'd never forget the feeling I had when we evacuated for Charley. I was driving through hell and high water across Alligator Alley, and didn't care at all about the stuff we'd left behind—the souvenirs of nearly four decades of marriage, the trinkets, the furniture, even the pieces with sentimental value that had been passed on from our parents and grandparents. But I regretted with all my heart that I'd left the photo albums. They couldn't be replaced. And, unlike the other stuff that I thought I cared about, the photos really mattered. It was a mistake I wouldn't make twice.

Late the next morning, we became part of an evacuation that shocked Salladé. What he discovered is that even members of his critical staff had taken off for North Georgia, North Carolina, even Tennessee. "I guess they couldn't handle the thought of dealing with another hurricane in so short a time." Ivan made it three in six weeks. That's a pretty good clip for an area that hadn't seen a hurricane since the early Sixties.

Cell phones have taken the joy out of convoying the way we did. No one—except maybe interstate truckers—bothers with a CB radio handle anymore. No one but the cops bother to learn the ten-codes anymore. There's no ten-fours, and "Roger that, good buddy" and "I've got your back door." When you want to find out what's going on with your friend, you hit speed dial on the cell phone and there he is. But it also eliminates any opportunity to engage in conversation with people you don't know, even though for the moment, they're part of your world. It's a shame, too, because when you're all running from a force of nature that could kill you, idle conversation about shared fears might not be a bad thing.

There were two things that made this road trip to Jacksonville really bothersome. First, almost as soon as we got there, we went online and looked at the National Hurricane Center's latest report on Ivan. The computer models were converging, but no longer were any of them indicating that the storm would follow Charley's path to Punta Gorda. In fact, we were completely out of the cone we'd been smack in the middle of less than twenty-four hours earlier. And you wondered why I call it the cone of stupidity?

Now, they were saying that it was going to go well out into the Gulf of Mexico before turning to the north. They weren't sure whether it was going to obliterate the Panhandle or New Orleans, or maybe even Galveston. But they were certain it wasn't going to hit us.

chapter 28
fly

We'd come all the way to Jacksonville, so we figured we might as well make a party of it. We blew some money at the local dog track and went sightseeing in St. Augustine, which under any other circumstance would have been a "delightful day during which to savor a much earlier time in the history of our adopted state" as the tourist brochures put it.

But three days of relaxation was more than I could handle. I was overjoyed to be back home, and I'm sure Sophia was happy to have me out of her hair. Enforced togetherness ain't all it's cracked up to be, especially when my brain was still tied in knots.

I was polishing *Inamorata's* teak rails when it hit me and I blurted out, "*Maron!* Why not?" I spent a buck to get Lacey Dewers' phone number and address from the thieves at cell phone 411, then called her. On the second ring she picked up and said hello in a voice that was phony Southern femme-fatale. When I introduced myself as Deputy Moscone of the Charlotte County Sheriff's Office, she reverted to Jersey Girl.

"Whattaya want wit me?"

"If it's convenient, I'd like to come over and speak with you about an ongoing investigation."

"Investigation of what?"

"It has to do with the death of Mr. Catlett."

"Oh, puh-leeeeeze. I've moved on."

"It'll just take a few minutes."

Fortunately, she caved. A good thing, too, because I was getting increasingly agitated and was afraid I'd slip and say something about her reputation around town.

Five minutes later, I knocked on the door of her apartment in the Miramar Condominiums. The building fronted on Bass Inlet where it entered Charlotte Harbor. While not primo waterfront, it was expensive because it was in walking distance to the shops and restaurants in Fisherman's Village. Her second floor unit was the smaller of the two on each floor, and under the location-location-location rule down here, she was in the center of the loaf, two floors beneath the building's upper crust.

When she opened the door I went mute. Lacey Drawers was living up to her reputation. "I'm going out, so we have to make this fast." She was wearing skin tight jeans with a top that nicely contrasted with her I-spend-a-lot-of-time-on-a-boat tanned skin. And there was a lot of skin. A *whole lotta* skin. And what wasn't exposed, was cupped in a lacy bra that was clearly visible beneath the top. The bra didn't hide much, especially considering that the AC in her place was set to nippy.

I was instantly sorry that I'd removed my sunglasses in the car. They would've provided some cover while I was checking her out. Hey, I tried not to look. I did. But sometimes, no matter how hard we try, we can't help it. We may be older, but we're guys. And Lacey caught me looking. But instead of being angry, she seemed pleased.

"You like the bait," she said, glancing down at what had to be the nicest pair of custom-made C-cups that I had seen since we moved to Punta Gorda from Orlando. "Perky, don'tcha think? Then there's the rear view." She pirouetted and cocked her hip so I got a good look at her well-carved ass. "My second husband was a plastic surgeon."

A dozen responses ran through my mind, but I kept my mouth shut; full credit to the sexual harassment lectures at the academy.

"You're not going to say anything?" Lacey said, moving close enough for me to catch a whiff of Chanel No. 5 drifting northward from the ample cleavage. "I'm going clubbing. I need to know that the outfit is working. You can tell me. Are these tits world class or what?"

I managed a cautious response, "They're very nice, ma'am. Everything is very nice. All of it."

"They're better than very nice. They're 360cc smooth round salines. These are the Bentley of implants. He wouldn't have put in anything less. He was a really nice guy."

I couldn't resist. "What happened to him?"

"Same thing that happened to Nelson Rockefeller. I guess three times in one night was too much for him. His ticker, ya know? And he was only sixty-five when it happened." She turned around and beckoned for me to follow her to the living room, where she pointed to a couch upholstered in a pink Florida floral that matched her blouse. "Sit."

"Wait one second Mr. Sheriff's Deputy." It was Sophia, and she'd surprised everyone on the boat by jumping in. "You mean to tell me that you went to Lacey Drawer's apartment? *By yourself?* And you never bothered to mention it to me?"

"Soph, it was nuttin'—I was just trying to find out about the Picasso. You're makin' it sound like I was doin' somethin' skeevy."

"Are you going to sit there and tell me that she didn't come on to you? That women would come on to a mannequin at Dillard's."

"You know her?" Jan Beiler asked, in a tiny voice.

"We *all* know her," responded Laura, glaring at Jinx for unexplained reasons. "She's a *nahf-kee*," Laura stated without hesitation, using the Yiddish word for whore.

I need to keep this from rolling completely out of control. "Soph, I had to ask her some questions about the dead guy, who was in line to be husband number four. She's a *scavad'oro*. No way do I have enough money for that gold digger. She wasn't interested in me. And more important, I got no interest in her."

Soph wasn't going to let this one go. I could tell by the look on her face. "Tell me again what was she wearing?"

"She was dressed up to go out. I don't know what she had on. I really didn't pay all that much attention. I had questions to ask her."

Big mistake. Oh, Jesus. Why did I say that? She's going to nail me.

"You're supposed to be a hotshot cop. You're supposed to pay attention. *I* wasn't even there and I could tell you what she was wearing. That *putan* had on a *see-through* low-cut top to show off the boobs one of her dead husbands bought for her…"

I caught myself. I was about to remind her that it was her second husband, the plastic surgeon. That would have done it. She'd throw me overboard.

"…and she was wearing jeans—stretch denim jeans so tight you could tell if she shaved her legs that morning…"

I shot a look at Jinx that said "keep your mouth shut or I'll throw *you* overboard."

"…or anything else." Sophia said it, not Jinx. I can't believe she said it.

"Soph! I can't believe you said that. You *never* say things like that."

"I'm sure that woman doesn't even own a pair of panties." It was Laura again. Our wives live in a parallel universe. Who knew they were just like guys, only worse?

Then Sophia unloads on me. "When my husband goes to some *putan*'s apartment by himself, all bets are off. So am I right? Is that what she was wearing? Tell me you didn't notice real good. Tell *them*"—she motioned to the others on the boat—"you didn't notice it all, real good."

When all else fails, throw in the towel. I shoulda done it as soon as Soph went after me. "Yes, dear. I noticed what the *putan* was wearing. You all obviously know more about her than I do. She insisted that I notice. But sweetheart, I went there on business. She mighta had some information about something that was stolen from the dead guy. I *had to go see her*. I'm sorry."

I can't believe it. My own wife is busting my agates in front of strangers. "He *had* to go see her," Soph mimicked me, looking at the Beilers and Aronsons who were sitting there in stunned silence taking it all in. Then she smiled. "I was just checking. Okay, go on with your story. You just sat down on her couch. Don't leave *anything* out. We're all ears."

Now what do I do? She had just tossed my brain like a Cobb salad. I thought for a second, finished off a Diet Dr. Pepper. Paused. "Okay, just so you understand. I'm tellin' it exactly the way it happened. Soph, promise me you won't read nuttin' into it."

She nodded. If I survive this, it'll be a friggin' miracle. But I resumed the story.

I sat down on the couch. Lacey perched on the arm of a chair, which meant that to avoid staring directly at her cleavage, I would have to look up at an uncomfortable angle. That's when I noticed the many-carat diamond solitaire nestling between the very tan 36-Cs. She caught me staring. "What do you want to know about John?" she asked. Her voice forced me to refocus on her face. I'm sure she was used to men talking to her chest. Hell, I'm sure she encouraged it.

I pulled out the newspaper photo of the late Mr. Catlett with the Picasso and showed it to her. "I assume you've seen this?"

"The photo or the Picasso?"

"The Picasso," I responded, weariness creeping into my voice.

"Yeah, of course I seen it. It was on the wall in John's bedroom. I spent lots of time there, you know."

"I didn't know, but I'll take your word that you two were close," I said. My thoughts were less than charitable; something to do with how unfortunate it was that she didn't get a chance to marry the guy and then screw him to death before Charley did him in. What I said aloud was, "When's the last time you saw it?"

"The last time we were together at his place. That Picasso was worth at least 75K."

I wondered how she knew the New York auction price of an obscure drawing, but let it go for the moment. "And when was that?"

"Why all these questions about a shitty little drawing? Doesn't that useless hippie attorney of his have it?"

"Ma'am, I'd respectfully say that if it's worth $75,000, it's not a shitty little drawing. And no, his attorney never saw it, never knew it even existed until I stopped by to ask." I didn't feel the need to tell her that I knew who had the Picasso. "When was the last time you saw it?" I repeated.

"The night before the storm." She paused. "Hey, now I know where I seen you before. You're the cop who threw John out of Dean's when that skanky Mexican bitch brought him a burned steak. You had some nerve."

"I'm sorry you feel that way, but he assaulted that waitress, and he had to leave or go to jail."

"Well aren't you mister knight in shining armor rescuing the damsel in distress." Her tone was off-putting. Sort of the anti-Viagra.

"No, just doing my job, ma'am. So you haven't seen the Picasso since the night before Charley?"

"No, ain't seen it. I told John I really liked it and he said that when he died, I could have it. But the stupid bastard never wrote it down. The hippie lawyer told me that I wasn't left *anything* in his will. Now you're telling me it's gone?"

"I'm just trying to find out what happened to it." It was the truth—not the whole truth, but close enough for volunteer work. I debated whether or not to tell her about my suspicions that Catlett didn't die accidentally, but decided there'd be no point.

"Well, I couldn't tell you. But if you find it, tell that attorney that I'll swear that John wanted me to have it. On a Bible." She looked at her watch, "Hey, I've got to run. It's Sinatra night and the pickings get slim if you don't get there before seven."

I thanked her, said I'd pass the message along to Attorney Thurmond and as I walked out the door, I didn't even bother with a last look at the twins. I got my pride.

chapter 29
fly

Back in the car, I felt stymied. Again. All I could do was go home and try to get hold of Vin because he might be able to point me in the right direction. I found myself shaking my head with the realization that I was such an amateur.

But instead of calling Vin, I drove over to Jinx's house, snagged two Diet Dr. Peppers which he keeps on ice just for me, sat down on the living room couch and related everything that had happened during the day, from figuring out that the artwork the kid sold to Westchester Gold came from Catlett's condo, to the meeting with Strom where I learned that Catlett had no insurance and no paperwork on his collection, to the fruitless though visually stimulating meeting with Lacey Drawers. And that was the good news.

"No," Jinx said, "the good news is that you thought a crime had been committed, and now you're sure—unless you think Catlett had a weak moment and gave some kid the Picasso to sell."

I wasn't buying Jinx's upbeat bullshit. "Next thing you're going to tell me is that I should look on the bright side, that every cloud has a silver lining, it's always darkest before the dawn…"

Before I could finish the cliché run, Jinx chimed in with, "And sit on a happy face."

"If you would've sung it, it might have been funny."

"My, aren't we cranky this evening, Mr. Moscone. What's wrong? Didn't get a nap? For a guy who had his way with the good hands man and is getting a brand new tile roof in the decorator color of his wife's choice, you are really grumpy." Jinx paused. "You're not armed right now, are you?"

"I'm equipped to thump you upside the head if you give me any more grief, you *stunad,*" I replied, grumpily. "Remember what you told me two hurricanes ago? That a mentor of yours had once told you to trust your instincts and not kill your own story."

Jinx nodded.

"Well, I trust my instincts, and I'm trying hard not to kill my own story, but it's not working. Unless I can locate the kid who sold the Picasso, I've got—what's the word you people use?— oh, yeah. *Gornisht.* Nothing. Nada. Zip. Zilch. G'boink. And the only way I'm going to find him is if he makes the crime reports because he flashed that cash and got rolled outside a Port Charlotte titty bar."

Then Jinx decided to get philosophical. "Fly, I'm no expert in hands-on law enforcement work, but I think you're going to have to let this one go. Maybe a lead will develop, maybe not. You said you hadn't called Vin yet. Why don't you go home, make the call, and see what he has to say?"

"So now you're trying to get rid of me?"

"If I thought it would do you some good to sit here and go over the same thing another three or four dozen times, I'd listen. But Laura is on her way home and I have to start dinner."

"You realize that in my house, my wife works, and she comes home and makes me dinner. It's the Italian way."

"And you realize that in my house, my wife works, and either I make dinner or she makes reservations. It's the Jewish way. Now get the hell out of here."

chapter 30
jinx

F ly, I'm tired of playing helmsman. You drive, I'll talk." Fly and I swapped places; we stopped the boat and just drifted while a couple of the ladies went below to use the head. Then, with drinks refilled and everyone back topside, Fly gave it gas and I picked up the story.

It took almost a week for reality to set in. My buddy was off the Catlett case, because without a lead to the kid, there was no case. He thought about discussing it with the captain who headed up the volunteer program, but the conversation he had with Vin—and then again with me—had served as a dress rehearsal for talking to the boss, and since the out-of-town tryouts had gone badly, there was no point in opening the show.

What Fly hadn't realized is how focusing full time on the pursuit of truth, justice and the American way had had a major positive impact on his personality. For the duration of his total immersion there'd been a turnaround. Unfortunately, it hadn't been permanent, because now he'd reverted to Mr. Grumpy. He also wasn't sleeping well, and couldn't tell whether that was cause or effect vis-à-vis the grumpiness. Bottom line: Fly was not very

pleasant to be around—and I'm talking more than his usual un-
pleasantness that you can see makes him so endearing.

After Fly's prostate cancer was diagnosed, he had been told to
take his meds, get regular checkups, and reduce the level of
stress in his life. He made the same mistake a lot of new retirees
do when getting orders like that from their doc: he assumed that
inactivity, or more precisely, non-productive activity was stress-
less. In truth, it was the opposite. Fly would sit in front of the TV
and curse out the politicians on C-SPAN who regularly drank at
the Kool-Aid fountain of the right wing broadcasters. Or he'd sit
in front of the computer, going from one news site to another
deliberately seeking out the stories and blogs that would aggra-
vate him. It seemed that no matter what he did, he couldn't relax.
To fill time, he'd go over to the local Publix and take his blood
pressure. The readings didn't help because they forced him to
choose between believing that either the machine was broken, or
his meds weren't doing the job. You can imagine what a delight
he was to be around. He was giving me agita.

One of his regular stops on the computer was the NOAA site
run by the National Hurricane Center. Three times a day they'd
issue reports on developments in the tropics. The best reports
were the briefest: no activity. It's when they spotted something
happening off the coast of Africa, or later in the season, in the
southern Caribbean, that things would get interesting. And when
that occurred, strangely enough, I could sense that Fly's stress
level went down, not up.

That's what happened on September 13. Tropical Depression
Eleven formed seventy miles east-southeast of Guadeloupe. For
those of you who never mastered "Where in the World is Car-
men San Diego?" that's southeast of Puerto Rico and just north
of Martinique. The depression—tropical, not Fly's—didn't waste
any time; the next day it was upgraded and named Tropical
Storm Jeanne. Two days later, it made landfall on Puerto Rico,
crossed the island and as it reached the eastern tip of the Domin-
ican Republic, it achieved hurricane strength.

Fly's response was to thank God because he could now focus
his worrying and begin to annoy me with matters of real sub-
stance. Unfortunately for him, my accusation that Chicken Little

was his role model proved to be correct when two days later, Jeanne was downgraded back to tropical depression. That wasn't as good as it sounds, because at this strength, Jeanne still managed to dump thirteen inches of rain over Haiti. And it wasn't even a tropical storm.

Three days later, Fly sat down to read the 8 a.m. update from the hurricane center. One glance, and he reached for the phone, hitting speed dial. It took four full rings for me to answer. "Morning," I said.

"Then we agree. Jinx, it's me."

"Who else would it be? Is this important, or do you just think it's important?

"It's important," Fly almost shouted. "The bitch is back."

"Pardon me?" He couldn't blame me for being confused. I had actually slept through the night and was pretty sure I sounded as though I'd just woken from a coma.

"Jeanne. She's a hurricane again."

"Am I supposed to care?" His grating voice had forced my brain cells to begin firing.

"They're not sure yet. The spaghetti is all over the place. They're reasonably certain the Bahamas are going to get smacked, but that doesn't necessarily mean it makes landfall in Florida."

"Fly," I said, with a weariness that I know occasionally creeps into my voice when I have to deal with him, "Couldn't this news have waited? I'm not asking for much. Just an hour. I was dreaming about a girl in a leotard at the gym. She had an incredible body, but her face was out of focus. I think I was just about to get a good look when you woke me up. She could have been that Punta Gorda ten we keep looking for." A Punta Gorda ten was a woman who might be a six in New Jersey where Fly came from, or a four or five in LA where I came here from. Fly wasn't buying it.

"*Mannaggia!* You're an ingrate. I save your life by warning you about the first hurricane. Now, I feel the need to talk with you about the fourth, and you want me to wait until some faceless woman in a dream blows you off, *off* being the operative word. Be real, you've got nothing more important to do than sleep in. So to answer your question, no, it couldn't wait."

Sometimes friendship—deeply felt, mutual friendship between two mature men—can be a real pain in the ass. I'm sure our wives would dispute the "mature men" part of that equation, but it's really none of their business. This is between guys.

I knew Fly could picture me sitting up in bed, then putting my legs over the side and feeling around for my flip-flops. Screw him. "You can wait a minute, or I'll call you back. Which?"

He said he'd wait. So I shuffled from our bedroom to my office. On the way, I practiced some deep breathing—in through the nose, out through the mouth—just the way I do it on the golf course. I hadn't shut the computer off overnight, so it took just a few seconds to put on my computer glasses, hit a few keys, and arrive at our favorite hurricane watching site. It only took a glimpse to see the problem.

"I'm looking at Weather Underground. This could get serious," I said, sounding serious.

"That's what I've been trying to tell you."

"But the consensus is that it's still several days away from making landfall on the east coast." I paused, thinking about what I'd just said. "Can you believe that Florida could be whacked by four major hurricanes in less than two months? I don't think that's ever happened before, I think it's too early to figure out what we're going to do. We just need to keep an eye on it. What're you going to tell Sophia?"

"The same thing you're going to tell Laura," he replied brusquely. "As little as possible."

"Sexist pig."

"Guilty as charged. But we share a sty, don't we? Look," Fly said rapidly, "I just can't deal with four days of unanswerable questions. I don't know whether it's going to hit here. I don't know when. I don't know how bad it'll be. I haven't figured out where we'll go if it does come here. I got no answers," he said in complete and total frustration. "Why is it that when there are no good answers, we're supposed to have all the answers? But when we actually do know something, the women aren't interested in hearing what we know?"

"It's perverse," I replied. "But we love them anyway." A pause. "We do, don't we?"

"Yeah. Tell me the truth. If it weren't for sex, would you put up with any of it?"

I didn't opt for the usual response—what's sex? Instead, I took a more nuanced approach. "It depends what day you ask me."

"How about today?" Fly pressed, wanting to pin me down.

"Today, I'll put up with it. Laura is really pretty good *in* a crisis. It's before and after the crisis that she's a pain in the ass."

"So you're saying that a blow-up doll with realistic orifices is something you could consider."

"No, Fly, that's what you're saying. I'm taking the Fifth. Or drinking a fifth. I'll see you at the Food and Friends dinner tonight. Call me if anything big happens. Otherwise, don't bother me, 'cause I'm on deadline with a piece for the *Herald-Trib*." And with that, I hung up on him.

chapter 31
jinx

Fly's brain was on overload, sort of like the control tower at Newark Liberty Airport about 5 p.m. on a stormy day. Staring into his eyes, you could almost see the sparks flashing. He was trying to psych out the hurricane, an impossible task, while fishing for a new entry into the Catlett case and feeling guilty for not doing anything to find the sniper, which is something the detectives who were getting paid to do also hadn't been able to accomplish.

With all that going on inside his head, Fly decided to call his roofing company. Actually, Sophia decided for him. She wanted a new roof on their house and she wanted it now. He tried to tell her that it was in the works, that thousands of other people were waiting just like they were. She didn't care about the thousands of other people, and it was his job to get it done. So he sat down, punched in the number, and listened to busy signals for half an hour while offering a prayer of thanks to the guy who invented the redial button.

The roofers had been relatively quick about tearing off the old roof and drying him in—putting down a layer of what they call ninety-pound—something like tarpaper but technologically superior—and then hot mopping it with tar. They'd managed to do the job with a minimum of tar sprayed all over the house and driveway. They'd even taken great care to pick up dozens of loose roofing nails on the driveway before they found their way into Fly's tires.

He had been a little queasy about the roofer taking the next step—and I didn't blame him. It involved delivering five thousand square feet of concrete tiles and loading them onto the roof in stacks of eight or ten. He'd tried to get them to commit to loading them on the roof and having the finishing crew standing by to lay them out and foam them in place. But they wouldn't do it. This may not sound like much of a problem, but we could have another hurricane blow through the place while we've got thousands of dollars worth of new tiles just stacked on the roof, waiting to be plucked off by gusts and tossed around the neighborhood.

"Don't worry, Mr. Moscone," the roofer had told him, "If another storm is coming, we'll pull crews off our east coast jobs, and send them over to wire the tiles in stacks." It's not that Fly didn't believe the guy, but he didn't believe the guy. Fly was shocked out of his pants when a truck from Stop-A-Storm Roofing pulled up on the day the Hurricane Center was preparing to give us the straight dope on Jeanne.

He was about to go outside and greet them when Sophia grabbed him by the arm and hauled him back down onto the couch. "Don't even think about going out there. There's nothing you can say that will improve our situation, and a whole lot that you can do to make it worse." Does that woman know her man, or what?

Fly argued that if he went out and talked to the foreman, he might be able to find out when they were going to get around to completing the roof. Sophia had a devastatingly logical response. "Did I miss something or have you secretly learned how to speak Spanish?"

"No, but…" Fly stammered.

She wasn't interested. "There's no one out there who speaks English…"

Fly interrupted, "No, there's no one out there who will *admit* to speaking English, except when it's convenient for them."

"My point is still the same," Sophia said firmly—more firmly than Fly expected. "You can't communicate with them. They don't know the answer to your question. Leave it alone. Why don't you go call your brother and bet on some football games? It'll keep you out of trouble."

Since Fly hadn't figured out his picks for the week, he wasn't ready to call his bookie. Instead, he went from window to window around the house, trying to see what the roofing crew was doing. As near as he could tell, there were half a dozen guys scampering up ladders and over the roof. Within an hour, the house was covered with stacks of eight or ten tiles, neatly tied together with baling wire. They weren't going to blow off the roof in a storm; they probably wouldn't even slide off the roof.

The roofer showing up as promised was proof enough for Fly that not only does God exist, but that He's keeping an eye on Paul Moscone & Family. Now, if only He'd take care of all of us and just send Jeanne somewhere else.

chapter 32
jinx

It was 5:30 in the evening and Laura and I were just getting ready to go pick up Fly and Sophia and head to the first Newcomer's Club potluck gathering since Charley whacked Punta Gorda upside the head. Just as we were going out the door, Fly called to say they wouldn't be going and asked us to stop by and pick up the dessert Sophia had been assigned to make. I listened for a few seconds, then said, "Sure. I believe it, Fly. You're bailing out on food and friends because Soph has the sniffles. It wouldn't have anything to do with the fact that it's at Jerry Renfroe's house and you can't stand him, would it?"

A second after I rang the doorbell at Casa Moscone, Fly offered me the same advice my own wife had given me just minutes earlier. "Try not to pick any fights, Be- Bop. Without me there, you're gonna be outnumbered forty to one—and they all can justify global warming, oil rigs in Charlotte Harbor and open season on manatees."

"If I can't fight, what the hell is the point of going? And don't think for a second I believe that crap about Soph being sick. You just don't want to have to smile that crooked smile of yours for three hours listening to them bragging about how they already got their insurance checks and their new roofs and how they're goin' to Europe with the money left over."

"You're right. But Soph really is sick. Otherwise I wouldn't miss the opportunity to mess with their heads. And the food *is* always good."

"Yeah, who knew hypocrites could cook? Hey, I just thought of something. With all the shooting going on, maybe I can borrow one of your guns. The little .38. What do you say?"

Fly shook his head, reached over to the table in their entryway and handed me a box. "Here, Clemenza, leave the gun. Take the cannolis."

Ten minutes later Laura and I walked through the front door of one of the newer and larger homes in the Isles. It had been built to the latest codes and had been hardly bothered by Charley. There was no rule that required a division of the sexes, but that's what happens down here: the women gather in the living room, and after filling a plate with food, the guys head for the lanai. My MO at these things is to blend in, listen, and wait for an opportunity to pull the pin and lob a grenade or two if the talk turns to national politics. But post-Charley conversation—as predicted—tended toward the status of insurance claims and the impossibility of dealing with contractors. The only political talk centered on the inadequacies of FEMA and the Corps of Engineers, which was reported to be doing more harm than good by nailing blue tarps to roofs, and there wasn't a good fight to be had over that.

I gravitated toward a group of guys who were listening to what appeared to be a lecture from the evening's host, the henna-haired Jerry Renfroe, who Laura and I both disliked from the moment we first heard him talk out of both sides of his mouth simultaneously. The schmuck was going on about how the insurance adjustors who'd been shot had probably deserved it because they were making dozens of lives miserable. While no one in the crowd seemed especially interested in defending the adjustors, there were some muted objections to his over-the-top stance, probably from some of the same people who for weeks had been bragging about ripping off their insurance carriers with phony claims.

I listened for a few more minutes, and then wandered back inside the house. The women were still yammering away about whatever it is women yammer about. No point in trying to pull Laura away from the group. As the hostess passed me on her way to the kitchen, I asked where the bathroom was. She pointed toward a doorway near the front of the house, and I headed in that direction. Down a short hall was the bathroom, which I used, and in no rush to get back to Renfroe's rant I began to wander.

Turning right instead of left, I opened a door and found myself in a game room. A billiard table occupied center stage, an old-fashioned *Playboy* pinball machine was to my right, and straight ahead were some sliding glass doors leading to a side patio. But what caused me to stop dead in my tracks were the hunting trophies on the walls. Elk, mule deer, Cape buffalo, lion, zebra, and Rocky Mountain sheep. All animals that were hunted with the scope-mounted rifles hanging on the opposite wall. "Holy shit!" I exclaimed out loud, and was shocked when a man's voice said, "Holy shit what?"

I wheeled around to face the doorway, hoping in the split second it took to pirouette that the voice wasn't that of the whack-job homeowner. Fortunately, it was a guy I knew from fishing club, Rich Calvo, so I was able to cover myself. "Get a load of those trophies. You think Jerry shot 'em all himself?"

"I know he did," came the response. "He used to go on safari every year." Calvo did a quick look back into the hallway, apparently to make sure no one was listening. "He bored the crap out of Lori and me one night with a slide show that went on till eleven o'clock. Even I wouldn't do that to company, and I shoot pictures for a living."

"Damn, that's two hours after Punta Gorda midnight. Did he at least have the decency to put some topless National Geo shots in there—just to keep you up, so to speak?"

"No such luck. You shoot pool?"

"I was in the army. Everyone shoots pool. Rack 'em up." We played Eight Ball, and Calvo killed me. Turns out, he was in the army, too. Vietnam, about the same time I was there. The problem was not that I can't shoot, but I really couldn't concentrate. What I wanted to do was go outside and call Fly, but there was no way I could just walk out on the guy. So I played, finally winning a game just as Laura came looking for me and said it was time to go home.

I was tempted to tell her what I'd discovered about Renfroe's little hobby, but decided that giving her any idea I was somehow involved in pursuing a killer with a gun—many big guns— would not be marriage-affirming. By the time we got home, I figured it was too late to call Fly. I'd have to tell him about my discovery in the morning.

chapter 33
jinx

The phone rang at 7:30, just as I was viciously slapping at the snooze button on my alarm clock. I picked it up—the phone, not the alarm clock—and said, "What?" It didn't even cross my mind that it would be anyone but Fly at that hour. "Still in bed nursing the after-effects of Boone's Farm and cranberry juice on the rocks? It's 7:30. Time to get up and tell me how miserable a time you had."

Unless it's an absolute emergency, no one should be required to carry on a conversation with Fly without first emptying his bladder, brushing his teeth, and fixing a cup of coffee. I told him to give me five minutes and hung up.

I had completed task one and was engaged in task two when the phone rang. I quick-walked from the bathroom to the kitchen while my electric toothbrush buzzed away, spraying a contrail of Crest, grabbed the phone and as I shouted "What?" managed to schpritz the screen that told me it was him again. I wiped the phone on my pajama top, looked at it, hit the button and yelled again. "What? I haven't had my coffee yet."

"I wanna know what went on last night."

"You'll never guess what I discovered in Renfroe's house," I said, spitting toothpaste into the bathroom sink. And then I told him about the rifles with scopes and the trophy animal heads on the wall in the game room. There was a moment of silence, during which I moved the phone away from my ear. I knew what was coming.

"Why didn't you call me as soon as you got home?" Fly screamed. He went on. And on. And on and on and on. I walked into the kitchen and set the phone on the kitchen counter. I could hear him without putting it on speaker.

When he stopped to catch his breath, I messed with his head. "You'll never believe what Renfroe said." Then I paused.

It was as though his brain was downshifting into a lower gear: listening.

"What'd the *giamoke* say?" That was his grumpy voice, not the screech that could break Waterford crystal.

"That maybe the insurance adjustors who'd been shot deserved it for messing with people's lives."

"He actually said that?"

"As God and twenty of your closest friends are my witnesses."

"*Ba fongool!* He's justifying killing insurance adjustors on his lanai, and down the hall he's got a room full of animal heads that pretty much proves he knows how to use a scoped rifle, several of which are coincidentally hanging on the wall." Fly's voice was rising into the range it often seeks when someone disagrees with him over matters he deems to be non-disagreeable. That's his term, not mine.

"Fly, he didn't justify killing insurance adjustors on his lanai."

"What? You're becoming my wife? You know what I meant. Don't act like a *jadrool*. Now I need to figure out what I should do."

"How 'bout you call Vin. Don't you think that would be the logical thing?" I asked.

"What's with you this morning? You're really getting annoying."

"*I'm* getting annoying? You're the one who woke me up just to gossip. You didn't know I might have something meaningful to tell you."

"Okay. Yeah. I s'pose calling Vin would be the logical thing to do. But…"

"But...what?"

"But I wanted to try and work this out without asking him for help. It's a pride thing, not that you'd understand that concept."

"My, my, aren't we getting pissy this morning. Look, Fly, digging into the theft of some artwork is one thing, but now you're messing around with a guy who's trying to qualify as a serial killer. How do you know that the homicide cops aren't already onto Renfroe and anything you do could screw it up?"

"So you're saying I should tell the cops?"

"You know you should call them. You just asked me for confirmation."

He hates it when he knows I'm right, so he just mumbled, "I'll talk to you later," and hung up.

chapter 34
fly

Fly pulled back on the throttles and the boat quickly came off plane. "There's a pod of dolphins over there if you wanna watch. Besides, where the story is about to go, I gotta tell it. This *jadrool* wasn't there."

An hour after I got off the phone with Jinx, I drove over to the sheriff's office and found the homicide boss, Lieutenant Lew Albert in the kitchen, pouring himself a cup of coffee.

"Loo Lew, I need to talk to you."

"Moscone, how many times I told you not to call me that? It's bad enough I got to take it from Sandler. What do you need?" he harrumphed, adding cream and sugar to the heavy ceramic mug that had a Red Sox logo on the side. I managed to avoid commenting, which for a Yankee fan, was hard.

"If you've caught the insurance shooter already, then what I have to tell you is a waste of time. If you haven't, then it's serious."

"Let's go into my office," he said, which I took to be a clear indication that they didn't have the killer signed, sealed and delivered to the county jail.

It took me less than ten minutes to explain why I thought Jerry Renfroe could be a POI—a person of interest. In addition to his skill with a hunting rifle and his toxic attitude toward insurance adjustors, I mentioned that on at least one occasion before a shooting, we'd seen the guy hanging out at Dean's, which coincidentally is where nearly all the adjustors working the Punta Gorda claims gathered for breakfast and lunch—making it easy for someone to find a target and follow him. Loo Lew listened carefully, asked a few questions, and promised they'd look into it.

"That's it? You'll look into it?" I said, my voice carrying a clear connotation of disappointment that left a bad aftertaste on the palate. It was probably bile.

"Fly, I said we'll look into it. Hanging out at Dean's isn't a capital offense. If it were, most of my squad would be under arrest."

"I gotta ask you a question," I said, knowing that it wasn't going to earn me the civilian volunteer of the month award. "When I told you that we heard the shooter's car lay rubber after he killed the Allstate guy, did your crime scene techs look for a sample of the rubber on the road?"

"I'd have to pull the file. But it sounds like you just watched *My Cousin Vinny* again. Am I right?"

"Great movie. Love Joe Pesci. And even Sophia would let me do Marisa Tomei, who is unbearably cute. Okay, well maybe Soph wouldn't. But that's beside the point. Did your guys do what I asked about or not? Because it would be simple to match the samples or tread pattern to Renfroe's SUV tires."

It didn't take a salesman's intuition for me to tell just from the look on Loo Lew's face that I'd pushed about twenty or thirty percent too far. So I thanked the lieutenant for his time, wished him luck with the search for the killer, and left.

"Okay, let the journey resume. Go ahead, Jinx, tell 'em what happened next."

chapter 35
jinx

On the morning of September 25, just six weeks after Charley, Hurricane Jeanne stopped meandering in the Atlantic, strengthened to a Category 3, and passed over Grand Abaco in the Bahamas on its way to Port Saint Lucie and Stuart, Florida, just two miles from where Hurricane Frances made landfall three weeks earlier. When Fly saw the bulletin on the Internet, he imagined hearing a very deep voice from up above saying, "I sent your roofer to keep his promise. I'm keeping an eye on you. Count your blessings."

It was clear from the cone of stupidity that Jeanne would not be visiting Charlotte County. Thinking that the lack of need to deal with storm shutters, laying in a supply of ice and drinking water, and soothing Laura might leave me with some free time, Fly called.

"What're you doing today?"

"I've gotta take some furniture and old clothes over to Goodwill," I replied.

"You better save that for late in the day so you have something to look forward to," Fly responded.

"That's why you called? To bust my balls?"

"It's what I live for. I repeat my question: what are you doing today?"

"Fly, you couldn't give a rat's ass what I'm doing today. Get to the point."

"Moretti's is back open. I haven't had a Caesar salad with Cajun fried shrimp in months. I'll drive." Offering to drive was the clincher. Moretti's is twenty miles away in Mat-la-*shay*—spelled M-a-t-l-a-c-h-a—an old fishing village on the road to Pine Island, which is what Sanibel could be if it didn't have traffic, tourists, Gulf beaches and a toll bridge. Moretti's has someone in the kitchen who knows that the surest way to turn shrimp into cat food is to overcook it. They also don't use breading, just a light dusting of flour seasoned with a mixture of stuff they refuse to reveal. The only downside is that the drive to Matlacha requires you to take your life in your hands on Burnt Store Road, a two lane highway overrun by dump trucks driven by guys who are paid by the load, not the hour. You haven't lived till you've driven sixty-five with a Kenworth sporting a Confederate Flag on its grille six inches off your rear bumper.

"Okay, pick me up," I said.

"Be there in ten minutes." Fly threw on a clean pair of shorts and a polo shirt, kissed Sophia good-bye, and headed over to my house. He'd just honked the horn for me when his cell phone rang.

"Fly, it's Steve at Westchester Gold."

"I'm not buyin' her the earrings till her birthday."

"Fly, I know who the kid is. You've got to come over here."

Now Fly was torn. How was he going to tell me that instead of Cajun shrimp at Moretti's we're going to Port Charlotte? He made a quick decision, which, of course, didn't take my feelings into consideration. "Steve, I'll be over there in fifteen minutes."

He was about to snap the cell phone shut when he heard Steve shouting his name. "Fly, we've moved. We're in the shopping center behind ABC Liquors. We're right next to the Thai place."

"Got it," he said, signing off and turning to me just as I was climbing into the SUV. "Change of plans. We're going over to Westchester Gold. Steve says he knows who the kid is. Bad news and good news on lunch. We're not going to Matlacha, but

Steve moved his place next to the Thai Café. I'll buy you all the Pad Thai you can eat."

"You're not getting off that cheap. I feel like crispy duck. And spring rolls. And Tom Ka Kai. And in your honor, Prik King. And a cold Singha beer. And we go to Matlacha next week. And you're still buying. And driving."

We left the Isles via Olympia Avenue, hung a left on 41, and headed north toward the bridge. Something—maybe fate, maybe a stiff neck—caused Fly to glance to our right just as we were passing Dean's. *"Ba fongool!* It's him."

I followed his gaze and the two of us watched Renfroe doing a fast-walk through the parking lot to his fancy Lexus SUV. Fly had about a quarter of a second to decide what to do, decided, and yelled "hang on" as he threw the car into a tight right turn onto Retta Esplanade.

"What're you doing?" I yelled, grabbing for the handhold.

"We're going to see what Renfroe is doing. There's no reason for him to be running through the parking lot." In a big city, a coincidence like this would be farfetched. But in a small town like Punta Gorda, we're always running into people we know—at the Publix, in the Walgreens, and at the relatively few local restaurants.

Fly drove past the alley that would have taken us into the un-paved parking lot, went to the end of the block, turned left, pulled into the lot adjacent to one of the local attorney's offices and found a spot where we could unobtrusively watch cars leaving Dean's.

"Slouch down," he ordered.

"For what?" I said. "Is that what they taught you in Crimestoppers 101?"

"Just do it in case he comes this way. And stop giving me any crap." At the same time he reached across me, clicked open the glove compartment, and pulled out his Glock. He released the magazine, checked it, shoved it home, and cranked a round into the receiver.

"Are you nuts?" I said firmly.

"We established that a long time ago. But in this case, not nuts, just prepared. Here comes a pickup." Fly had made an almost instantaneous transformation from Jersey Guy to professional cop. It scared me 'cause it impressed me.

Pulling out of the alley and making a right, which was going to take it past where we were parked, was a red Ford F-150. On the driver's door—and presumably on the passenger door—was a magnetic sign telling everyone that Nationwide was on their side. The pickup stopped at the corner, and then turned right onto Nesbit. "Look who's tailing him." It was Renfroe, following slowly, about a hundred feet behind the Ford. "Let's see where he goes."

chapter 36
jinx

Fly waited until Renfroe had turned onto Nesbit, then eased onto the street and up to the stop sign, turning right in time to see the Ford take the corner onto westbound Marion, with Renfroe not far behind. "Shit," we said simultaneously, watching the light at Marion turn red. The intersection was marked by the only No Turn On Red sign for miles. Fly pulled up to the corner. We looked to our left, saw no traffic approaching, and both said, "Fuck it." He made the turn.

The insurance guy and Renfroe caught the green light at 41 North, and rather than risk losing them if they turned down a side street, Fly hit the gas and made it through on the yellow, immediately backing off as he passed Punta Gorda's mini-restaurant row.

"You have a plan? You've thought this out ahead of time?" I asked, "Or are you making it up as you go?"

"The only thing I planned for is to make sure I always had the Glock with me. Other than that, we're winging it. Do me a favor," he said, as he handed me his cell phone, "Call Steve and tell him it may be an hour or two, but we'll be there. His number is in the contacts list." While I made the call, Fly tried to practice everything he'd learned about tailing cars from watching Clint Eastwood movies.

The insurance guy was clearly heading for the Isles, and Renfroe was staying on his tail. He probably figured that he could stay close, since it wouldn't be unusual to have an ad hoc caravan of cars heading from US 41, westbound on Marion. "Okay, here's what we're doing," Fly said to me in an annoyingly competent tone of voice. "I'm guessing that the insurance guy is going to pull into someone's driveway, and the odds are that Renfroe is going to drive past that driveway, and sooner or later he'll park, with the tailgate on his car facing his target. We're going to drive right past him and keep going until we're out of sight..."

"What happens if he parks in a cul-de-sac?"

"I don't know. We'll have to play it by ear."

"That's not a comforting answer, Fly, not when both sides are playing with guns."

"It's the best I can do. If you don't want to come along, I can pull over and drop you off. But I'm betting that Renfroe is going for another kill, and we've got a chance to prevent it, and catch the SOB."

"You're not dropping me off—but if I get killed, Laura is going to own your ass. Got it?"

"I got it."

"And your boat."

"I said *I got it*."

"Would you consider calling the cops who are investigating the murders?"

Fly looked at me with a disgusted expression on his face.

"Okay, I take that to mean you think it would be a waste of time." I paused for a second and looked down at the Glock that was resting in his lap. "You're the one who knows how to shoot that thing, so I think if we can make the switch, I should be driving. Yes?"

We continued making plans as we tailed Renfroe deep into the Isles. When he made a left onto Islamorada Lane, following the adjustor down a street that I knew was more than a mile long, I began to breathe a little easier. "If we're lucky, no cul-de-sac." Less than a minute later, we could see the red Ford pull into a driveway on the right. Renfroe tapped his brakes a couple of times, then drifted past the driveway, stopping what looked to be six or eight houses beyond the one being visited by the insurance man. Fly had slowed up so we were still more than a block away.

"You want to park here, or risk driving past him?" I asked.

"Let's stick with the plan. I'll drive past him without slowing down. You don't even look in his direction. Islamorada has no outlet. The only way he's going to get out of here is by turning around."

About a quarter mile past Renfroe's car, Fly pulled into a circular driveway on the right, going all the way around till the car was just a few feet from the street. He hit the button to unlock the tailgate, then yelled, "Switch." We both got out and walked around the back of the car, giving him a chance to grab the binoculars that he kept there. Once back in the vehicle, he handed them to me. "See what you can see."

I futzed with the focusing ring, took a few seconds, and then said, "I can see his car. The tailgate is up, but he must be inside. I can't see him."

"Can you see the insurance guy—or the front door of the house?"

"There's a palm tree blocking my view of the front door, but I'll be able to see the guy before he gets back to his truck."

"If Renfroe is the shooter and he sticks with the pattern, he won't shoot until the guy is sitting still at the wheel of his truck. Why take a moving target if you don't have to? And if he's laying flat in the rear of his SUV, there's no way he can even take a shot until his target gets to the front of his truck. How long do you think it will take you to cover the distance between here and Renfroe's car?"

"That's a stupid question. How fast will I be driving?"

"Hey, cut me some slack, I'm new to this. I assume if you floored it, you could be there in under ten seconds. But if we crawled…"

"Why don't you try thinking out loud? What's going through that *fercockteh* mind of yours?" I asked.

"I'm thinking that if we don't start moving until you see him clear the palm tree, can we get to his car before the target is sitting in his truck with the door closed?"

"That's cutting it close, isn't it?"

"Yeah, but if we try and bust him before he's set up to take the shot, he can make some half-assed legitimate excuse for being there. We've got to catch him in the act."

"I hope you know what you're doing," I said, as I took another look through the binoculars. "What I'm thinking is that we should pull out of the driveway and park across the street, facing in Renfroe's direction. I'll have even a better view of the situation from there. We have to assume he's already in the back of his vehicle, he's not looking in our direction."

"Okay, then you have to make the call on when to move," Fly said, amazing both of us that he could give up control at a moment like this.

"I just thought of something," I said. "You wouldn't have remembered to bring your sheriff's radio by any chance? 'Cause it would sure be nice to call for backup if this thing really does go down."

"No such luck. We were just going for lunch and dropping by Westchester Gold. But if this goes the way I think it's going, as soon as I get out of the car, dial 911 and tell them 'officer involved, shots fired.' Then give 'em the address."

"Even if you don't have to shoot him?" I asked, a quizzical look on my face.

"Absolutely. I'll apologize for breaking the rules later. Just do what you can to get help on the way. I don't have my cuffs with me and I'm not going to be happy holding a gun on this guy for a long time. One other thing. Take a look at the steering wheel so you know where the horn is. Just in case our timing is off, I want to throw as much commotion into this as we can. Maybe it'll fuck up his aim."

"You realize that if this plays out, I hope you're not thinking that you're going to be the beloved hometown hero. Because it's fifty-fifty whether Renfroe is seen as a bad guy, or just someone doing what a lot of guys wish they had the balls to do."

"I'll live with it, however it goes down. And if anyone wants to argue with me about it, I'll beat the crap out of them. How can these law-and-order types cheer for a guy who commits murder?"

"That's just one long notch up from cheering for guys who commit felony insurance fraud—and they don't have a problem doing that."

"Point taken," Fly said, looking at his watch. "It's been about fifteen minutes since the guy went in. Let's pull onto the street. And leave it running."

I put the 4-Runner in gear and slowly pulled out of the driveway, parking on the opposite side of the street.

We sat there for a few seconds, both of us in deep thought. Fly broke the silence. "I wish this thing were a Hummer. Then we'd just ram the *strunz* and knock him unconscious."

"Funny you mention that," I said. "I was wondering how you'd feel if things moved fast and I opted to ram him. I'm not sure how this car would do in a head-on with a Lexus SUV, but I can bet it wouldn't be pretty."

"How I'd feel isn't nearly as important as how Soph would feel. She wouldn't be impressed with you arguing that it made sense at the time."

I was scanning with the binoculars, not responding to his comment. "You see something?" he asked.

"Here he comes," I shouted, dropping the binoculars over my shoulder into the back. I put the car in gear, and began moving, slowly at first, then picking up speed.

Fly started issuing last second instructions. "When I yell, hit the horn. I want you to pull up even with his car; just don't go past it because it'll put me in the line of fire." He tapped the button that unlocked the doors, checked the Glock one more time, unfastened his seatbelt, and cracked the door open. As he saw the insurance guy open the door to his pickup, Fly yelled, "Horn!"

I laid on it, and sped up a bit—probably to about 20 MPH, taking my foot off the gas as we approached the Lexus, and then slammed on the brakes. Fly didn't wait for the car to stop, but bailed out as it drew even with Renfroe's vehicle. As he jumped out he yelled, "Police, drop your weapon," and shocked the crap out of me when he fired a shot into the grassy swale.

It had the desired effect. The insurance guy threw himself across the seat of his truck, so he was now out of sight. Fly heard some jumping around in Renfroe's car, and looking through the tinted glass could see him trying to turn so he could get a shot at him. He yelled, "Drop your weapon!"

Renfroe was trying to sit up so he could aim the rifle at Fly through the side rear window. But before he could take a shot, Fly stepped in front of the open hatch and put a round into the back of the right passenger seat, just a foot or two from Renfroe's head.

"Don't shoot, don't shoot," Renfroe screamed.

"Drop the rifle, Jerry!" Fly yelled back. "Jinx, the back door."

I had already gotten out of the car, and yanked the rear door of the Lexus open, reached inside and grabbed the rifle butt, pulling it away from Renfroe.

"Now, crawl this way, scumbag," Fly shouted, adrenaline clearly getting the upper hand. "One false move and I'll put a bullet in your stupid fuckin' head," he added gratuitously. Then he shot a quick glance at me. I was on the cellphone, talking excitedly. Seconds later, I yelled that help was on the way.

By this time, Renfroe was on his belly, his head hanging out the back of the SUV. Fly walked over, grabbed him by the back of his shirt and dragged him out, letting him fall onto the pavement.

"Don't shoot me, just don't shoot me," Renfroe begged.

Now, Fly was at a loss for what to do until the cavalry arrived. He didn't know whether the shooter was crazy enough—or desperate enough—to go for his gun. Then it struck him. "Lie on your back," he said.

Renfroe complied.

"Now unbuckle your belt and push your pants down around your knees."

Once again, he did what he'd been told to do.

"Now roll over on your belly."

We watched him do it. I glanced down the road to the pickup truck. The insurance guy was just climbing out of the cab.

"Hey, what's your name?"

"Brian."

"Well, Brian, you got anything in there Deputy Moscone can use to tie this guy up?"

"How 'bout a roll of duct tape?"

"That'll work just fine. Bring it over here," I said. He did, and I pointed at Renfroe. "You wanna do it?"

He didn't need to be asked a second time. We watched as Brian wrapped Renfroe's ankles with half a dozen turns of a man's second best friend. "Now, we wait."

Noticing that the insurance guy had turned pasty white and was shaking, I put an arm around him, helped him to the back of the Lexus where he sat down. "You really think this guy was going to kill me?" he asked.

"He wasn't here to shoot antelope," Fly said. Then he looked back down at Renfroe. "Why? Why'd you do it?"

"Because they're scum! My father got a heart attack and died at forty-two because scum insurance adjustors screwed him over. We lost our house when the Mississippi flooded, and they wouldn't pay. We ended up losing everything, dad lost his job, and we had nowhere to live. Moved to St. Louis, and then dad had a heart attack and died. I hate insurance guys. And most of the people around here agree with me. Ask your asshole buddy. He heard them at the party. They're scum. They don't care whose lives they ruin. The ones I kill aren't going to be ruining any more lives."

At that point we'd heard enough, and Fly didn't want to get into any hot water with the brass by looking as though he was taking down a confession without Mirandizing the bastard. "Just shut the fuck up. You'll have plenty of time to tell your story."

That's when we heard the first sirens approaching, and within seconds, there were three squad cars screeching to a halt.

chapter 37
jinx

Three hours later, Fly, Brian the intended target, and I had finished giving our statements at Punta Gorda Police HQ.

The county sheriff himself had come over to sit in on the questioning, and when it was all over, he told Fly that he'd done well, but that he wanted to see him the next day. That's when Fly looked at his watch, saw that it was not quite five, and abruptly excused himself, motioning for me to follow.

As soon as we were out of the interrogation room, Fly pointed at his watch. "Jinx. The time! Let's go."

I looked at him like he was nuts, but I followed him at a trot out of the building.

"What?" I said.

"Steve. I almost forgot. Give me my cell phone back."

As we were climbing into his car, Fly got Steve on the phone, told him we'd been delayed, and asked him to wait for us. "We'll be there in five minutes."

We headed south on US 41, went past Dean's where the afternoon's adventures had begun, and crossed over the Peace River, heading into Port Charlotte. The harbor was almost flat and there were only a couple of boats fishing the bridge pilings.

"Fly, I thought you were just going to put on the sheriff's uniform, help kids and little old ladies cross the street, and keep peace in the Publix parking lot. What happened?"

"What happened is I got a chance to do something important."

"Well, you did it. Can't you let this other thing drop?"

"Trust me, Jinx. If what happens in the next fifteen minutes doesn't convince you that this is worth doing, I'll give it up. Promise."

"I'm not sure how you can reprogram your brain to go from arresting a murderer to tracking down a kid who stole a drawing or something. Haven't you had enough excitement for one day?"

"Just trust me, okay? I really feel like I'm doing what I should have been doing my entire life, okay?"

Frankly, I was shocked that he had any adrenaline left in him. It had been one hell of an afternoon: a rolling surveillance, firing his weapon which I was betting is what the sheriff wants to see him about, disarming and busting a would-be serial killer. Maybe busting criminals is like eating potato chips. You can't stop at just one. But he had a feeling that if he could track down the kid, he could put him in the condo around the time of Catlett's death.

"You know, Jinx, I might never be able to prove that the *stugatz's* death was anything other than accidental—but I know that something happened in that condo that wasn't kosher, and dammit, I wanna find out what it was and see that someone is locked up. Do the crime, do the time."

We walked into Westchester Gold exactly five minutes later. The new digs were actually nicer than the original store that Charley blew out and a lot nicer than their first post-Charley location, but one thing was still missing—the parrot. "Where's AJ?" Fly said to anyone within shouting distance.

Steve's wife, Barb, answered first. "Dr. Bevins said that allowing him to associate with riffraff like you on a regular basis could be bad for his health. So we're keeping him home." Andrea Bevins is the vet who takes care of AJ, Fly's mutt, my Alfie, and the pets of just about everyone else we knew in Punta Gorda. The only problem with her office is that she's staffed it with all women. There isn't an ounce of testosterone in the place, and I get the feeling that they all secretly smile when someone brings a dog in to have him neutered. The day I accidentally nailed Alfie with a fishhook in the mouth—I told you they don't call me Mr. Jinx for nothing—and brought him in to have it removed, the women decided that on the ten-point scale of stupid things husbands do, this only merited a three. They only stopped dumping on me long enough to have me bring Laura in from the car so they could tell her that a three wasn't so bad. I suppose I should have been grateful.

As soon as Steve heard Fly, he waved us behind the counter to his desk, where that day's edition of the Charlotte *Sun* was spread out. "Took you long enough to get here. I expected you at lunch time."

"Steve," Fly said, "something came up and I was otherwise engaged. You can read about it in tomorrow's paper. I'll make it up to you." I think that's the moment it dawned on Fly that solving the mystery of the Picasso theft was more important to him, personally, than nailing a killer. Crazy, huh?

"Never mind making it up to me," Steve said. "Look at the front of the sports section." We did. It featured trading card photos of each starter on the Charlotte High Tarpons football team. Steve pointed to a photo in the top row, then tapped it for emphasis. "That's the kid who brought in the Picasso. No doubt."

Fly picked up the paper and looked at it closely. "You want a loupe?" Steve teased.

"You're sure this is the kid? Absolutely?"

"I'm sure. So is Barb." He took a folded sheet of paper from his pocket and tossed it onto the desk. "Compare it to the phony driver's license picture."

No question. They matched. The caption said the kid's name is Tony Duarte, a senior running back who is the second leading scorer on the team. "Now I have to figure out where to find him," Fly said, mostly to himself. But Steve heard him, and shaking his head in amusement, he pointed to the two-inch high headline above the picture that Fly's eyes had passed over. It read, "Homecoming Tonight."

I pointed at a little box near the top of the page. "See this?" Fly hadn't noticed. It said that the governor would be at the game for the coin toss. So finding Duarte wasn't going to be a problem. But busting a hometown hero on the Friday night of homecoming, which also happened to be the first home game since Charley wiped out Charlotte High School's historic building and football stadium, could start a riot.

So just when Fly was feeling the weight of the world lifting from his shoulders because he'd finally ID'd the kid, it dropped on him again.

"Jinx, we're going to a football game tonight." He turned toward where I'd been standing behind him, only to discover I was gone. I'd wandered into the pawnshop corner of the store and was hefting a red Hohner Bravo 72 accordion.

"Fly, I've found your new hobby. No guns necessary. Except maybe for self-defense when you murder 'Lady of Spain' on open mike night in Gilchrist Park."

I fished some sheet music out of the instrument case. "Look! It comes with 'Seventeen Italian Standards Arranged for Accordion.' 'Come Back to Sorrento,' 'Oh, Marie,' and the ever popular 'Funiculi, Funicula.' Sophia'll go crazy for it. Steve, what kind of deal can you make him? He'll be a whole new Fly."

Fly wasn't amused. "I said we're going to a football game tonight. *We*. Got it?"

"You're just no fun any more." I looked at the time. "I got it. But first, you're buying me dinner. They've got a crispy duck next door with my name on it."

"Can we take it to go?" Fly asked, seriously.

"Not a chance. But I won't linger."

chapter 38
jinx

We pulled into the parking lot outside the recently repaired Tarpon Stadium a few minutes after six, a little less than two hours before game time. Fly had debated back and forth over whether to go home and put on his uniform or drive straight to the game wearing civvies, and chose the latter. No matter how he dressed, I was not especially thrilled to be along for the ride on this one.

As we were getting out of the car, a familiar white Ford Expedition with "Charlotte County Emergency Management EM-1" on the side pulled in right next to us. Wayne Salladé, wearing his Tarpons cap and T-shirt exited. "Nice outfit," Fly said, snarkily.

"Every game, for twenty-two years," Wayne replied, ignoring said snarkiness. "I hear you had some excitement today. Nice work."

"Thanks. I'll tell you all about it at lunch. You can buy." Then Fly pointed to his T-shirt, "You're that much of a fan?" he asked, incredulous that a grown man could pay so much attention to a game ignored by Vegas odds makers.

"Yes, I'm a fan. But I've been the stadium announcer all that time. Ever since I got out of broadcast school and came home to Charlotte County."

I was standing back, quietly observing the byplay. At a break in the conversation, I stepped forward. Wayne saw me coming. "If it isn't Mr. Jinx. You're not sitting on our side of the field tonight, are you?"

"Not to worry, Wayne. The jinx only kicks in on a fishing boat or a golf course."

"That's what he says now," Fly responded.

"Wayne," said Fly, looking serious, "if you're calling the game, you must know all the players."

"Of course I know them all. I start meeting them when they make the JV, and stay in touch with the starters all through the season."

"You know a kid named Tony Duarte?" Fly asked, pointedly.

"Of course I know him," replied Wayne. "He's a starter, a running back. I can check my stat book but I think he's the second or third highest scorer on the team this year. Of course we've only played three games. What's your interest in Duarte?" he asked, getting suspicious. Fly's poker face wasn't as good as it had been sitting in a college dorm playing five card stud with a bunch of potheads, causing Wayne to suddenly lose his normally outgoing, friendly nature. "This have anything to do with you working for the sheriff's department?"

"Wayne, maybe we shouldn't discuss this right now," Fly responded weakly. He'd been riding a white horse on this search for justice, and suddenly, he saw that sometimes the good guy had to wear a black hat. Or ride a black horse. Something like that. Wayne wasn't going to walk away.

"C'mon, Fly. We nearly died together. What's going on with Duarte?"

Fly was uncomfortable having this conversation in the parking lot, but it was still early and we were alone. "Wayne, I'm pretty sure that the kid took something that wasn't his, and sold it." As soon as he laid out that moronically simplistic version of the crime, he wanted to kick himself. He'd made a fifty grand heist sound like the kid stole a candy bar from the drug store. Salladé just looked at him.

"Okay, I'll give you the short version."

"You just did," responded Wayne, a grim look now on his face. "Try again."

"The kid sold a Picasso drawing to Westchester Gold for fifty grand. It belonged to Catlett, the dead guy…"

Salladé cut him off. "I know who Catlett is."

"Of course you do." He was still picking his way through the conversation. Maybe it was time to let it all hang out.

"Wayne, I was the first cop to get into the condo where Catlett died. It was a fluke." He took a couple of minutes to explain how it all happened, concluding with, "I got there and found him dead in the bed. He'd bled out. But there were footprints in the ceiling insulation that covered the floor. Someone had been there ahead of me. I thought it was the neighbors, the ones who called it in. But they said no; they didn't go upstairs to look. When I got there, they were still shell-shocked, so I figured it was *possible* they didn't. But something just didn't seem right. Truth is, for a long time I thought the *stugots* might have been murdered, that the death wasn't an accident. But I couldn't figure out a motive. He had a fifteen thousand dollar Rolex on his wrist. If robbery was the motive, it woulda been gone."

We could see Wayne was getting impatient, and more cars were filling up the parking lot. "What's a *stugots*? And you still haven't told me how the kid fits in," he said firmly.

"It's Italian for pile of shit."

"And how the kid fits in?"

"I'm coming to that," Fly answered. "Catlett left all his stuff to the Catholic Church here in Punta Gorda, all the antiques, artwork, real estate, boat. But a month or so ago, the kid comes in to Westchester Gold with a Picasso drawing that he sells to Steve for fifty thousand dollars. Steve did his due diligence; the piece had never been reported stolen. The kid told him it had been in his family for a long time. And he gives Steve a photo ID that later turns out to be phony.

"Steve knows I'm into being a detective, and he's given me some tips before on petty theft stuff. So he calls me to tell me about the Picasso, just because it was so odd. I go over and take a look at it, and something clicks." Fly pulled the newspaper clipping out of his wallet and showed it to Salladé. "It was part of Catlett's collection. It should have gone to the church. How'd the kid get it if he didn't steal it from the condo?"

Wayne was visibly upset. "Oh, man. Your timing couldn't be worse. Tonight's homecoming, it's the first home game since Charley. The governor is here. And Duarte is key to our offense. You don't have to do this tonight, do you?"

Fly looked at me, but I had nothing to say. I just gave him the shrug and the don't-ask-me-this-is-your-problem look. It was clear that Fly was in over his head.

Wayne jumped into the silence. "Fly, Tony is a good kid. His mother teaches here. His father is a disabled vet from the Gulf War. He's not going to run away. I'll make you a deal. Don't say anything before the game. When it's all over, I'll introduce you to his parents."

"They'll be here?"

Wayne gave him the you're-kidding-me look. "Their kid is a star. They'll be here. I'll introduce you to them after the game, and you can see how you want to play it."

Fly nodded agreement, and Salladé took off for the press box. I looked at my friend, the wanna-be detective and said, "You don't have a clue, do you?"

chapter 39
jinx

I was about to go on when Sophia stood up and yelled at her husband to stop the boat. "What it is? What's wrong?" Fly said to her.

"There's nothing wrong, if you don't count trying to get yourself killed."

"But Soph, I was careful. I never got in front of the business end of that *stunad*'s rifle. We planned our moves, and it went down just the way we planned it. And we stopped a murder."

"I'm not talking about *that*. I can't believe you were even *thinking* about arresting a kid on Charlotte High's football team *before* their homecoming game. Are you crazy? Do you care whether we can keep living in this town? You're not in Orlando any more. It's Punta Gorda. Everyone here knows everyone else."

Fly was dumfounded. His wife wasn't upset that he had to fire his gun to prevent a murder and arrest a killer. That wasn't the problem. Busting the star running back or whatever the hell he was before homecoming—*that* was his mistake.

He looked over at me for support. I was behind Soph and she couldn't see me shrug my shoulders.

"Honey," Fly began, "I *didn't* arrest the kid before the game."

"But you thought about it," she insisted.

I looked at the faces of the other three guys on the boat. We were all thinking the same thing—even Beiler, who I'd pegged as a weenie. *If we can get busted by our wives for what we're thinking, life ain't worth living.*

"Yeah, Soph, I *thought* about it!" Fly had given up on the apologetic tone and was going on the offensive. "Remember the workshop we once went to with Father Tim, about how the church made *wanna* a sin. 'I wanna do the nasty with her.' I didn't do it, but I *wanna*. Oops. Sin. Might as well have done it. Remember what Father said? If I recall, it was *fuhgedaboutit.*

"You can't bust me for *wanna*. You already know I didn't screw up their homecoming game. Why don't you sit back, have another glass of wine, and hear what happens? Okay?"

That's when Rich Aronson opened his mouth. "I don't want to take sides, here, but it seems to me that even though you didn't actually arrest the kid before a big game, your timing wasn't so great." Big mistake.

Fly climbed down from the captain's chair, did a 360-degree scan to determine that we wouldn't get into any trouble just drifting, and then motioned for Aronson, Beiler and me to huddle up away from the wives. "I need to tell you about my cousin Mario," Fly whispered. "Mario and I grew up together; he was a couple years older. And he taught me Man Rules. There's a long list of 'em. I broke one of 'em once. I sided with the wives against Mario and the other husbands over what movie we were gonna see."

Beiler interrupted. "What movie did the wives want to see?"

Fly's eyes flashed, and he snapped, "That's not important. Man Rules says you never—I mean never—ever side with the wife against a buddy." It could be a big thing or a little one. It don't matter. That's how the game is played. He looked intently at Aronson. "I broke that rule once—just once—about thirty years ago, and Mario still busts my agates over it." Then he swiveled his head in order to make contact with each of us. "*Capisce?*" He paused. "The wives wanted to see *Ordinary People*, and I sorta wanted to see it, too."

"What'd the guys want to see?" Aronson asked.

"*Blues Brothers*."

I held my breath, hoping neither of the newbies would say a word. Fortunately, they didn't.

Fly turned, grabbed another DDP from the cooler, popped it open, took the wheel, and waved at me to resume the story as he pushed both throttles forward. The boat surged ahead, bow high, then slowly settled onto a smooth plane.

Okay, so Salladé walks away and I give Fly a shot—cuz he didn't have a clue what he was going to do now.

"Jinx, I'm going on instinct here," he said. "I spent thirty-five years reading people, figuring strategy and keeping my head above water. None of it's paying off right now."

"Sure it is," I said, being uncharacteristically supportive at a time that provided an opening for big time ball busting. "Just slow down and think it through. You'll be okay."

Fly knew I was being way too solicitous and supportive, so he waited for the zinger, but it never came. He was about to thank me for my support but it's hard to talk when your jaw has just dropped open. A pickup truck pulling into the parking lot caught his eye. He'd seen it before, on Marion, just before he got to the condos and discovered Catlett's body. A kid wearing a baseball cap pulled low over his head was driving. I could tell that he'd stopped paying attention to me. I turned and followed his gaze.

"What?"

"The pickup. It's the same truck I saw coming from the condos after the storm."

The kid parked the truck, got out and walked to the back, leaned over and pulled a wheelchair out. He rolled it around to the other side, out of our sight."

"Let's walk," he said to me. We casually walked to where we could see what was going on. A woman who looked to be in her forties had gotten out, the kid positioned the wheelchair, then the two of them helped a very gaunt man out of the truck and into the chair. The kid slammed the truck's door, leaned down and kissed the man, then kissed the woman on the cheek. She gave him a hug, and after grabbing a duffle out of the back, he took off toward the locker rooms while the woman—I presume she's the kid's mom—began pushing the wheelchair toward the stadium.

"Meet Tony Duarte and family," I said. The sympathy I'd shown Fly just minutes earlier was gone. "Yeah, he looks like a real juvenile delinquent. What was it you said? Do the crime, do the time."

The last thing Fly needed just then was crap from me. "Let's go watch a football game. I can't wait to hear what the gov has to say."

chapter 40
jinx

Friday night high school football is a time for people to pull together, to enjoy being part of a community. Homecoming is usually the best of times for a small high school. Homecoming in the shadow of a historic building that's being held up by an exoskeleton of steel because Charley gutted the place is bittersweet. But winning the game sure helps everyone forget the bitterness and just enjoy the sweetness of the moment.

To our immense displeasure, the governor exhibited perfect pitch with his remarks. No overt politicking, other than the obvious fact that he made the trip to Southwest Florida from Tallahassee. What good is a speech by a politician if you can't make fun of it?

Fly's heart sank when they called the team co-captains out for the coin toss, and the kid he was ready to bust for grand theft ran onto the field and shook the governor's hand. Fly wanted to be a cop to lock up scum—just like he'd done that afternoon—but this wasn't playing out the way he'd imagined.

When the game ended with a Tarpons' victory, we waited a few minutes, and then made our way to the press box to meet up with Salladé. The huge smile on his face evaporated when he saw Fly. "Talk about buzzkill," Wayne said.

"I don't understand," said Fly, somewhat confused. "What's buzzkill?"

"You really are old. Buzzkill is something that causes a high to deflate. I'm high on our victory. I see you. My high is deflated. Buzzkill. Got it?"

"Aw, Wayne, you been hanging out with these high schoolers too long. I'm just doin' my job. Can't you see it that way?"

"No, Paul, I can't." When he used Fly's given name, it was obvious that he was sore. "You don't have to be doing this. Charlotte County's got an over abundance of scumbags for you to track down. Why go after a good kid?"

"Look Wayne, it's not like I picked this kid first and then tried to attach a criminal act to him. It's just the way the chips are falling into place. You're a decent, law abiding guy. You're even Catholic. Your church was supposed to get that artwork, or the money from it. But somehow, Duarte got hold of it and sold it. Those are the facts. They'll hold up in a court of law."

"All I'm telling you is that there must be an explanation. This is a good kid. Can you try and keep an open mind?"

"I can try. You gonna introduce me to the family? 'Cause I'm ready."

Frankly, I wasn't sure how true that was. Fly might have been putting on a good show, but I know him like a brother. He was faking it.

It was a typical October night in Punta Gorda. At ten o'clock it was still in the high eighties, still humid as hell, for which Fly silently said, thank God. His shirt was soaked with flop sweat, and his palms were slippery enough that he had to keep wiping them on his pants. The good news was that everyone else was also sweaty, so maybe it wasn't too much of a tell.

Salladé scanned the field till he found Tony Duarte's dad in his wheelchair, waiting for his son to emerge from the locker room. Mrs. Duarte was nearby talking to parents also waiting for their victorious kids. Reluctantly, Wayne began climbing down the bleachers, then mumbled a weak, "Follow me."

When we got to within a few yards of Mr. and Mrs. Duarte, Wayne turned and asked Fly to wait till he spoke with them. A minute later, he waved Fly over. I hung back. This was going to be painful.

"Mr. and Mrs. Duarte, this is Reserve Deputy Paul Moscone," he said to them. "Meet Jessica and Armando Duarte. I told them you had some questions for their son, and that you were a reasonable guy. Don't make me look bad."

Wayne backed away as Fly shook hands with the mom first, and then with the dad. Up close, the kid's father looked even worse than he had at a distance. His grip was weak and his voice was soft. "Wayne tells me there may be a problem with Tony. I don't understand."

Fly looked around and could see that they were being observed by half a dozen sets of parents who could tell that this was not a typical after-game congratulatory conversation. Fly looked at me, and I slowly shook my head from side to side. Fly got the message.

"Folks, I need to talk to your son, but Wayne tells me you're good people, and so is Tony. Can I come by your place tomorrow morning and we can have this conversation then? I'm assuming Tony is going to be there, right?"

The mom spoke first. "Of course Antonio will be there. I'm not sure how much sleep we'll get tonight worrying about what this is about, but you're right, in the morning would be better."

She gave Fly their address; they again shook hands all around. Fly and I walked away. He nodded at Salladé who was watching from a distance.

As we got to the car, I said, "You're on your own tomorrow. Laura's got things for me to do. And even if I weren't busy, I'd be busy."

"Great friend you are. Look, even if there's extenuating circumstances, there's nothing that can justify a seventy-five K theft. And that's what I got the kid on. I saw him coming from the dead guy's place, and Steve and his wife will absolutely ID him as the kid who sold the Picasso for fifty thou in cash. I know for certain that it belonged to Catlett. It should have gone to Sacred Heart. If ever something was black and white, this is."

"Yeah, I know," I replied in a moderately sarcastic tone, "do the crime, do the time. How much time does someone get for a seventy-five thousand dollar heist? Do you know?"

"As a matter of fact I do. I looked it up. Second degree grand theft is a class two felony. For a first offense, fifteen years more or less.

All I said as we climbed into the car was, "Uh huh." Fly reached for the radio, turned it on, and tuned to the public station. He figured music would be better than the cold shoulder he knew I'd be giving him. He was expecting classical music, but it was Friday night, after ten. Time for Mona Golabek and The Romantic Hour. I couldn't handle it. "Can you turn that crap off?" I added a grudging, "Please." Fly tapped the scan button with his index finger and suddenly the car was filled with mariachis. "No!" I said. He hit the button again. Rap music. Again. Chainsaw rock. Again. Organ music backing some preacher promising hellfire and damnation.

"Just turn it off." Florida radio. Yecch.

chapter 41
jinx

We were passing Marker One, a couple miles off the entrance to the Punta Gorda Isles canal system, when another pod of dolphins swam by. Fly eased *Inamorata* off plane and came to a stop. Just off the starboard bow we could see fishermen in a couple of flats boats throwing cast nets near the marker for baitfish. A lumbering V-formation of brown pelicans—the Punta Gorda Air Force—went by us less than ten feet above the water, then climbed, spotted a school of fish and began diving on them. It was one of those moments when you look around Charlotte Harbor and realize how lucky you are to live here. "We own it," I said to the newbies. "And now you do, too." Sophia had gone below; when she returned, she announced that coffee and dessert would be ready in fifteen minutes. "In that case," said Fly, "let's just drift here while I tell you the rest of the story."

He looked over at me and said, "*I* gotta tell it, 'cause there's stuff that happened that I never told you about." Hearing no objection from me, Fly took over.

fly

As I walked into the house after confronting the Duartes at the stadium, I began wrestling with another problem, one that Jinx and I had discussed at the Thai place. How much or how little do I tell Soph about the things that happened in the last few hours. The homicide bust was sure to be in the morning papers. And she knew I was obsessed about the stolen Picasso. She hadn't been terribly interested in the day-to-day details of what I'd been doing, except when she could tell it was getting me upset, causing stress and raising my blood pressure—which she insisted I check every night.

About once a week she gave me the "why do you have to be involved?" lecture, even though she knew all the reasons. Women don't accept there are certain things some men need to do, even if the consequences of doing them are net negative. Maybe some guys can change their nature, but I can't.

Sophia was sitting on the couch watching TV when I got home. As I passed her on the way to the fridge to grab a Diet Dr. Pepper, I tried a cheery, "Hi there." It didn't work.

"What's wrong? What happened tonight? You haven't gone to a high school football game since we moved here," she observed. "Was Jinx with you?"

"It's too complicated to explain. I gotta go out early tomorrow morning to interview some people. Maybe it'll all be over tomorrow and I'll be able to tell you the whole story. If you make me go through it again now, I'll just get aggravated and it'll drive my blood pressure through the roof."

"You'll be aggravated at *me*? Why would you get aggravated at me?" she said. See what I mean about women? It's always about them. You know what? She should get a job at the vet's office. She'd fit right in. But all I said was, "Not at you. The situation is just aggravating. Okay, you wanna know what's bothering me? Here it is in a nutshell. With this law enforcement stuff—how long have I wanted to be a cop?—How long? Since you've known me, right?"

I figured there was no point in waiting for her to answer rhetorical questions, so I pressed on. "All that time, I wanted to be a cop because they deal in right and wrong, black and white. Truth, justice and the American Way. So what happens if you've believed something your whole life, and then you find out it might not be right? That's what I'm dealing with. And right now, I've got to deal with it alone. Try to understand. And by the way, my name is going to be in the paper tomorrow morning. I arrested the guy who killed that one insurance adjustor and shot the others. It's Jerry Renfroe. But I'd rather not talk about it any more tonight, okay?"

"Jerry Renfroe!" she almost screamed. "We were supposed to go to his house for dinner!"

"Yes, dear. You got sick and we didn't go, but Jinx went, saw Renfroe's collection of hunting trophies and his rifles. That's when he figured out Renfroe was the guy. Jinx called me the next morning. This afternoon I stopped Renfroe from shooting another insurance adjustor. But honey, I just don't want to talk about it right now. It's been a rough day."

She didn't say anything at all, no response. That's a bad sign. I gulped down the soda, then took the mutt out for a walk. By the time I got back, Soph was already in bed and the bedroom lights were out. I showered, put on my pajamas, crawled in next to her, and tried to fall asleep. But I couldn't. So I nudged her. "Soph, my feet are cold. What should I do?"

"Do what you usually do with your feet," she'd said, "put them in your mouth."

chapter 42
fly

A half hour before my nine o'clock appointment with the Duarte family, I parked just down the street from their house.

They lived on the other side of the tracks from the Isles—way on the other side of the tracks—in a poor neighborhood not far from the high school that most of the folks who live in the Isles never think about. The cracker cops in the county call the neighborhood *The Quarters*. Draw your own conclusions. The buzzword since the hurricane destroyed thousands of residential units in Charlotte County has been *workforce housing*. That's what I was looking at here. But somehow, this little pocket off of Cooper Street had managed to avoid the ravages of Charley.

As soon as I knocked on the door, Mrs. Duarte and her son stepped outside. "I know why you're here, but I want to talk to you away from my husband. Can we sit in your car?"

I was a bit surprised at her forthrightness, but quickly agreed. They both got in the back seat, and I got in the front passenger seat, and turned as far as I could to face them. Maybe this wasn't going to be so tough after all, except on the bulging disks in my cervical vertebrae. On the drive over I'd tried to review some of the techniques Vin had taught me, but since it appeared that I was going to get some cooperation, I opted to just let them tell the story with minimal prodding. I pulled out a mini-cassette tape recorder and told them I was going to tape the conversation. They agreed. I recited the time and date into the recorder, said I was sitting with Mrs. Jessica Duarte and her son, Antonio "Tony" Duarte. I pulled out the little card the department gave us with the Miranda warning on it and began to read it. Mrs. Duarte interrupted, "We'll waive the right to remain silent, I'll waive it for my son, and we'll waive our right to an attorney." I felt like thanking her right then and there, but I acted like I knew what I was doing and began with the obvious. "Why do you think I'm here?"

The kid spoke up immediately. "It's about the Picasso. What do you want me to tell you?"

"How about everything. Start at the beginning, and if I have questions, I'll ask."

"It was easy getting into the condo after the storm. I saw the Picasso and knew it was worth a lot of money from the article in the newspaper. So I took it and drove home. I didn't tell mom about it for a long time."

At that point the kid hung his head, glancing sideways at his mother, who had her hands clasped and was rhythmically squeezing them together. The kid went on. "Actually, I didn't tell her about it until I sold it at Westchester Gold. She didn't know anything about it. Even when I came home with the money, I didn't tell her for about a week. That's all there is to tell." Mom unclasped her hands, put both arms around the boy's neck, and hugged him to her.

My head was spinning. I hadn't dealt with teenagers for a long time and had completely forgotten that their brains aren't wired the same way ours are. Tony wasn't holding back; he believed he'd just told everything there was to tell. Letting the kid set the pace clearly wasn't going to work.

"Tony, let's back up and I'll ask you some questions. Why were you over at the condo after the storm?"

Before he could respond, his mom spoke up. "I sent him over there."

Now I was really confused. She didn't know about the Picasso, but she sent the kid to the condo? Either I wasn't hearing right, or I was missing a major piece of the story. "You sent him over there right after the hurricane? Why would you do that?"

"Because I wanted him to check up on my father—his grandfather."

Now my head was doing a full Linda Blair. "Who's your father?"

"Was," she said. "John Catlett was my father. We were estranged. He was Antonio's grandfather, but he never had anything to do with my son. When the hurricane was coming, I just knew that my father would be too stubborn to evacuate. He'd want to stay there with his stuff." Just the way she said *stuff* was a commentary on the man's entire life.

"He always thought the stuff made him important. The stuff and the money. So as soon as Charley passed, I told Tony to drive over there and check on his grandfather. We'd driven by the condos when Tony first started to drive, and that's when I first told him about his grandfather, so he knew where to go."

I looked at the kid. "You drove over there—in your pickup?"

"The wind was still pretty bad when I left the house, but yeah, I drove over there. I parked in front and went up the stairs to the fourth floor."

"What did it look like?" I asked, more to buy time to think than to get information.

"The building was trashed, but still standing. There was this white ceiling insulation all over the place on the top floor. That's how I knew someone had gone up there before me."

"What do you mean?"

"There were tracks in the insulation, like someone had walked down the hall and into my grandfather's apartment. The tracks went all the way to the bed. Or they came all the way from the bed back to the door and into the hallway. They were pretty messed up, but it was obvious that someone had come in and had gone back out."

"So you walked into the apartment. What did you do next?"

"I hollered for my grandfather. I yelled, 'Mr. Catlett, Mr. Catlett.' Of course no one answered. So I followed the tracks into the bedroom, and that's when I saw him laying on the bed." His eyes were tearing up as he remembered the scene.

"I'm sorry, Tony, for putting you through this, but I've got to know everything that happened."

"There was a lot of blood on the floor. It was obvious he'd been bleeding from his thigh. I thought I saw a chunk of glass sticking in him, but I didn't want to touch anything, so I can't be sure. I looked around, and that's when I saw a blood trail from the living room. I followed it over to a broken slider that opened onto a little balcony overlooking the harbor. You didn't need to be a genius to figure out what happened. He was standing in front of the slider when it got busted. He got cut bad, made it to the bedroom where he wrapped a towel around his leg—I forgot to mention the towel before."

"That's okay. Just go ahead."

"He had a towel wrapped around his leg, probably 'cause he thought he could stop the bleeding. And he lay down and just bled to death. Served the son-of-a-bitch right."

"Antonio, he was your grandfather. Don't talk that way."

"Yeah, mom, but he was your father and he cut you off like you were nothing to him. We live in this shithole"—he gestured toward the house—"and he's over there in a fancy condo, with all that money, with a boat and *stuff*." It must be genetic; the way he spit the word out said it all.

The kid continued. "You saw the article in the newspaper, about all the stuff he had. And he cut you off." Then he began sobbing quietly, clearly not out of grief for his dead grandfather. His mom pulled him to her again and hugged him close.

"Mr. Moscone—or do I call you deputy?"

"Mr. Moscone is fine. Please go ahead." I checked the recorder to make sure it was still running.

"My father was a complicated man. He was raised with certain beliefs, and I was a rebellious daughter and went against those beliefs." She stopped to gather her thoughts. I debated whether to prod her along, or just wait. I opted to wait. Yeah, I know that's not like me. Who says you can't teach an old dog new tricks?

"I was in college in Gainesville, in my senior year, when I met Armando. We fell in love and wanted to get married. I knew there'd be a problem because—this is difficult to say now that he's dead—my father was a racist. There's no nice way to say it. He hated blacks and he hated Mexicans, actually all Hispanics. My dad came up there for graduation—mom had died several years before—and after I got my diploma, I introduced Armando Duarte to him as my fiancé. He went nuts, my father did. Right there in front of Mondo he said that if I go ahead and marry him, he'll cut me off. I'll never see a penny of his money; he'll never have a thing to do with me. And that's what he did."

chapter 43
fly

Once again, my mind was reeling. What had seemed as though it would be a simple story had whipped well beyond *Days of Our Lives* to turn into Shakespearean tragedy. "If you were cut off by your father, why did you come back to Punta Gorda—or is this where your husband is from?"

"No. Mondo put himself through college by joining army ROTC. When he graduated, he owed them four years. So I became a military wife and Mondo and I lived at Fort Benning. In Georgia. That's where we had Tony. Then the Gulf War came, and his unit got orders to go over there. Rather than stay at Benning, where I really wasn't close with anyone, I came back to Punta Gorda. I'd grown up here. I went to Charlotte High where I teach now. A lot of my friends were still here and I was pretty sure I could get a job. It was strange sometimes, seeing my father around town, but if he saw me, he never let on.

"Mondo's military pay was enough for us to get a tiny apartment, and I began taking courses to get my teaching certificate. About six months after the war ended, Mondo's commitment to the army was up and he was discharged."

Having seen her husband shrunken to almost nothing and wheeled around in a chair, I drew the obvious conclusion. "Your husband was hurt in the war?" Wrong again.

"He didn't get wounded if that's what you mean. But not long after he got home he began getting sick. You've heard of Gulf War Syndrome?"

"Yes, but I'm sorry I don't know very much about it."

"Well it's just like Agent Orange was for the Vietnam vets. The government and the VA fought for years against admitting that our guys were exposed to something that could mess them up so badly. They still haven't acknowledged all the stuff that Gulf War Syndrome does. What it's doing is killing Tony's dad. It's killing him slowly."

I felt as though I'd completely lost control of the interview. It was hard to listen to their story without being touched. "Mrs. Duarte, I need to come back to something that's troubling me. Can you tell me again why you sent Tony over to check on your father after the storm, I mean, after the way he'd treated you and your family?"

"He's my father. We go to church, to Sacred Heart. So did my father. One time I talked to the priest there about him. In confession I told Father Tim how angry I was at my father. And he said I've got to find forgiveness. It was hard, and I don't think I was able to do it. But with the storm, I knew that the right thing to do was to look after him. He was almost eighty-five years old. So I sent Tony."

As she was talking, I remembered back to my first encounter with Catlett, the time when Jinx and I were having lunch at Dean's and the bastard caused such a stink. "Mrs. Duarte, a couple of months ago, just a day or two before Charley, did you have a phone conversation with your father?"

She looked at me in complete surprise. "How do you know?"

"Please," I said, "Just tell me."

"I called him on his cell phone. We were desperate. I needed some special medication for Mondo. It's a drug that some of the Gulf War vets found helpful but the VA wouldn't give it to him, and since it wasn't in my insurance company's formulary, they wouldn't provide it for him either. And it was expensive. So I called my father to ask if he'd help me pay for the drug." Her voice dropped to a whisper. "He wouldn't."

"I know. You reached him when he was at Dean's. I was there. Everyone heard him screaming at you." The moment I said it, I regretted it. The woman flushed with embarrassment. I immediately decided not to tell her about what had happened a few minutes later with the Hispanic waitress.

Instead, I turned back to the kid. "Son, let's go back to what happened in the condo. You knew your grandfather was dead. What did you do next?"

"I was about to leave when I saw the painting or drawing or whatever it is. The Picasso. Somehow the wind hadn't blown it off the wall. I don't know how, but it was hanging there, all crooked. And I remembered seeing the picture of him with it in the newspaper, and it made a big deal about it being an original Picasso and how it was worth all sorts of money. I knew mom could use the money to help dad, so I took it off the wall, went looking in the closet for a blanket I could wrap it in. And I left."

"Wait a second. When your grandfather died, he had a very expensive wristwatch on his arm. Why didn't you take that?"

Tony looked at me in horror. "You mean like rob his body? I couldn't do anything like that."

It was another brief insight into the reasoning power of American teenagers. It's okay to swipe a Picasso off the wall, but not a Rolex off a dead guy's wrist. I couldn't stop the conversation to try and figure it out, so I followed Vin's rules of interrogation. "What did you do next?"

"I went down the stairs—didn't see anyone—got in my truck and left. There was no one on the road—except as I was coming over the bridge, there was this SUV coming toward me. I ducked down. I think the guy driving it waved at me."

I couldn't resist. "He did wave at you, but you just kept going. That was me. Your grandfather's downstairs neighbors had called 911 because…" I almost screwed up and told them about the blood dripping through the ceiling, but caught myself. "They'd called 911 and I was the closest deputy. I was in the apartment just minutes after you left. I'm sorry for interrupting you. What happened next?"

"I got home and hid the Picasso in the garage. Then went inside and told mom about her father. But I didn't tell her about the drawing."

"Why not?"

"Because I wasn't sure what she'd say. I knew she was going to be upset that her father was dead, especially the way he died, all alone. And I know my mom. She'd have all sorts of problems with me taking the Picasso. She'd say it was stealing, even though I don't think it was. It's her father who owned it. She's his daughter. How can it be stealing if I gave it to her? And we needed the money for dad's medicine."

Mrs. Duarte hadn't spoken for several minutes. I could tell by the look on her face that she knew that what her son had done was stealing. I reached down and turned the tape cassette over. Then hit record. "Mrs. Duarte, when did you find out about the Picasso, about what Tony had done?"

"Maybe a month or a little more after the hurricane. Tony asked me to go for a walk with him, and that's when he gave me the money he got for selling it. Can you imagine how I felt when he explained where the money came from?"

Tony piped up, "She really let me have it. Mom never yells at me. Okay, maybe sometime, like when I'm screwing up in school or something. But this time, she let me have it."

"Tony couldn't understand why I was so upset. He knew we needed the money. He knew that his grandfather was gone. Basically, he was saying, 'Who did I hurt?' I didn't have a good answer. I should have. But standing there in South County Park, watching the herons and egrets wading, listening to the sounds, holding a plastic bag with fifty thousand dollars in hundred dollar bills and knowing how much that could help Mondo, help our family, I didn't have a better answer. I just told him that his father is to never know about it, and that he should never talk about it to anyone. Never. Ever. And he said he wouldn't."

The three of us sat there looking at each other. I glanced at my wristwatch and realized we'd been talking for nearly an hour. "Is your husband going to wonder where you are?"

"No, it's okay. He had a bad night. He's probably still asleep. It's what he usually does after he takes his meds in the morning." She paused, looked at Tony, then back at me. "Mr. Moscone, what are you going to do?"

I had been dreading the question, mostly because I didn't have an answer. Not a good one; not a bad one. Jinx was right when he said I didn't have a clue. What I needed was to get some advice from someone without foreclosing any options. So asking anyone at the sheriff's department was out. It was pretty clear to me that the kid had committed a major felony. His mom was probably also guilty. I had a very brief fly-on-the-wall moment, looking down at a conversation I'd had with Vin, where I was saying, "It's black and white. Do the crime, do the time," and Vin telling me that life is shades of gray.

"Mrs. Duarte, I'll be honest with you. I'm not sure what I'm going to do. I just trust that you're not going anywhere while I think about it. I'm sorry for everything you've gone through, but..." I couldn't finish the sentence. I looked at the two of them. "I should go now. I'll be back in touch with you."

We all got out of the car. Mrs. Duarte hugged Tony and started to walk with him toward the house. I watched them for a few seconds, then walked around to the driver's side, got in and started the engine. I hadn't seen her send the boy back to the house alone and return to the car, which was why I was startled when she leaned close to the open window and spoke to me. "I'll pray for you, Mr. Moscone. I know this is difficult for you."

chapter 44
fly

I wasn't happy when I drove away from the Duarte's house. I should have been, but I wasn't. I'd proved that a second degree felony punishable by up to fifteen years in prison had been committed. Actually, it's worse than that. Since the property was stolen while we were under a declared state of emergency, and the perpetration of the theft was facilitated by conditions arising *from* the emergency, it's now a *first* degree felony and the mandatory minimum is twenty-one years in the slammer plus a $100,000 fine. See—I was paying attention at the academy.

The big problem is that I felt like I was the one in the box, when it should have been the kid.

Since I was already on east side of town, I drove over to the sheriff's headquarters, which had finally been cobbled back together with popsicle sticks, duct tape and Elmer's glue after the beating it had taken from Charley. I just sat in the parking lot. I needed time to think.

The mere fact that I was feeling the need to make a decision rather than just break out the cuffs was troubling. I tried to think logically. No question that a crime was committed, a major felony. But black and white had morphed to shades of gray, just like Vin said it could. And that was causing me to ask a question that the law books ignore—except for crimes against children: who's the victim of this crime?

The guy the Picasso was stolen from, John Catlett, is dead, buried, and if there is a God, by all rights the bastard is trying to keep cool in a very hot place. He wasn't going to miss the artwork. The victim, then, had to be the guy's heir, and that would be the church. But the church had gotten everything else that Catlett owned—a big boat, four condos, the Rolex, plus the other artwork and antiques that hadn't been trashed in the storm. That made it a seven figure payout for JC, tax free.

I was sitting in the car staring blankly at the now repaired building when a voice startled me. "Reminiscing?" It was Captain Sandler.

"Nah, just thinking."

"That can get a guy in trouble," he said, as he headed toward the front door.

Maybe it was the brief interruption that cleared my head, sort of rebooted my brain. It helped me figure the solution to part of the problem: God was the beneficiary; God stands to lose on this deal. It's God's problem; let God solve it. I looked at my watch. It was early afternoon. At least one of the priests at Sacred Heart would be there, either hearing confessions or preparing for the 5:30 mass which was always a sellout. I suddenly felt something I hadn't felt in a long time, even though Sophia and I were regular churchgoers: a need to sit down and talk to a priest.

A few seconds later, I was on the phone with a very pleasant woman in the rectory at Sacred Heart Church. Introduced myself and asked if one of the priests would be available a bit later in the afternoon. She said that Father Tim would be there in about an hour, and she was certain he'd be happy to see me. I made the appointment, snapped my phone shut, and then looked at my watch again. I needed to take care of one other thing: I wanted to have a little talk with Walter Forrester, the asshole in apartment 3B who had lied about going up to the dead guy's condo. It was possible that Walter and his wife hadn't yet moved back into their damaged place, and if that was the case, I'd have to do some work to find out where they were staying. On the other hand, there was the off chance that they were visiting their place just to annoy the contractors who were supposed to be working 24/7 to fix it up.

Figuring that it would only take me fifteen minutes to get all the way down Marion to the condos, I decided it was worth a shot. If Forrester is there, I'd deal with him. It might mean postponing my appointment at the church until tomorrow. If he isn't there, I'd still have time to get back to Sacred Heart. As far as time management goes, the plan sucked, but by now, you know me. I couldn't help myself.

I grabbed my uniform and gear from the SUV and ran inside to change. No matter who I ended up talking to, I wanted to look official. On the way out of the building, I grabbed the keys to one of the squad cars assigned to volunteers. Might as well dress up and give 'em the reverse Full Monty, so to speak.

Minutes later I pulled up to the front of the condo building where I'd found the body. Despite the fact that it was Saturday, an assorted gaggle of contractors was working. I looked for an overseer with a bullwhip because I couldn't figure any other way that could be happening, but these guys actually seemed happy to have the work.

The place looked a lot better than the last time I'd seen it. For one thing, all the apartments actually had doors that appeared to lock, the soggy carpeting was gone, and I could see where new sheetrock had replaced sections that had been damaged. I couldn't resist running my hands over the wallboard. That's when I noticed an almost obscure logo stenciled across it. "Damn, what happened to U.S. Gypsum?" I asked myself. "This stuff's from China."

Someone had marked apartment numbers and names in thick black marker on the unpainted walls next to each door. When I got to the one that said Forrester, I pulled the Maglite off my belt, flipped it around, and pounded a couple of times on the door. I didn't want to be confused with Officer Friendly on this visit.

I was about ready to put a couple more dents into the veneer when the door opened. There he was, the weaselly lying *stugots* himself. "Remember me," I said between gritted teeth.

"Yeah, you were the cop who showed up right after Charley."

"You got a good memory. Strange that it didn't seem to be working so good that afternoon."

The look of confusion, bordering on panic, that crossed his face already made the trip here worth it. "I don't understand. What do you mean?"

"You know what I mean. What did you tell me when I questioned you that afternoon? Let's see how good your memory is."

"I told you that I was the one who called 911 when blood started dripping through the ceiling, right around the vent in our bedroom." It didn't take Dr. Phil to figure that this time I had him off balance. Maybe he was teetering on the verge of truth.

"What else did you tell me?"

He looked down at the floor, then up to the right—anywhere but directly at me. "I told you that I hadn't gone upstairs."

"Was that the truth?" I didn't shout it directly into his ear, but he still flinched.

"No." Finally, the *jadrool* caved.

"Tell me what you did. And this time, try keeping it real."

As this confrontation was taking place, Forrester kept backing away from me. By the time the weasel crumbled, we'd pas de deux'd our way through the entry hall and all the way across the living room, ending up near the sliding glass doors overlooking the harbor. "Okay, we saw the blood coming through the ceiling right after the storm passed. It came through the bedroom ceiling. We'd been hiding in the bathtub with a mattress over us, my wife and I. She started screaming. I mean, can you imagine the sight of blood dripping down from the ceiling? It's like something out of a Stephen King novel.

"Catlett's apartment is right over ours. The penthouse. The one that he lives in. Lived in. I told Diane that I was going to go upstairs and see. So I went upstairs. You know what it looked like."

I wasn't letting up. "Pretend I don't, and tell me."

"There was all the insulation down from the ceiling, and the doors were blown open just like on our floor. I got to the door of his apartment—4B, right over ours. I stepped inside the door and yelled his name, I yelled 'Catlett, John Catlett. You in here?' He didn't answer. So I went in farther. The place looked like a hurricane had gone through it."

I looked to see if he was making a joke. He wasn't. "Keep going," I said. "What'd you do next?"

"I walked to the doorway to the bedroom. That's when I saw him laying on the bed. I could see a bloody towel on his leg—up here." He pointed to his thigh. "And I walked closer. His eyes were open, but I don't think he was alive."

"Why do you say that?"

"Because I yelled his name again, and then I poked him in his shoulder. He didn't say nothing."

"Did you check to see if he was breathing? Did you see if he had a pulse, a heartbeat?"

"No, I didn't!" he screamed. It caught me off guard. "If he'd been breathing, I would've just stood there and watched the son-of-a-bitch die." Forrester saw the look of surprise on my face. "You heard me right. But he was already dead. We called 911. We did everything we were supposed to. He didn't deserve any help. It's his fault all this happened to us in the first place." He was shouting, and he was crying at the same time. And what he'd said didn't make sense. How could it be Catlett's fault that a hurricane hit Punta Gorda? I'd heard him correctly—'cause the *giamoke* repeated it. "It's his fuckin' fault."

I backed off a bit. "Mr. Forrester, calm down. What do you mean it was his fault all this happened?" I had no idea where this was going.

"When you pulled up, did you notice the building next door to ours? It was built at the same time. But it didn't get destroyed. You know why? I'll tell you why. Because they voted—the owners of the units—to put hurricane shutters on all the windows and the sliding glass doors. You see any shutters on our building? No. You want to know why?"

In a much quieter voice I assured him that I did.

"Because Catlett voted against it."

"Did the other owners vote for it?"

"Of course we did. You think we're stupid? There are sixteen units in this building. But he owned four of them. The condo documents say that eighty percent of the units have to approve any assessment for things like hurricane shutters. With his four votes, he vetoed it. We'd gotten a couple of bids. It would have cost each condo owner eight thousand dollars. It would've cost him thirty-two thousand. He didn't want to pay it."

"Why couldn't you each have taken care of your own unit and to hell with him?"

"You never lived in a condo, I'm guessing. The covenants prohibit it. They change the appearance of the building. We couldn't do it, even though every other owner wanted to." Now the guy was really crying, and I was beginning to feel sorry for him.

"Did he tell you why he didn't want the shutters—I mean any reason other than the money, 'cause he had plenty of money. It just doesn't make sense."

"He said Punta Gorda hadn't been hit by a hurricane since 1960. He'd be dead before another one hit here. Why should he pay?"

I wanted to say that Catlett was pretty much right—his timing was just a little bit off, by maybe two or three minutes, and he had the sequence reversed. But I bit my tongue.

"Mr. Forrester, aside from poking Mr. Catlett a couple of times in his bed, you never touched him? You never did anything to him?"

"You think I killed him? Officer or deputy or whatever the hell you are, I hated his guts, but I'm a law-abiding citizen. I'm a good person. So I lied to you. I didn't want to be involved. What happened happened. Nothing was going to bring him back."

Forrester took a couple of deep breaths, and this time, he was looking me right in the eye. "I didn't kill him. God did. And God chose right."

chapter 45
fly

On the drive from the end of Marion to Sacred Heart, I finally gave up my quest for John Catlett's murderer. I had to kill my own story. I'd been wrong—not that something hadn't gone down in the dead guy's apartment that broke the law. I was still nagged by the voice of the ex-New York cop who'd told me that if you want to commit murder and get away with it, do it here. Nevertheless, I had to admit that the medical examiner was right. Catlett's death was accidental, but the real cause was gross stupidity.

Now I had to deal with the crime that actually went down, the crime I'd uncovered. And I was beginning to worry that I might be wrong on that one, too. Not that the law hadn't been broken, but on the whole black-white-gray thing.

Charley hadn't been kind to Sacred Heart Catholic Church. The main sanctuary had been red tagged. Fact is, they'd already torn it down and were beginning to struggle with how to rebuild. For the duration, services were being held in an annex that was a plain vanilla auditorium. The parish served a large geographic area and a diverse community. The 5:30 Saturday evening service was usually filled up with retirees. During the season when all the snowbirds were down here, it was kneeling room only. Ditto for the early service Sunday morning. And then there was the Saturday night Spanish language mass that served the community of permanent residents and the migrants who worked on the area farms and groves as well as making up much of the blue collar work force in this part of Charlotte County. That's the mass Tony Duarte went to with his parents. It guaranteed that he would have never, ever accidentally run into his grandfather.

Word had gone out that they had already hired an architect to begin designing a new sanctuary building. But the bigger news was that Sacred Heart Parish would be required to foot the bill— the entire bill. The diocese would not be sending a Brinks truck to their rescue. There hadn't been any publicity about Catlett leaving his entire estate to Sacred Heart. My guess is they were holding back on the announcement in order to use it to jump start the fund raising campaign. Nothing like setting a goal that seems impossible—say five or six million bucks—and then telling everyone that because of the generosity of one fine man, you're almost halfway there.

I hadn't talked to any realtors, but I estimated that Catlett's four condos with their unobstructed views of the sunset over Charlotte Harbor would average at least half a million bucks each, even if they were sold as is. His art and antiques maybe another million. Then there was his yacht. Before he got involved with this mess, long before Charley, Jinx and I had seen the yacht up close. If you went to an event at the PGI Civic Association, Catlett's boat was moored right in front of the windows that overlooked the Isles Yacht Club basin.

For anyone into power boats, she was something to slobber over. First of all, she was the biggest, most expensive yacht docked there, a fact Catlett apparently made a point of mentioning whenever he entertained on board. A fifty-five foot Viking convertible isn't something you see too often. Fewer than 200 were built. He must have bought it when Viking introduced the model. I don't know what he paid then, but now, almost seven years old, I figure in round numbers it's still worth a million bucks. The church will probably give it to a yacht broker to sell, and even paying a ten percent commission, they'll net 900K minimum. That ought to buy them a few new pews.

What I was beginning to understand is that even though the kid ripped off a piece of artwork that would probably net the church sixty to seventy thousand if sold at auction in New York, as a percentage of what they got from the estate, it wasn't significant—Jinx would say *bupkes*. And as a percentage of what they had to raise to rebuild, barely *bupkes*. That's not to say it's insignificant. Even during the height of the season, the monthly take from the collection plate didn't come anywhere near fifty K— and the Venice diocese raked a percentage off the top of that.

I walked into the church office right on time, only to be told by the same pleasant voice I'd heard on the phone that Father Tim hadn't returned yet, but that she expected him momentarily. My assumption that the priest was off performing some pastoral duty was obliterated a few minutes later when he walked in and put his golf bag in a corner of the office. I know priests have down time, but I hadn't expected to be meeting with a guy wearing flip-flops, Bermuda shorts and a robin's egg blue polo shirt.

"How'd you do?" I asked, hoping that I'd masked my surprise.

"High eighties," he said. Then he looked heavenward, "Okay, low nineties with a few mulligans. You play?"

"Not any more. I had to play for work—you know, take clients to fancy courses and let them win. I vowed that when I retired, I'd never set foot on a golf course again."

"That's too bad. It's really a great game. Frustrating, but enjoyable." He sat down in one of the pull-up chairs in front of his desk, and motioned me to take the other. "I read about you in the paper this morning. You've made a lot of people down here feel much safer by taking that man off the streets."

"Maybe, but I'm sure there are a lot of folks here in the Isles who liked Jerry Renfroe. They aren't very happy with me right now." I really didn't want to launch into a discussion of the murders, so I took a left turn with the conversation. "I suppose you've heard every golfing priest joke there is." I figured it was worth a shot to loosen him up before I got into the reason I came to see him.

"I'm always up for a new one. Go for it," he said.

"Okay. A young guy is playing golf with a priest. At the par three, 150-yard third hole, the priest asks, 'What are you going to use on this hole, son?'

"The guy says, 'An eight iron, father. How about you?'"

"The priest says, 'I'm going to hit an easy six and pray.'"

"The young guy hits his eight iron and puts the ball on the green, pin high. The priest tops his six iron and dribbles the ball a few yards in front of the tee. The young man looks at the ball, then at the priest, and says, 'I don't know about you, father, but in my church, when we pray, we keep our head down.'"

Father Tim looked at me with a grin. "Sounds like you might have been out there watching me this morning."

Okay, enough small talk. Even after thirty years in sales, I never did learn a gracious way to move from meaningless yammering to the real purpose of the meeting. What it meant is that over the course of my life I had to endure countless hours of absolute, mind-numbing bullshit—with a smile on my face. It was Father Tim who provided the segue. "So, what brings you here, Paul?"

"First, Father, I just want to make sure that whatever I tell you stays between us. I mean, can we do this in your office, or do I have to go into the closet?" He assured me that wherever I talked with him as a priest, the conversation was privileged. Satisfied with that assurance, I took a deep breath and said, "This is going to take a few minutes," and I launched into the whole story, start to finish. The priest never interrupted me once, just sat there listening. I concluded with what I'd just learned in my confrontation with Forrester, about how Catlett may have actually been responsible for his own death by refusing to put shutters on the building. Father Tim just sat there, looking at me.

"That's some story," he said quietly. "I knew there was bad blood between John and his daughter, but until just this moment never knew the reason for it. It's sad."

I nodded in agreement, but said nothing. I wanted to see where the priest was going to go.

"It's uplifting to know that even with hard feelings between them, Jessica still loved her father enough to send her son to see if he needed help after the storm. But tell me, Paul, why did you come here?"

"Because I don't know what to do, Father. I'm sworn to up-hold the law. The kid and his mother broke the law. But I don't believe they're bad people. That's what's tearing me apart. All my life I thought of lawbreakers as scum, rotten people society would be better off without. Lock 'em up and throw the key away. Now…this."

I paused, hoping Father Tim would say something, but he sat there, mute. I could hear a phone ringing in the outer office, a truck rumbling down southbound 41. Even birds outside the window.

"If I arrest them—and knowing what I know, I could—their lives are ruined. She'll lose her job at the high school. It'll kill any chance the kid has of getting a college scholarship."

"What's the sentence if they were to be convicted?"

"Under normal circumstances, probation to fifteen years. But since the crime was committed in the aftermath of a natural dis-aster, a hard-core judge could double it. Truthfully, I can't imag-ine a judge putting either of them in jail. But even probation pretty much destroys their lives."

The priest appeared troubled, and he looked down momentari-ly. "You're talking as though you have a choice. Yet a few minutes ago, you said you were sworn to uphold the law. Do you have a choice, Paul?"

"That's what I'm trying to figure out. It's up to me whether I arrest them, or look the other way." I stopped for a second, try-ing to remember something that was just out of my reach. Then it came to me. "Father Tim, remember a sermon you gave about character? You said character is what we do when we think no one is watching. Something like that."

"Close," said the priest, with a smile. "Let's back up for a mi-nute. I think the reason you're here, or at least one of the reasons, is that you think Sacred Heart Parish is the victim of this crime. The estate was left to the parish, the Picasso was part of the es-tate, young Duarte stole the Picasso essentially from the church. Is that about right?"

"That's exactly right."

"But you're not asking me whether we'll press charges."

"No, not right now. That's not my job. I did the investigation. I know a crime was committed. I have suspects. After I make an arrest, I suppose the prosecutor would get around to asking about pressing charges. Honestly, I don't know how it works because I haven't been doing this that long. And I can't go and ask anyone at the Sheriff's office for help, because then I won't have any choice. I'd have to arrest them."

"Paul, let's set something aside right now. You're thinking about the money the church has lost, right?"

I nodded yes.

"It's not an issue."

"But father, seventy-five K is a lot more than a month's take in the weekly collection. And that's when the snowbirds are here."

"Paul," he said, in a tone that was a chilling reminder of the priest who was principal of my grammar school back in Newark, "the money is not the issue. It's not important. What's important is the anguish I hear in your soul. You're a good person. You want to do the right thing."

"But I don't know what the right thing is. I got two bad choices. If I do the right thing and arrest them, two people who I really believe are good could go to jail. If I don't arrest them, I violate the oath I took when I signed up to be a cop. It should be easy. Right is right and wrong is wrong. But…" The *but* just sort of hung there, like a cloud of foul-smelling smoke from a cheap cigar.

"There's a concept that the clergy call pastoral sensitivity. All denominations recognize it. We try and teach it in seminary, but it can take years to learn how it really works. Only experience can teach it. What they try and get us to understand is that the world is made up of dozens upon dozens of glorious shades of gray." He paused and reflected for a moment. "Paul, what does your soul tell you that you want to do?"

"I want it to go away. You know the Duartes. They're not criminals."

"Remember the lesson of the story about the woman caught in the act of adultery, then brought to Jesus Christ?"

"Of course. Let he who is without sin cast the first stone."

"Right. But do you know what came next?"

I was drawing a blank, and shook my head.

"Jesus refused to condemn the woman. He said to her, 'Go, and sin no more.' If it worked for him…"

I didn't know what to say. "What are you thinking?" Father Tim asked.

"It seems like such a simple solution."

"I'll lend you my six iron. You can pray on it. Just keep your head down."

We both stood. "I'll try."

"Can I hug a cop without getting busted?" he said.

I took a step toward him, and the priest put his arms around me. "Paul," he whispered in his ear. "You're a good person no matter what they say about you."

For the first time that day, I smiled.

I walked out to the squad car, and then drove slowly back to the sheriff's office. On the way, I continued wrestling with his dilemma. I had to do mental gymnastics to keep my focus off the amount of money involved and on the higher ethical questions. My choices weren't between good and evil. A kid could make that choice.

When I was a kid, I used to complain that the church, the Roman Catholic Church, had too many rules. Everything about the church was an absolute, no flexibility, no room to think about what religion means to an individual or how he wants to practice it. The nuns and priests teaching in Catholic School spelled it out and enforced it, and that's the way it was.

By the time you become an adult, you went one of two ways: you're either locked in and continue to be a strict Catholic, or as a result of exposure to a lot of people who weren't raised that way, who think differently and believe differently and—here's the toughest part—can give you lots of good reasons for doing so—you drift away from the church.

I found myself sort of in the middle. After my brush with cancer I thought a lot about the afterlife. It's a place I want to get to, so I set about consciously doing what was probably the bare minimum as far as the church was concerned to make it past the gates. But after my conversation with Father Tim, I realized how much easier it would be if the church today were still doing things the way it did them in the 1950s. It would have been a whole lot easier if father had just said, "Paul, this is what you must do. Anything else is unacceptable, a mortal sin. You will be punished."

But except for the extremists, I saw that there were no longer any of those hard and fast rules. I'm not sayin' the Catholic Church was into situational ethics. But the way I see it, it now gives out enough rope so's we can hang ourselves. As I switched from the squad car to my SUV, I almost couldn't help but look around the parking lot for a healthy oak tree.

On the way home, I began thinking about how much I was going to tell Sophia—about both cases. I didn't want to have to explain everything all over again, in fact, I was pretty sure that she'd be better off not knowing all the gritty details. But it would piss her off if I told her that I couldn't talk about it, at least not yet.

Sure as hell, I walked into the house, kissed her hello and said I was taking the dog for a walk. "You've been gone all day on a Saturday, my day off, and you're not going to tell me what you've been doing? I have to read about it in the newspapers like everyone else?"

chapter 46
fly

I rushed out the door with the mutt, who was only too happy to have my undivided attention. We walked down the block for a while, the dog taking care of his business, me thinking about mine. Finally, I pulled out my cell phone and dialed Vin's number.

Caller ID gave me away, because after two rings I heard Vin's hearty voice asking, "How goes the pursuit of truth, justice and whatever the rest of that crap is?"

"If it were going well, why would I waste my time calling you?" I said, realizing that it had been a long time since I'd been able to bust anyone's agates purely in jest.

After I had learned about the painting and had the conversation with Strom Thurmond, I'd talked with Vin, so the guy was up to speed on all that. But I spent the next ten minutes taking him through the last twenty-four hours. The arrest of Renfroe. The football game. The meeting with Tony and Jessica Duarte. The confrontation with Forrester and what I'd learned about what a *stugots* Catlett was and how he probably brought his demise on himself by being such a cheap, rotten bastard. And finally, my meeting with Father Tim. Vin listened without interrupting, for which I was extremely grateful.

When I had finished, he said, "I suppose you want to know what I think about the Duarte kid."

"You suppose right."

"Okay. Nice job on the Miranda warnings. And taping the conversation was smart. Who taught you to do that?" It was a rhetorical question. "Fly, I'm going to cut to the chase. You're operating in the grayest of gray areas. You ever heard of investigative or prosecutorial discretion?"

I hadn't and told him so.

"I'm working narcotics and we bust a dealer, a really bad guy. Let's say that when we grab him, he's got his girlfriend with him. And just to make it interesting, let's say that she's the one actually holding the drugs, they're in her purse or bra or crotch, wherever. We know that he's the bad guy, and it usually doesn't take much to figure out that she's carrying the drugs because she was told to. Does she know it's wrong? Sure. Did she have a choice? Who knows? But if we get a feeling that she's a decent person who got caught up in some bad shit—maybe even a bad life—as long as we got her boyfriend, we can exercise our discretion and tell her to get lost."

"Wait a second. You caught her with drugs in her possession, maybe she was even hiding them, but you chose not to bust her?"

"That surprises you—why? She wasn't our target. Getting her off the street and into jail is not going to make society safer. It's not even worth a discussion."

"And you're telling me this because…?"

"Because police work is about knowing the book, but thinking for yourself. I know, they don't teach you that at the academy, but take my word. Let's take a tougher example. Yesterday, you could have put a shot right into that guy's head and gotten away with it. But in the moment, you decide you don't want to do it, that it's not necessary to doing your job. Doesn't mean you're afraid to shoot, or that you won't do it the next time. Your brain does the computations and decides that in this particular case, you don't want it on your conscience that you blew someone away, even if it would have been a righteous shooting. Take it one step further. Suppose you don't shoot and the bad guy gets away. It's okay. If he's really a bad guy, he's going to wind up in the same situation again, and maybe then, he gets shot. And don't tell me that in the mean time, he might hurt someone. I'm trying to make a point here, not get into a philosophical debate with some Jersey refugee who pronounces beautiful as a four syllable word."

"I'll let that pass for now, but that remark will come back to haunt you." I was seriously trying to figure this out, and it was tough. "I see where you're going. Do I think this kid or his mom are going to turn into cat burglars if they get away with this one? Not a chance. They're decent people. They deserved better than they got, both from her father and from the army."

"Okay then. Anything else you want to talk about? Because I've got something to ask you."

"No, I'm good. I've got to sit down and do something think-ing." I stopped talking for a second, and then said, "What's up?"

"You doing anything Monday morning? 'Cause I could use some help."

"I'm yours. What're we doing?"

"I'll meet you at your house around nine. If you can pick up a squad car, that would help. Wear your uniform. Bring your handcuffs. We're doing one your way."

Suddenly, my entire outlook on life brightened. If Vin was ready to have me bust someone, the perp had to have done some-thing to deserve it. "Do I need to clear this with my boss?"

"Nope. Already took care of it."

"You son-of-a-bitch. You played me."

"Yeah, I did, but you're so predictable it wasn't even a chal-lenge. See you Monday at nine."

chapter 47
fly

You've heard the expression *high on life*? That's how I feel right now. I'm on the flying bridge of *Inamorata* with Jinx and my two new friends, Robbie and Rich. The four wives are down below, pouring coffee and laying out the dessert. We'd had a great meal at Hickory Dickory. The sky is blue, the harbor is flat, I've got a good supply of Diet Dr. Pepper, and all's right with the world if your world happens to be Southwest Florida.

Y'know, this is the first time I've had the boat out on a day cruise since Charley whacked us, and I'd forgotten how good it felt to be at her helm. Take a look around. One…two…three other boats. It's truly a wonder. Right now, like I say, we own Charlotte Harbor.

As soon as the girls climbed topside, Jinx said, "Okay, Officer Grumpy, tell us what happened yesterday morning with Vin."

I plucked a piece of Laura's homemade apple strudel off the tray and stuck it in my mouth. It was wonderful and the smile that crossed my face said so.

"Glad you like it," Laura said.

Sophia had broken out into a big smile as well. "My God," said my wife, "maybe the morose creature who's been living in our house for the last couple of months is actually gone. C'mon, you wouldn't tell me yesterday when I asked what happened.

You said you wanted to save it for the boat. We've heard the whole story, except for the epilogue. We're waiting."

"Okay, picture this," I said, wiping strudel crumbs from the corners of my mouth, "Guy has a forty foot Trojan that he can no longer afford. Instead of trying to get a broker to peddle the boat, which could take some time, he decides he'll sell it to his insurance company."

"I thought only restaurant owners did that. Usually a 'fire of suspicious origin,'" interrupted Jinx.

"No, but come to think of it, a fire would have been a better choice than what this *giamoke* did. Here's the story he told us. The boat survived Hurricane Charley with some cosmetic damage. Frances blew it around a bit and tore some canvas. He filed a claim. Ivan was supposed to cause real problems, but turned out to be a bust. But then along comes Jeanne. Jeanne, he says in his final claim, battered his boat so badly that it sunk right at the dock. He must've dreamt of Jeannie with the large single eye."

"I suppose that's a hurricane joke. But the last storm wasn't Jeannie; it was Jeanne. Stephen Foster might forgive you, I won't," said Laura.

"Friends are supposed to be forgiving. Do you wanna hear what happened, or not?"

"We all want to hear," said Sophia. I knew I could count on my wife.

"Anyway, the boat sinks while still tied to his dock, and he blames it on Hurricane Jeanne."

"We walked the dog during Jeanne," Laura shouted. "I think the Nieberlines took their sailboat out in it."

"The insurance investigators knew that. They pulled the weather data and it didn't add up. So they hired a marine salvage company to bring up the boat."

Jinx couldn't resist putting in his two cents. "Was that guy stupid or what? He didn't think you were going to let it sit on the bottom—at his dock, in a canal that might be eight feet deep at high tide. Or did he?"

"Maybe, maybe not. May I continue?"

All of them nodded.

"Anyway, they raised the boat with slings and a forklift, stuck it on a flatbed, and their salvage expert climbed aboard to take a look. It took him about two minutes down in the bilge to see that someone had taken a hacksaw to the water intake hoses for the engines. The owner wasn't there when this was going on, so they just took the boat to a yard up near Tampa, where their forensic guys went over it.

"They confirm it. Someone cut the hoses with a hacksaw without bothering to close the sea cocks. And the boat sinks. They do some more checking and find that the guy had stopped making payments on the boat, and that he just got sued by his business partner. All the paperwork came together last week, and yesterday morning, we busted the guy."

"I don't understand," Jinx interrupted. "I thought you said insurance companies just want claims to go away. Isn't that what Vin told you? I remember you getting all upset with them not wanting to lock up the crooks."

"Usually that's true," I answered. "But there's no way they were going to shell out 300K for a boat the guy sunk himself. At least Vin has a little self-respect left.

"Vin actually let me slap the cuffs on the *stunad*. When I did it, I told the Boatman of Alcatraz he made three mistakes. And the *jadrool* actually asks me what they were.

"I said, 'Your first mistake was buying the boat. Your second mistake was sinking the boat.' And he says something about me telling him the obvious. I looked at him and said, 'You know what your third mistake was?' He said he didn't know. So I said, 'Your third mistake, captain, was not going down with the ship.'"

I looked around and was really disappointed that no one had convulsed in laughter. "Hey, it was funny at the time, trust me."

Jinx looked at me, not smiling. I wasn't sure what was coming. "Fly, you okay with the way it all turned out? Not the schmuck with the boat. The big stuff, Catlett's death, the stolen Picasso. I mean, c'mon, you're Mr. Law and Order."

"I'm okay with it. I did nail Renfroe for the murder, and you and I prevented a killing. That was big. But the resolution of the Catlett thing still leaves me—I don't know—I just wish I felt more enthusiastic. There was something Father Tim said that really helped. He said I should do what I think is right."

Jinx started laughing.

"What's so friggin' funny?"

"That's what I used to tell my son when he was a kid. He hated it. But he usually did the right thing. You think what you did is the right thing?"

"Yeah," I responded. "It's not necessarily what the law says, and I used to believe that following the letter of the law was always the right thing. I mean, what kind of society do we have if everyone decides for themselves what laws they'll obey and what laws they won't. Now, I'm not so sure. But uncertainty isn't necessarily a bad thing."

"But I thought you were against situational ethics," Jinx said, still working at busting my agates.

"Yeah, I was. Until I got into a situation. Who woulda thought I'd be learning new stuff at sixty?" I turned to Sophia and said, "Do me a favor?"

"What?"

"Just don't tell our kids. They think I already know everything."

"Honey," my wife said with a smile, "You're delusional."

acknowledgments

After a life spent in non-fiction television, and then writing non-fiction books, the transition to my first piece of book-length fiction was bumpy. The problem was that I was hung up on facts. I need to thank my agent, Matt Bialer, for giving me the advice that got me through it. "Mike," he said, "I'm going to give you the secret of writing fiction. Here it is. It's fiction. You can make shit up." After that, while not quite a piece of cake, the writing went much easier.

I want to thank my friend Mark Porzio who inspired the Fly character, but to be clear, the only things the two of them really have in common are an inexplicable addiction to Diet Dr. Pepper and the consequences of growing up in Newark. Thanks to the real Wayne Salladé—not the guy in this book— and the Charlotte County 911 operators for reliving their Charley experiences with me.

Also thanks to my friends Todd Katz and Ira Furman, and my daughter Jennifer Weisberrger, for commenting helpfully during *Fly*'s gestation, and to Leslie Sewell and Peter Herford for their ongoing encouragement and moral support. My gratitude goes to a veteran Florida insurance fraud investigator who wants to remain anonymous, for teaching me—and Fly—the ropes. Pastor Tim Stewart of Punta Gorda's Burnt Store Presbyterian Church served as my theological advisor, and helped me see the way to give peace of mind to Fly.

Immeasurable appreciation goes to my editor and publisher at Antenna Books, Doug Grad, who thought it would be worth his time and effort to get to know Mr. Jinx and Fly, and who helped turn my first draft into my first published novel. Thanks to Jill Boltin who designed a cover that captures the spirit of the book, and to Karen Lauziere and Lauren Cooley at Createspace, who put it all together.

And last, as always, my thanks and love to Karen, who still says that I'm "playing on my computer," even though sooner or later the damn thing spits out a book. Jinx told me not to fight it; he says there are some things women—wives—will never understand.

Readers are invited to write to me at:

FlyandJinx@gmail.com.

Author photo by Karen Hirsh

about the author

A Chicago native and lifelong journalist, Michael Hirsh served as an Army combat correspondent with the 25th Infantry Division in Vietnam. He spent most of his professional life in non-fiction television, reporting, producing, writing, and directing documentaries and specials that aired on PBS, CBS, ABC and HBO. Among the programs he's produced are the twentieth anniversary special "Memories of M*A*S*H," a series on the prevention of child sexual abuse, documentaries on the American funeral industry, teen pregnancy, political advertising, television censorship and college suicide.

He's received the Peabody and Writers Guild Awards, the 2010 Vietnam Veterans of America Excellence in the Arts Award, as well as many other honors that his wife, Karen, says she's tired of dusting. He's written seven non-fiction books. *Fly on the Wall* is his first novel. He and Karen live in Punta Gorda, Florida, and quite often run into Fly and Mr. Jinx at Dean's South of the Border.